Courage,
The Adventuress
&
The False Messiah

Courage,
The Adventuress

The False Messiah

BY

HANS JACOB CHRISTOFFEL
VON GRIMMELSHAUSEN

TRANSLATION AND INTRODUCTION BY
HANS SPEIER

Princeton, New Jersey
Princeton University Press
1964

Publication of this book has been aided
by the Whitney Darrow Publication Reserve Fund
of Princeton University Press.

Printed in the United States of America
Princeton University Press
Princeton, New Jersey

Acknowledgments

MY FRIEND Herbert Goldhamer has read various drafts of the translation and the introductory essay. I am very grateful to him for his help and for many valuable suggestions. I wish to thank also Maria Paasche, who for many years has assisted me in my studies of 17th century German literature.

I should like also to acknowledge the gracious and generous help of Yale University Library in providing the reproduction of the frontispiece from the first edition of Grimmelshausen's *Courage, the Adventuress.*

H. S.

CONTENTS

Courage,
The Adventuress
&
The False Messiah

Explanation of the Engraving
or
Courage Addressing the Gracious Reader

Behold th' accessories of folly scattered here
Which were so precious to me and so very dear.
I've thrown them down but wholly unimpeached by shame:
My occupation now is such and such my fame
That I need neither rouge nor powder for my hair;
My ointments and my salves are for the lice to share.
What else? you ask. I say that naught gives more delight
Than money or assailing *Simplicem* with spite.

INTRODUCTION*

IN Germany, Simplicissimus is a folk figure like Till Eulenspiegel and Dr. Faustus. The popularity of this deceptively simple man goes back to the year 1669 when *The Adventurous Simplicissimus* was published. The book was an immediate success. It bore the subtitle "True Description of the Life of a Strange Vagabond, named Melchior Sternfels von Fuchshaim," and contained the grimly humorous story of a young boy growing up to mature manhood during the Thirty Years War or, to be exact, from 1622 to 1650, two years after the conclusion of the Peace of Westphalia. The editor of Fuchshaim's alleged autobiography, which consisted of five parts or books, called himself German Schleifheim von Sulsfort. In the same year, 1669, a *Continuatio* or conclusion of this work was published both separately and as the sixth book of *The Adventurous Simplicissimus*. This *Continuatio* was signed by another editor with the initials, H.J.C.V.G.; he declared that the story of Simplicissimus was not an autobiography, but a piece of fiction written by Sulsfort, partly in his youth "when he was still a musketeer" in the Thirty Years War. According to H.J.C.V.G., Sulsfort's true name was Samuel Greifnson vom Hirschfeld, a name that he had concealed by transposing its letters to make up the anagram Melchior Sternfels von Fuchshaim (Fugshaim). But H.J.C.V.G. were not the initials of an editor who

* The Introduction is based on two of my essays, "A Woman Named Courage," in *The Arts in Society*, ed. Robert N. Wilson (Englewood Cliffs, N.J.: Prentice-Hall, Inc., 1964) and "Grimmelshausen's Laughter," in *Ancients and Moderns. Essays on the Tradition of Political Philosophy, in Honor of Leo Strauss*, ed. Joseph Cropsey (New York: Basic Books, Inc., 1964). I am indebted to both publishers for their kind permission to use in this volume an abridged version of the essays.

[3]

pretended to know and reveal the identity of the author; instead, they were the initials of the true author, Hans Jacob Christoffel von Grimmelshausen. In his youth he had indeed been a musketeer in the long war, and it was established later that various passages in his novel reflected actual experiences in his life. Samuel Greifnson vom Hirschfeld, German Schleifheim von Sulsfort, and Melchior Sternfels von Fuchshaim—all were different anagrams of the author's true name. In the course of his literary career Grimmelshausen used no less than seven other pen names. Only three of his works were published under his real name, namely, two conventional novels, *Dietwald und Amelinde* (1670), and *Proximus und Lympida* (1672), and a small unimportant, anti-Machiavellian treatise, *Ratio Status* (1670). Only these writings were dedicated to aristocrats though with less than customary obsequiousness.

Grimmelshausen's identity was reestablished in 1837, a hundred and sixty-one years after his death.[1] When Goethe and Lessing read *The Adventurous Simplicissimus* they did not know that its author was Grimmelshausen, and in a learned edition of 1836 authorship was still attributed to Samuel Greifnson. And yet Grimmelshausen had not only hinted at his identity through the initials H.J.C.V.G., but had also prevailed upon three "poets," named Sylvander, Perikles, and Urban, to praise him under his true name as the author of novels that he had published or was going to publish under some pseudonym. To complete the mas-

---

[1] Another major figure of 17th century German literature, Johann Beer, was even more successful in hiding his name behind a large number of pseudonyms. His identity was rediscovered only 232 years after the author's death by Richard Alewyn in his *Johann Beer, Studien zum Roman des 17. Jahrhunderts*, Leipzig, 1932.

querade, these poetic commendations of Grimmelshausen and of his Simplician writings appeared in the prefatory material of the two novels which the author published under his own name, and much later it was discovered that Sylvander, Perikles, and Urban were all one person: Grimmelshausen himself!

When he wrote commendatory poems on his own behalf he followed, as it were, the advice laughingly given by the friend to whom Cervantes complained about his misfortune in not having an illustrious poet to help *Don Quixote* on its way: "Your difficulty, respecting the want of sonnets, epigrams, or panegyrics by high and titled authors, may at once be removed simply by taking the trouble to compose them yourself, and then baptizing them by whatever name you please."[2] Probably Grimmelshausen panegyrized himself, because he had no trusted friend among the literati to render him this service. His praise was so fulsome, however, that there can be little doubt of his interest in satirizing the complimentary style of commendatory poetry while at the same time he was blowing his horn for his own works.[3]

Grimmelshausen wrote three additional brief continuations and a *Zugab: Simplicissimus als Arzt* ("Addendum: Simplicissimus as Physician") all of which he included as "side stories" in the 1670 edition of *The Adventurous Simplicissimus*,[4] and three other important novels: *Die Land-*

[2] Miguel de Cervantes, *Adventures of Don Quixote*, tr. Charles Jarvis, "Author's Preface."

[3] Cf. Hans Ehrenzeller, *Studien zur Romanvorrede von Grimmelshausen bis Jean Paul.* Basler Studien, Heft 16, Bern, 1955, pp. 99-106.

[4] These three additional continuations were published also separately in annual almanacs entitled *Simplicianischer Wundergeschichten Kalender* ("Simplician Almanac of Curious Stories") for the years 1670, 1671, and 1672 respectively. Interestingly enough, this almanac continued to appear well into the 19th century.

störzerin Courasche (*Courage, The Adventuress*) (1670), *Der Seltsame Springinsfeld* ("The Strange Skipinthefield"), (1670), and *Das wunderbarliche Vogelsnest* ("The Enchanted Bird's-nest"), Part I (1672), and Part II (1675). Together with *The Adventurous Simplicissimus*, which consists of six books, these novels form a larger unit, the Simplician cycle, comprising ten books, Grimmelshausen's main literary achievement.

Although each of these four novels is an independent unit that can be read and appreciated without knowledge of the other three, Grimmelshausen himself said in the second preface to *The Enchanted Bird's-nest*, Part II, that the four novels or ten books formed a unit and that only those readers would understand his work who were familiar with the whole cycle. This statement has been variously interpreted by those critics who have taken it seriously.

The four novels are interlocked in the sense that Simplicissimus, Courage, and Skipinthefield appear in several books of the cycle, and not only in the novels which carry their names in the titles. For example, Courage, a woman more adventurous, more evil, and considerably more interesting than Defoe's Moll Flanders or Brecht's Mother Courage, is introduced to the reader first in a minor episode of *The Adventurous Simplicissimus*, when the hero, at a watering place in the Black Forest, meets a lady who pretends to be a noblewoman. He is attracted by her, but soon she strikes him as "more mobile than noble,"[5] since for due payment she readily grants him the favors he seeks. Later, not long after his marriage to a young peasant

---

[5] *Grimmelshausens Simplicissimus Teutsch*, ed. J. H. Scholte, Tübingen, 1954 (hereafter cited as *Simplicissimus*), bk. v, chap. 6.

girl, he finds a newborn son of his abandoned on his doorstep.

Courage, the Adventuress, the seventh book of the Simplician cycle, is the autobiography of the wily harlot whom Simplicissimus met at the watering place. She discloses her whole adventurous and dissolute life allegedly for the sole purpose of taking revenge on her lover, for she has never forgiven him (although her name was not mentioned in his tale). The original German title of her story begins with the words *Trutz Simplex* . . . ("To spite simplex . . ."), Simplex being a short colloquial version of the name Simplicius Simplicissimus. Courage reaches the height of her furious triumph when she reveals the true identity of the baby that she had ordered her maid to leave in front of Simplicissimus' house. The baby was not the son of her lover, nor even her own child, but a bastard born to her maidservant. In her malice Courage wanted not only to cause trouble between Simplicissimus and his wife, but also to force him to bring up a bastard as his own son.

In *The Strange Skipinthefield*, the eighth book of the cycle, Courage's story is developed further. A young Swiss clerk to whom, it now turns out, she dictated the story of her life reminisces about the beautiful, evil woman who had taken revenge on Simplicissimus. The Swiss tells the story in an inn with the aged Simplicissimus and Skipinthefield, an old veteran maimed in the war, listening to his tale. Readers of the preceding books of the cycle remember Skipinthefield as he was in his younger days, a reckless comrade of young Simplicissimus in the war. They recall also that, like his famous companion, he, too, once loved Courage.

When Simplicissimus learns from the Swiss of Courage's

base revenge by forcing a bastard child upon him, he replies calmly that the woman failed: the deceiver was deceived. For at the time when Simplicissimus had known Courage he had in fact seen less of her than of her maid-servant, and the child left on his doorstep was, unbeknownst to Courage, his own son after all. Thus familiarity with various books in the cycle is necessary to reach a full understanding of the "plot" and of the individual events and actions that occur in any one of them.

Such intricate interlocking of the parts of a long work in order to cast light on past events from various vantage points was a standard compositional practice in the conventional baroque novel, which presented the world as enigmatic,[6] conveying this notion by unexpected reunions, incidents based on disguise and mistaken identity, startling disclosures of unexpected blood relationships, and in many other ways. The popular "comic" novels of Grimmelshausen reverberate with echoes from the conventional baroque world. The origins of both Simplicissimus and Courage are at first obscure to the reader and disclosed only slowly to him; disguise and mistaken identity play a prominent role in their lives, including their first sexual experiences.

It is not only with reference to such literary techniques that the ten books of the Simplician cycle form a unit. It might also be said that no single book, but only the cycle as a whole discloses the author's full view of the nature of man and of his life in this world. In order to understand the nature of man, the nature of woman must be considered, and the latter subject is a central theme only in *Cour-*

[6] The "enigmatic" character of human relations in the baroque novel ("*Verrätselung*") has been discussed in the brilliant book by Clemens Lugowski, *Wirklichkeit und Dichtung*, Frankfort/M., 1936.

age, the Adventuress. Similarly, in order to understand the nature of life in this world, both peace and war must be represented, and apart from the sixth book of *The Adventurous Simplicissimus*, only the two parts of *The Enchanted Bird's-nest* deal with life in peacetime; all others books of the cycle are put in a war setting. Finally, and most importantly, the meaning and consequences of Simplicissimus' two renunciations of the world, occurring at the end of the fifth book, and again at the end of the sixth, are bound to be misunderstood unless the sequels are read.[7]

[7] Extending an earlier inquiry into the structural balance of *Simplicissimus* (Johannes Alt, *Grimmelshausen und der Simplicissimus*, Munich, 1936) Siegfried Streller has attempted to show that Grimmelshausen wrote the whole Simplician cycle most carefully according to principles of number composition, so that the specific number of chapters into which the author divided his novels, and the allocation of certain topics to positionally and numerically important chapters conveyed secret meanings. This interpretation suffers from certain intrinsic implausibilities and in consequence of severe criticism has in the meantime been almost entirely withdrawn. (Cf. Siegfried Streller, *Grimmelshausens Simplicianische Schriften*, [East] Berlin, 1957; Horst Hartmann, "Bemerkungen zu Siegfried Strellers Theorie der Zahlenkomposition," *Zeitschrift für deutsche Literaturgeschichte*, 1959, v, pp. 428-436 and Siegfried Streller's reply to Hartmann's criticism, "Spiel oder Forschungsgegenstand," *op.cit.*, pp. 437-440. For reasons other than those advanced in the controversy, Streller's original view is probably false. According to Streller, Grimmelshausen was an orthodox Catholic in that all numerical symbols in his work call for an interpretation in the tradition of Christian number symbolism. Streller's original interpretation indeed relies heavily on St. Augustine. But the orthodoxy of Grimmelshausen's Christian faith is questionable. The Simplician writings contain many heretical and blasphemous allusions. To accept Streller's original view one would have not to disregard, but to dismiss as irrelevant, the meaning and double meaning of Grimmelshausen's words in many of his tales. (Cf. below, Introduction, and Hans Speier, "Grimmelshausen's Laughter," *Ancients and Moderns. Essays on the Tradition of Political Philosophy, in Honor of Leo Strauss*, ed. Joseph Cropsey, New York, 1964.)

Neither Grimmelshausen's views of nature nor his religious beliefs can be inferred from any single book of his but only from his work as a whole. Least of all is it safe to take any of his Christian admonitions at their face value or to attribute a particular view to Grimmelshausen merely because Simplicissimus can be shown to have held it at some time in his life. If the author resembled the main character in his works he must have been capable of many different things: solemnity and laughter, veracity and dissembling, moral preaching and cynicism, compliance with the demands of the Church and something close to blasphemy. By taking the hero's views uncritically for those of the author one merely raises the question as to what kind of man Grimmelshausen really was.

GRIMMELSHAUSEN: MAN AND AUTHOR

Grimmelshausen led an uneventful life which, when compared with the adventurous careers of the main characters in his writings, appears almost dull. Grimmelshausen was born as Hans Jacob Christoff in Gelnhausen at the foot of the Spessart mountains, probably in 1621 or 1622. He was a small child when his father died; his mother remarried in Frankfort/M. in April 1627. The child grew up in the care of his grandfather Melchior Christoff, a stern Lutheran who had lived in Gelnhausen as a baker and tavern keeper at least since 1588. In 1613 he was involved as a radical on the side of the burghers against the suppression of their civil rights by the councilmen of the town. He accused one of them of having homosexually abused his young son, Grimmelshausen's father.[8] It is not known whether Grimmelshausen ever learned about the incident;

___

[8] Gustav Könnecke, *Quellen und Forschungen zur Lebensgeschichte Grimmelshausens*, Weimar, 1926, Vol. 1, pp. 110-111.

but since his grandfather testified before a commission that had been appointed by the Elector Johann Wilhelm to settle the civic conflict, this possibility cannot be dismissed.

The circumstances of Grimmelshausen's early life were shaped by the Thirty Years War. He was drawn into its maelstrom when he was still a small boy, but in 1648 he had advanced only to the position of a regimental secretary. In that year, when peace was finally concluded, he seems to have reclaimed the old family name von Grimmelshausen, which his grandfather had given up. At the age of 26 or 27 the young man, now no longer a commoner but the bearer of a fuller and more distinguished name, became a steward for various members of the Schauenburg family. Serving these local barons in a war-ravaged part of Southern Germany was the closest Grimmelshausen ever came in his life to the upper layers of European society, a long way indeed from its summits of power and splendor. As a steward he collected taxes from the peasants and brought recalcitrant debtors to court. For a while he also acted as host in a local tavern that belonged to one of the barons, and he sold horses to add to his income. In 1660, when Grimmelshausen quit his job, he was in debt to his employers for land bought with their funds.[9] Thus at the age of about 40, after many years of military and civil employment in the service of provincial noblemen who outranked him, he had failed in preserving his honesty as well as in attaining security. By that time he was the father of a large family.

A year later he was employed for a while as steward of a castle belonging to a rich physician, Dr. Johannes Rüffer, who had a prosperous practice in Strasbourg. The doctor was an admirer of the arts, a friend and patron of

[9] *Op.cit.*, Vol. II, pp. 152 ff.

important writers and poets like Moscherosch and Rompler, a member of the influential Tannengesellschaft in Strasbourg (a language society), and a poet of sorts himself. Grimmelshausen failed again. He did not get along at all with Dr. Rüffer. The association lasted only until the spring of 1665, although Grimmelshausen was involved in legal quarrels stemming from this employment until 1672. Nor did he establish closer contacts with the other members of the language society in Strasbourg. Throughout his literary career he lacked any friends among the respected writers of his time and he took furious issue with those among them, like Christian Weise and Philipp von Zesen, who criticized his works.

After another two years as tavern keeper in a small house at Gaisbach he was appointed bailiff of Renchen, a small place in the Black Forest area, under the jurisdiction of the Bishop of Strasbourg. Thus with the help of his father-in-law, who put up the required security for him in 1667, Grimmelshausen finally reached a position that freed him of financial worries and gave him at the same time enough leisure to write. His income consisted in large part of a share of the revenues from Renchen, and much of the payment was made in kind. Not long before his death on August 17, 1676, he was drawn once more into a war, the war between the French, the Dutch, and the Germans. At the time of his death, Renchen was virtually depopulated, and the roads were again as unsafe as they had been in the Thirty Years War.

Throughout his life Grimmelshausen remained a child of the lower middle classes. He was at home in taverns rather than at court. He knew beggars and soldiers but no great merchants or important officials. He was familiar with peasants and lowly people in small towns and villages, with camp followers and jugglers, but with only a few members of the aristocracy. His relations with polite society were tenuous; nor did he belong to any literary clique. His wide knowledge was acquired autodidactically, mainly with the help of compendia. He read much, but he did not travel abroad. His Latin was faulty and he probably spoke no foreign language.

Small wonder that Grimmelshausen was unsuccessful in trying to meet the standards which the acknowledged literati applied to the historical-political novels of his day. They regarded such novels as "real schools for the court and the nobility, which ennoble the soul, the mind, and the manners and teach refined, courteous speech."[10] Grimmelshausen referred to the subjects of the conventional novel as "high things," and "high things" were not his strength. His genius was satirical. The Simplician writings proved him to be an unsurpassed teller of stories that dealt with the "low things" in life. The relation of these writings to the conventional novel resembles that of comedy to tragedy, and Martin Opitz's description of comedy in his *Book on German Poetry* fits the Simplician writings well, though not perfectly. He said that "comedy consists of low (*schlecht*) things and persons; it deals with weddings, festivities, gambling, fraud and roguery of knaves and vainglorious soldiers, with love affairs, the frivolity of youth, the miserliness of the aged, with procuring and other matters that occur every day among common people."[11]

Grimmelshausen's main characters in the Simplician

[10] Anton Ulrich von Braunschweig, *Die Durchleuchtige Syrerinn Aramena*, Nürnberg, 1678, "Voransprache zum Edlen Leser."

[11] Martin Opitz, *Buch von der deutschen Poeterei* (1624), ed. Wilhelm Braune, Tübingen, 1954, p. 20.

[13]

writings are no heroes whose will and reason triumph in adversity. In their adventures as soldiers, camp followers, highwaymen, and the like they are ensnared by the physical needs of the body, by passion, and by evil. They do not love but fear their neighbors, just as the courtier in the conventional novel fears his rival, and they see the hand of the Devil in everything unexpected that happens. They are concerned not with dignity, but with survival. They are extremely superstitious, particularly with regard to the chance of suddenly getting rich and the risk of violent death. Indeed, Grimmelshausen's Simplician writings are valuable as source books on popular beliefs in 17th century Germany.

The belief that certain persons are magically protected against bullets was widespread at the time and by no means confined to the uneducated masses of the population. Courage is "bullet-proof," but in her time many famous military leaders had the reputation of invulnerability. Tilly's troops were thought to be "frozen" or "proof" against leaden bullets, and "Christian of Brunswick actually employed his ducal brother's workers in glass to make balls of that material to be used against Tilly's troops."[12] Toward the end of the Thirty Years War special amulets, or so-called Passau tickets, for protection against bullets were widely sold. The technology of firearms sustained such superstitions. Bullets weighed ten to the pound, their penetrating power was low, and many of them missed their aim. Only a very small fraction—perhaps five per cent—of the staggering loss that the Thirty

[12] A.T.S. Goodrick in his "Introduction" to his (incomplete) English translation of *The Adventurous Simplicissimus*, first published London, 1912, and reprinted in a paperbound edition by University of Nebraska Press, Lincoln, 1962, p. xvi.

Years War inflicted on the population resulted from violence in battle.

The difference between the Simplician writings and the
conventional novels extends to the use of language. The
Simplician writings abound with proverbial expressions,
dialect and colloquialisms of the lower classes, whereas
the style of high or learned society is formal and precludes
proverbs; even Grimmelshausen's own two conventional
novels are virtually free of them.[18]

The liberal use of proverbs is only one of many features
which Grimmelshausen's Simplician writings have in
common with the popular literature of the folk books.
The affinity emerges also in the descriptive chapter headings and in the "oral style" of delivery, originally borne
of the custom of having the folk book read out loud. In
Grimmelshausen's work the oral style is most evident
when the narrator, who tells his tale in the first person,
interrupts himself to inform the reader directly that he
should listen to the next adventure. This device, which
Grimmelshausen employs frequently in *Courage, the Adventuress*, creates the illusion of an almost physical presence of the listeners sitting around the story teller. As in
all folk books and folk tales, Courage's and thus Grimmelshausen's "public" seems to be listeners who hear a
story they are being told.

Grimmelshausen conceived of "high and low things"
as opposites, but he contrasted the "Simplician" or "comical" (*lustig*) style not with the style of the conventional
baroque novel but with the "theological style," that is with
the form and content of sermons and serious devotional
books. Young Simplicissimus "becomes pale" when he sees

[18] Martha Lenschau, *Grimmelshausens Sprichwörter und Redens-
arten*, Frankfurt/M., 1924, p. 11.

[15]

a parson read "his" book, *Der Keusche Joseph* ("The Chaste Joseph"), a work of Grimmelshausen published in 1669, and the parson censors the lengthy treatment of the alluring beauty of Potiphar's wife. But Grimmelshausen feels no compunction in introducing the aged Courage, a former camp follower, into the company of Secundatus, a nobleman, who presides over the conversation in *Rathsstübel Plutonis* ("The Council Chamber of Pluto"), and this nobleman admits freely to having read the scandalous story of her life. The difference between Grimmelshausen's conventional novels and his Simplician writings is more clearly visible in subject matter and style than it is in the social status of his readers.

While it is extremely difficult to gain reliable insight into the social composition of Grimmelshausen's audience, it is almost certain that the author wished to have among the readers of the Simplician writings members of the aristocracy and of the learned. Some instances of such readership can be definitely proved. Thus the Duchess Sophie of Hannover wrote to her brother Karl Ludwig, Elector of the Palatinate, that she had someone read to her *Simplicissimus*; she found its beginning very pious in character. She was also pleased with *Courage, the Adventuress*. Nor did all learned readers reject the Simplician tales because they contained so many moral admonitions or because they were "vulgar." Such objections were raised by some of Grimmelshausen's literary colleagues who enjoyed social respectability (and did not hesitate as Protestants to write panegyrical poetry in praise of Catholic rulers). By contrast, men of freer spirit, like Leibniz, found *The Adventurous Simplicissimus* delightful reading. He wrote to the Duchess of Hannover that the work approached the genius of Charles Sorel's *Histoire Comique*

[16]

de Francion.[14] This is high praise indeed, both because of the intelligence of the critic and because of the comparison he made.

Grimmelshausen began his literary career with extraordinary self-consciousness. In an age when poets were proud to be scholars he seems to have been keenly aware of his lack of erudition, and may have feared criticism and ridicule. Thus, perhaps in order to protect himself, he not only masked the authorship of his first book, *Der Satyrische Pilgram* ("The Satirical Pilgrim"), but also criticized his own writing in the first preface to that work. Then in the second preface, entitled "The Author's Re-

[14] On *Simplicissimus* and *Courage, the Adventuress* being read by Duchess Sophie of Hannover cf. J. H. Scholte, *Der Simplicissimus und sein Dichter*, Tübingen, 1950, p. 144; the relevant passage in Leibniz's letter (of April 1688) to her is quoted by Manfred Koschlig, "Das Lob des 'Francion' bei Grimmelshausen," *Jahrbuch der deutschen Schillergesellschaft*, Stuttgart, 1957, Vol. I, pp. 33-34. Attacking the older view that Grimmelshausen's *Simplicissimus* was influenced by Spanish picaresque models in German translation, Koschlig tries to show the debt Grimmelshausen owed to the comical novel by Charles Sorel. By contrast Günther Weydt, in "Don Quijote Teutsch. Studien zur Herkunft des Simplicianischen Jupiter," *Euphorion*, 1951, Vol. LI, pp. 250-270, and before that in his essay "Zur Entstehung barocker Erzählkunst.—Harsdörffer und Grimmelshausen," *Wirkendes Wort*, 1952, Sonderheft I, has proved Grimmelshausen's indirect indebtedness to Cervantes by way of various intermediaries; of these Harsdörffer, the industrious translator and adapter of picaresque and other foreign tales, was especially important. Koschlig correctly assesses the common function of Grimmelshausen's and Sorel's humor, but seems to overstate the influence of *Francion* on the character of Grimmelshausen's Jove. Koschlig also fails to comment on the significant differences between the French and the German work. Sorel dealt with the upper classes as well as university life and the lowly elements in society. The social scope of his observation is larger and the fervor of his early nonconformism greater than Grimmelshausen's. Sorel wanted to teach people "to live like Gods." Cf. Charles Sorel, *Histoire Comique de Francion*; cinquième livre, ed. Emile Roy, Paris: librairie Hachettes, 1926, Vol. II, p. 123.

buttal," he proceeded to attack the imaginary critic on behalf of his readers, characterizing them as "simple-minded
people like myself"; this second preface also contained a
defiant statement to the effect that he had not written his
book for gain: "otherwise I would have dedicated it to
someone."[15]

Grimmelshausen masked the authorship of all his tales
written in the earthy and popular Simplician style, but
with mounting literary success he gained self-assurance
and hinted obliquely at his real name. At the same time
he insisted that his Simplician works were not merely
written to entertain and instruct the vulgar but to benefit
everyone, regardless of social status.

Grimmelshausen's understanding of himself will always
remain a matter of conjecture, but writing *The Third Continuatio* of *The Adventurous Simplicissimus* may have
been a moment of self-recognition for him. "If my critics
say so loudly that I am an ignoramus, why don't they
leaf through my *Everlasting Almanac* and many other
thoughtful little treatises remembering how often a phi-
losopher wears an uncouth cloak. Similarly, it happens
sometimes that under a simple-sounding name and behind
the printed words that deal with insignificant things
something else is hidden which evades discovery by many
a reader."[16]

WAR—SEX—RELIGION

If any three motifs of universal human concern were to
be singled out for the poignancy with which Grimmels-

---

[15] The Prefaces to *The Satirical Pilgrim* have been reprinted in Hans
Ehrenzeller, *op.cit.*, pp. 203-207.

[16] *Grimmelshausens Simpliciana*, ed. J. H. Scholte, Halle, 1943 (hereafter cited as *Simpliciana*), p. 43.

hausen treats them, they could be either folly, inconstancy, and laughter; adventure, evil, and despair; or war, sex, and religion. Consideration of any one of these triads leads to the center of Grimmelshausen's world.

In his war novels, Grimmelshausen describes many acts of wanton cruelty, which soldiers commit against peasants, peasants against soldiers, and men against helpless women. All of these atrocities are known from other evidence to have indeed occurred at some time or other in the Thirty Years War. Stripping a slain enemy of his clothes was common practice and considered to be as permissible as taking his weapons, horse, or money. At one occasion Simplicissimus remarks quite incidentally that at the conclusion of an encounter he did not plunder the dead; the emphasis is not on the moral worth of his conduct, but merely on the fact that he had "no time" to do otherwise. Skipinthefield re-equips himself twice by means of murder. Pouring liquid filth into the mouth of a victim became known in Europe as the Swedish drink. Incidents in which peasants are roasted over a fire or in an oven are reported in other sources as well. So are the use of pistols for thumbscrews and many other hideous tortures, not to mention rape and mutilations.

Nevertheless, Grimmelshausen's Simplician writings can be used as source material by historians of war only at their own risk. They must remember that the author's treatment of reality was highly selective. Compared with the writers of conventional novels, in which common people were "the vulgar" or at best shepherds, Grimmelshausen was a "realist," but he gave undue prominence to lawlessness, cruelty, and filth, to the weird and the wretched, to soldiers, beggars, whores, and highwaymen. He neglected many moral and social aspects of reality.

Grimmelshausen can be cited in support of the orthodox opinion that war is a scourge, sent by God to punish
sin, but he knew that in war the innocent suffer with the
guilty. The dynastic interests in the Thirty Years War did
not concern him; in his view, it was "an internal war and
a conflict between brothers."[17] Even many years after the
Peace of Westphalia was concluded he seems to have been
of the opinion that the rivalry among the Christian
churches stood in the way of lasting peace. This is at least
the argument which Simplicissimus offers to the mad
character who thinks of himself as Jove and has come to
establish eternal peace.

Grimmelshausen presented many of his general views
on war, as on other subjects, in the form of proverbs. This
includes the saying, "Young soldiers—old beggars," also
to be found in *The Pentameron*[18]: it is the main lesson
contained in the life of *The Strange Skipinthefield*. Again,
"boys who fail to obey father and mother follow the drummer, if not the hangman";[19] an elaboration of this theme
is *Der stolze Melcher* ("The Proud Melchior"), one of
Grimmelshausen's last writings, in which he equated turning soldier with joining a gang of loud-mouthed, hard-
drinking gamblers, robbers, and seducers of maidens.
Grimmelshausen was of the opinion that war attracts especially the rotten elements in society. They drift into the
armies. "Oh, Jove," says Simplicissimus, "if you send a
war, all the evil fellows and daredevils will join it and
torment the peace-loving, pious people."[20]

[17] *Simplicissimus*, bk. III, chap. 7.
[18] *Ibid.*, bk. III, chap. 19. Cf. also Basile, *The Pentameron*, tr. Sir
Richard Burton, London, 1952, p. 96.
[19] "Simplicissimi Galgenmännlin," in *Grimmelshausens Werke*, ed.
H. H. Borcherdt, Berlin, Leipzig, Wien, Stuttgart, 1921, Vol. IV, p. 305.
[20] *Simplicissimus*, bk. III, chap. 3.

"In war," Courage observes, "most people become worse rather than better,"[21] and she attributes this fact to the company which soldiers and camp followers keep. The point is worth noting. Grimmelshausen was not of the opinion that any abstract conditions account for human vice and depravity. It is quite concretely the example given by other men—what they do to you and others—that is corrupting. Such corruption—by bad example, by temptation, and as in the case of Courage, by humiliation—cannot occur without corruptibility, a general quality of human nature. Precisely for this reason man should avoid bad company. "Avoid bad company" is one of three pieces of advice given by a hermit to his son Simplicius, the young ignorant boy. War, to Grimmelshausen, meant above all, a tempting opportunity for young people to keep especially bad company.

Grimmelshausen depicted the disorder and corruption of the world, in peacetime as well as in war. He showed man in his blindness, his cruelty and suffering, and as a liar to both others and himself. He plumbed the depths of man's terror in this world. But time and again in his work, Grimmelshausen presented also fantasies of a good moral order. Sometimes such a dream emerges from the satirical depiction of the real, corrupted world. An example is the grand speech at the end of *The Council Chamber of Pluto*, in which Simplicissimus condemns the luxury, ostentation, and wastefulness at the courts.[22] At first glance this speech may seem to be but a high point of moralizing ardor, but the significance of the passage is thrown into relief by the absence of similar criticism in the conventional novels of the period. For example, Philipp von Zesen,

[21] *Courage, the Adventuress* (hereafter cited as *Courage*), chap. 9.
[22] "The Council Chamber of Pluto," *Simpliciana*, pp. 114-126.

[21]

in his *Assenat*, the story of Joseph, praised as exemplary statesmanship the usurious exploitation of the middle and lower strata of society during the seven lean years.

Sometimes the image of the good order emerges from the ironical ascription to the various professions of virtues they do not possess, as in the account of life on earth that Simplicissimus gives to the king of the submarine beings who inhabit the Mummelsee:[23] no priest is given to lust, all theologians resemble Hieronymus or Bede, the merchant is free of avarice, the innkeeper serves selflessly those who suffer hunger and thirst, the physician never seeks profit, but only the restoration of his patients' health, the craftsman is honest, the soldier does not rob and ruin the people but protects the fatherland.

What is the nature of the good order? When Simplicissimus comes to Switzerland, he holds the mere state of peace to be "paradise on earth,"[24] but Grimmelshausen was deeply convinced that the good order is utopian, because man is beyond reform. His evil nature asserts itself inexorably in peacetime as well as in war. This can be seen most clearly in the sixth book of *The Adventurous Simplicissimus* and in *The Enchanted Bird's-nest*. In no respect does man in these three books of the Simplician cycle, which depict life after the conclusion of the Peace of Westphalia, appear more contented than in the other books, where everything happens in the setting of the Thirty Years War. Of course, peace is preferable to war, but life is not essentially different, because man is neither better nor less subject to folly in peacetime than he is in war. It is this "pessimism" which gives to Grimmelshausen's portrait of man and to

[23] *Simplicissimus*, bk. v, chap. 15.
[24] *Ibid.*, bk. v, chap. 1.

his picture of war a perspective that eludes the children of the age of enlightenment.

When the captain of a Dutch ship discovers Simplicissimus on his paradisaical island and urges him to sail back to civilization, Simplicissimus, calling himself "a free person not subject to anyone"[25] refuses to return to Europe. "Here is peace, there is war," he says, and embarks upon an eloquent denunciation of civilized life. It becomes clear from this passage that Simplicissimus, the recluse, does not juxtapose the peace of the island with war in Europe, but with "civilized" life in general, whether in times of war or in peacetime: from the vantage point on the island, even peace in civilized or "real" life is a form of war. He says, "When I still lived in Europe . . . everything was full of war, fire, murder, robbery, looting, raping of women and girls. But when God in his goodness took away these scourges along with the terrible pestilence and the cruel hunger, giving to the poor and hard-pressed people noble peace, all the vices of lust made their appearance, such as eating, drinking, and gambling, whoring, sodomy, and adultery, and they brought on the whole swarm of the other vices until finally a condition was reached in which everyone publicly tried to become great by suppressing someone else, and no ruse, no fraud, no political artifice were spared; nor have I mentioned the worst: no hope for things to turn better remained. . . ."[26]

Grimmelshausen was of the opinion that man's nature makes the realization of the good order impossible. No other view of his work can be seriously entertained.

In Grimmelshausen's Simplician writings, as in the works of other satirists of the age, love is presented with

[25] *Continuatio*, ed. J. H. Scholte, Halle, 1939, chap. 26.
[26] *Ibid.*, chap. 27.

[23]

an uncompromising antifeminism which is Christian and middle class in origin. Love appears to be either utterly sinful or utterly ridiculous. Sexual activity is inevitable rather than enjoyable, even as the woman is indispensable for the propagation of the race, whereas love is nothing but rape, debauchery, filth, a carrier of disease, and the root of inconstancy and many vices. In general, the physical sphere is grotesquely enlarged, whereas the conventional novel of the baroque era in Germany tended to contract it. "The heroic-gallant novel never reaches love because of too much virtue, the naturalistic novel never does because of too much vice."[27] There is no parallel in 17th century German literature to Mme. de Lafayette's *La Princesse de Clèves* (1678); even in France it took about fifty years until the sensitive and lucid analysis of love in this extraordinary novel was matched.

Some critics have said that Grimmelshausen's "grossness" has no parallel in any Spanish novel and that his realism "knows no subdual of detail."[28] This opinion is incorrect on both counts. His so-called realism slights or suppresses whole regions of reality—landscapes, architecture, family life, all of upper-class life and large sectors of the life of the lower classes, including work. Grimmelshausen does not describe 17th century society. He is as little realistic as are the authors of the picaresque tales in Spain.[29] His realism, such as it is, is exaggerated, burlesque,

[27] Richard Alewyn, *op.cit.*, p. 172.

[28] Frank Wadleigh Chandler, *The Literature of Roguery* [1907], reprint New York, 1958, Vol. I, p. 30.

[29] The point that Grimmelshausen's Simplician writings are not "realistic" has been made most convincingly by Richard Alewyn, *op.cit.*, pp. 208 ff. On the difference between the picaresque and the realistic novel cf. also Antoine Adam, *Histoire de la Littérature Francaise au XVIIe Siècle*, Paris, 1956, tome I, pp. 138 ff. He says, "par plusieurs de

and obscene for the purpose of throwing his fantasies and his moral and religious concerns into relief.

The impression of grossness and "realism" is perhaps created in large part by the prominence of scatological imagery in Grimmelshausen's writings. In order not to misinterpret this aspect of his work it must first be understood that the inclusion of such material violated no moral taboo. Scatological imagery was vulgar and hence comical. It appears not only in many folk books, but also in comedies of the period that were written by distinguished poets like Gryphius,[30] and seen by the same audience that attended performances of tragic plays by the same authors. All satirical, comical, and picaresque writings emphasize the physical functions of man and abound with such imagery. Examples can be found in Quevedo's *Buscon*, if not in Aleman's *Guzman*, in Sorel's *Francion*, and in English tales of roguery.

In Grimmelshausen, and in the picaresque novel as well, scatological incidents furnish the most powerful scenes of humiliation. It seems that they do more than merely ridicule social distinction by pointing to common human frailties and natural functions that all men share alike. The victim in such scatological scenes is frequently re-

---

ses aspects les plus importants, le roman picaresque n'est pas réaliste." Nor are the *histoires comiques* realistic.

Richard Alewyn has also pointed out the difference between the picaresque novels and Grimmelshausen's Simplician novels. In the picaresque novel characters other than the picaro himself are strictly episodic. Simplicissimus is flanked by at least two important characters, Heartsbrother and Olivier. The typical picaro goes from one adventure to the next without any development of character. Courage's character changes.

[30] Andreas Gryphius, *Horribilicribrifax*, in *Die Deutsche Barock-komödie*, ed. W. Flemming, Leipzig, 1931. On the use of scatological humor in Gryphius cf. also the "Introduction" by W. Flemming, p. 18.

duced to a primitive state of helplessness. He is dragged through excrements and in this regard the fiercely aggressive function of 17th century comical literature leaves nothing to the imagination. Everything is presented in the most blatant directness to the senses: excrement is smelled, felt, heard, and even tasted. When it is felt, it is often by the face as if the noblest part of the human body is the preferred target of degradation.[31]

It is only in a social environment in which the demands of Christian morality do not interdict erotic pleasures that these scatological interests recede. Most writers who deal with erotic subjects do not indulge in descriptions of vomiting, flatulence, and soiling oneself or others. For example, the Renaissance novella, which explored the erotic freely, shunned on the whole the scatological realm.[32]

Grimmelshausen's description of all natural functions of the body fit the image of man as an animal that but for the power and grace of God would be devoid of spiritual life. At the same time, this spiritual life has an ethereal and synthetic quality in the Simplician tales, as though it could well be a superstitious delusion, whereas these same tales

[31] See, for example, *Courage*, chap. 17; *Des wunderbarlichen Vogelsnests Zweiter Teil* in *Grimmelshausens Werke*, ed. H. H. Borcherdt, Vol. 3 (hereafter cited as *Bird's-nest II*), chap. 7; cf. also *Francisco de Quevedo, The Life and Adventures of Don Pablos the Sharper*, tr. Mack Hendricks Singleton and others, in *Masterpieces of the Spanish Golden Age*, ed. Angel Flores, New York and Toronto: Rinehart Editions, 1957, p. 112; and Gryphius, *op.cit.*

[32] In his comments on Johann Beer's *Das Narrenspital* [1681], Hamburg: Rowohlts Klassiker, 1957, Richard Alewyn relates scatological humor "from the later Middle Ages to the end of the baroque" to "a repressed sexuality" (p. 147). The "hero" in *Das Narrenspital* may claim unique distinction by an unsurpassed performance in breaking wind. The point on repressed sexuality as an explanation of scatological humor was already made by Richard Alewyn in *Johann Beer*, pp. 174-175.

make it quite clear that there is nothing illusory about eating, vomiting, flatulence, defecating, and fornication. The pain of childbirth is the reality which remains of the woman's belief that she will give birth to the Messiah; dreams of peace on earth vanish in an itch that is caused by vermin; theological discussions end abruptly with a narrow escape from death; beauty is disfigured by syphilis; plans of marriage are thwarted by sudden loss of testicles or by unexpected threats of murder.

Grimmelshausen was, of course, neither an atheist nor a torchbearer of enlightenment. In many regards, the spirit of his Simplician tales points back, rather than forward, to religious skepticism and political disaffection in earlier times. It is related in spirit to *Reynke de Voss*, which Goethe called an unholy Bible of the world, and to *Till Eulenspiegel*, who when asked by his mother on his death-bed for a last word of wisdom gave her the most cynical advice that ever came from the mouth of a dying man.[33]

Grimmelshausen changed not only his name but also his religion. Some time between 1638, the first year which he spent in a strictly Catholic environment on the Upper Rhine, and 1649, the year of his marriage, he left the Lutheran Church. Neither the exact date nor the reasons for his conversion to Catholicism are known, but from the church records in Offenburg it is certain that he was a Catholic at the time of his marriage to Catherina Henninger, the daughter of a lieutenant of the guard. It does not seem prudent to attribute too much importance to his conversion.

[33] "Die muter sprach ach lieber sun gib mir dein süss ler da ich dein bei gedenken mag. Ulenspiegel sagt ia liebe muter wan du wilt deins gemachs thon, so ker den ars von dem wind so gat dir der gestank nit in die nass." (*Till Ulenspiegel* [1515], ed. Herman Knust, Neudrucke deutscher Literaturwerke, nos. 55-56, 1884, p. 140.)

Grimmelshausen's religious beliefs have been the subject of much controversy. Some have considered his work to be inspired by Protestant thought, many other critics have read him as a Catholic whose works are filled with the spirit of the Counter Reformation.[34] In one excellent study, the influence of Pelagianism has been detected in the Simplician writings and Grimmelshausen has even been called a nihilist,[35] whereas another eminent critic has found in his works "irenical understanding for the equal value of all faiths."[36] One student has taken Grimmelshausen for a man, who, like the lower classes of his epoch, was still engrossed in medieval ideas of the world as a realm of the Devil, of a united Christendom, and of Christian zeal to convert the infidels.[37] Still another student has stressed his progressiveness, saying that among all German satirists of the 17th century Grimmelshausen was the only one who looked forward to the unification of the Christian churches.[38] This meant attributing to him a spirit akin to

[34] Jakob Grimm (1785-1863) thought that Grimmelshausen's views were Protestant. J. H. Scholte, op.cit. (in Der Simplicissimus und sein Dichter) and many others are of the opinion that his writings reflect the Catholic spirit of the Counter-Reformation.

[35] Paul Gutzwiller, Der Narr bei Grimmelshausen, Bern: Francke Verlag, 1959, p. 90; on Pelagianism, p. 106: "kein wirklich religiöser Geist . . . nur äusserlich christlich"; on nihilism, p. 108: "Fast immer steht hinter dem Lachen das Nichts."

[36] Friedrich Gundolf, "Grimmelshausen und der Simplicissimus," Vierteljahrsschrift für Literaturwissenschaft und Geistesgeschichte, 1923, Vol. I, p. 354. About irenical tendencies in Gryphius, cf. Carl Viëtor, Probleme der deutschen Barockliteratur, Leipzig, 1928, p. 30; in Harsdörffer: ibid., p. 47.

[37] Siegfried Streller, op.cit.; cf. also James Franklin Hyde, "The Religious Thought of Johann Jacob Christoffel von Grimmelshausen as Expressed in the Simplicianische Schriften." Dissertation, Indiana University, 1960 (typescript).

[38] Hildegarde Wichert, Johann Balthasar Schupp and the Baroque Satire in Germany, New York: King's Crown Press, Columbia University, 1952, p. 112.

that of men like Calixtus[89] and Leibniz instead of seeing him as a superannuated crusader.

His work contains several striking passages in which the quarrels between the Christian churches are ridiculed. One of these passages occurs at the very end of the Simplician cycle. On a journey up the Rhine a Catholic priest and a Protestant minister join forces in an attempt to convert a Jew who accompanies them. "Although this fellow had studied a lot and was well informed, he did not really want to argue. He said that the Christians should glue their own schisms together before trying to convert to their religion the Jews who were united. For even if one of them wanted to become a Christian, he would not know which Christian he should turn to, since each claimed to be the best."[40]

There is almost general agreement that Grimmelshausen had little use for the established churches. If anything, he regarded the hermit, rather than the priest or the monk, as a true Christian, but then in baroque literature the hermit often is a sage in Christian garb. Grimmelshausen presented neither priests nor monks as venerable characters. At one point old Simplicissimus bursts out in anger that he would rather have his son become a soldier than see him enter a monastery.[41]

The Christians whom Grimmelshausen admired most were not those who belonged to any of the established churches, but the Hutterian Brethren, an anabaptist sect, founded in Switzerland in 1525, which suffered much

[89] On Calixtus cf. Ernst Ludwig Th. Henke, *Georg Calixtus und seine Zeit*, Halle, 1853.

[40] *Bird's-nest II*, chap. 27.

[41] *Grimmelshausens Das wunderbarliche Vogel-nest, Erster Teil* (hereafter cited as *Bird's-nest I*), ed. J. H. Scholte, Halle, 1931, p. 111.

[29]

persecution well into the 18th century. Their faith forbade them to bear arms, private property was abolished in their communities, the sexes were separated, and they developed a communistic system of rearing children. Grimmelshausen described the life and institutions of the "Hungarian" Hutterites in loving detail and with astonishing accuracy.[42] It has been suggested that his information may have come from an itinerant member of the sect.[43] Simplicissimus declared that their heretical life, which he called "seemingly Christian," "excelled the monastic one." As the most learned critic of Grimmelshausen's views on this subject has said, his references to heresy and the mere appearance of Christianity among these anabaptists were probably made "pro Ecclesia et Pontifice."[44] Simplicissimus declared that he would have liked to live like a Hutterite brother, if it could only be done, "under the protection of the authorities," adding that as one of its members he would gladly have surrendered all his worldly possessions to such a community. But his stepfather, a peasant, warned him that he would never succeed in getting enough people to join!

More than any other passage in Grimmelshausen's writings, the chapter in *The Adventurous Simplicissimus* which describes the life of the Hungarian anabaptists is convincing testimony of the author's attachment to Christian moral teaching, but even this chapter proves nothing about Grimmelshausen's belief in any Christian dogma. His admiration is confined to matters of practical conduct. In all his Simplician writings, Grimmelshausen has little to say about God's mercy or justice, and nothing to say

[42] *Simplicissimus*, bk. v, chap. 19.
[43] A. J. F. Zieglschmid, "Die ungarischen Wiedertäufer bei Grimmelshausen," *Zeitschrift für Kirchengeschichte*, Vol. 59, pp. 352-387.
[44] *Ibid.*, p. 386.

about the Holy Trinity, the revelation of truth, the sacraments, or about the power of faith. He wrote as though "acts of God" cannot be anything but disasters rather than causes of joy like the song of the nightingale or a good meal. Whatever he says seriously about religion is pale and dry compared with the lively colors to be found in his humorous tales and anecdotes.

If Grimmelshausen was cool toward the organized religion of the Christian churches he seems to have had nothing but smiles for various facets of Christian theological doctrine which conflicted with the observation of nature, with common sense and self-interest. A certain measure of such folk-blasphemy, as it were, has lived through the ages in proverb, song, and euphemism. On a few matters of great relevance to Christian theological doctrine, Grimmelshausen's views bordered on blasphemy. This fact is concealed from plain sight by a cloak of orthodoxy[45] and even the moral rigor of the man was tempered by grim laughter and by fascination that natural, rather than moral, behavior, exerted upon him. He wrote about man as he naturally is.

COURAGE

On the title page of *Courage, the Adventuress*, Grimmelshausen indicates that in this novel the reader will find the account of a descending life. As a young woman Courage is the wife of a cavalry captain, then she marries a captain of foot soldiers, then a lieutenant, thereafter she becomes a sutler-woman, next the wife of a musketeer, and finally a gypsy.

[45] See Introduction, below, and Hans Speier, *op.cit.*

Different from the heroes of the picaresque novel, who proceed from one adventure to the next without change in character, Courage does change under the influence of experience. In the early part of the novel she is not the evil woman she later turns into. To be sure, in part it is her native endowment that makes her a lustful creature, envious, greedy, and vindictive, but in part the evil in her emerges from senseless misfortune and in response to the cruelty of men.

Courage's exploits equal or excel those of men. In battle she is more valiant than her male companions, on marauding expeditions more daring, as a thief more resourceful and cunning. In most of her enterprises she is mistress, rather than helper; often she directs men to assist her. Her vitality is inexhaustible. When at the end of her career she has reached the status of an outcaste, she remains a queen, if only of the gypsies, aged, but still beautiful in appearance, her spirit unbroken and her skill unrivaled.

Whenever she fights men, whether with her fists as a young girl, with sword and pistol in battle later, with a cudgel after one of her many wedding nights, with a knife in the woods, or with wit, false tears, and pretty words— she almost always wins. Almost without exception men who oppose her are beaten up or humiliated, taken prisoner, killed, duped, or exploited by her. Courage is as much an amazon as a harlot.

Indeed, she has many of the qualities of the heroines in the idealistic novels of the baroque era. Like them, she is a manlike, vigorous creature, a virago in the sense in which Pope still used this word:

> To arms, to arms the fierce virago cries
> And swift as lightening to combat flies.

The virago was the ideal of the Renaissance, fashioned after illustrious ancient models. Viragos appear not only in Ariosto's and Bojardo's heroic poetry, but also in life: women like Caterina Sforza—"prima donna d'Italia" to her contemporaries—or Isabella d'Este, the wife of Marchese Francesco Gonzaga, were admired for both their beauty and their courage in meeting the formidable risks of their careers.[46] The third book of Castiglione's *Cortegiano* contains the portrait of the perfect lady at court and the Renaissance tribute to the civilizing influence that women exerted on men, but it also presents many great ladies in contemporary Italy, as well as in antiquity, who showed "virtue and prowess" in "the stormes of fortune."[47]

In the German idealistic novel of the 17th century, the Renaissance ideal is still potent: many heroines are amazons.[48] Even the middle-class Protestant, Andreas Heinrich Buchholtz, shows Valisca, his heroine, to be the equal of man in the fields of science and music as well as in battle. Disguised as a beautiful young man on a journey to Prague, she "does miracles" fighting off the highwaymen who assault her. At the Persian court, again in men's clothing, she shines in the arts of fencing and shooting with bow and arrow. She cruelly kills three Persian servants, defends her honor against the attack of a lover by thrusting her "bread knife" into his heart, and slays robbers with lightning speed. She fights gloriously as a general in battle, her beautiful hair falling down to her shoul-

[46] Jacob Burckhardt, *Die Kultur der Renaissance in Italien*, ed. Walter Goetz, Leipzig: Kröner Verlag, 1925, 14th edition, p. 271.

[47] Baldassare Castiglione, *The Book of the Courtier*, Done into English by Sir Thomas Hoby, anno 1561 (Everyman's Library), p. 218.

[48] For the following discussion cf. Antoine Claire Jungkunz, *Menschendarstellung im deutschen höfischen Roman des Barock*. Germanische Studien, Heft 160, Berlin, 1937, pp. 42, 78-90, 189, 220.

[33]

ders, a precious sword and a quiver of arrows at her side. In Buchholtz's novel, not only is Valisca a vigaro, but also Hercules himself has female qualities: for all his manliness, he is beautiful, like a young girl, dances daintily, and sometimes fights clad in the garb of an amazon.

Viragos appear also in the novels of D. C. von Lohenstein, who gave this description of Thusnelda through the eyes of Marbod, her lover: "The day before, Marbod had looked admiringly at Thusnelda only (!) as a woman, but this day he saw her on horseback as a valiant heroine. He had honored her as a half-divine being, now he was compelled to worship her as a goddess, for she sat astride her horse as a true amazon; in the race and in the shooting contest she did better than all, and she slew twice as much game as anyone else. For no stag was too swift for her, no bear too cruel, no lynx too terrible."[49]

Anton Ulrich's Aramena, too, at one time goes to the field leading a group of her female court attendants, "a marvellous host of the most beautiful ladies in the world." The amazon motif recedes in Anton Ulrich's second great novel, *Die Römische Oktavia*, as it does in H. A. von Zigler's *Asiatische Banise*, and Philipp von Zesen's novels. Johann Beer abandoned the heroic, idealistic mood and discovered new subjects of everyday life for literary treatment. But even in Beer's works amazons reappear, though with less bombast and fanfare. For example, in one of Beer's major works "a strange cavalier," his visor closed, suddenly enters the scene to help the noble friends who fight the villain and his evil companions. The stranger wounds and captures the wicked man, and when the friends, rejoicing about their victory, want to thank the stranger, he lifts his visor. Then, the friends all grow pale.

[49] Quoted in *ibid.*, p. 88.

They behold "the beautiful Amalia, disguised in knightly armor." Needless to say, beautiful Amalia is loved by one of the cavaliers whose valor she excelled so impressively in the fight.[50]

If the modern reader is amused by this theatrical display of heroism, just as he might be amused by the theatricality of the heroes and heroines in distress—when they pray with tears streaming down their cheeks or lift their eyes up to the Heavenly Father in martyrdom—he is in a mood which Grimmelshausen seems to have shared. For Courage is at least as much a caricature and mockery of the amazon to be found in the conventional baroque novel as she is a picaresque character. Her relation to the ideal virago resembles that of Don Quixote to the knightly code. Like the once much-admired ladies who populate the idealistic novel, Courage is an amazon, but she is a counter-heroine. She displays the qualities of a wild virago, in the modern sense of that term, while still retaining all the physical features of the ideal: radiant beauty, physical prowess, intelligence, and manlike energy. Like the amazons in the conventional novel, she is indestructible in trial and misfortune. But in three respects she is a counter-heroine.

First, despite her noble, if somewhat tainted, origin she moves in a socially undistinguished milieu, resembling in this regard all of Grimmelshausen's main characters. She is never at court, and when she meets an ambassador, spends some short time at a nobleman's castle, or lives for a while like a woman of means in town, it is for her sexual enjoyment and the amassing of a fortune.

Second, it is not virtue that is put to test after test in

[50] Johann Beer, *Kurtzweilige Sommer-Täge* [1683], ed. Wolfgang Schmidt, Halle, 1958, p. 116.

[35]

Courage's life, as in the conventional heroic career. If anything is tried, it is her ability to survive as a victim of a
blind and impenetrable destiny. A plaything of senseless
fate, which tosses her up and down in quick and violent
motion, Courage is flung back and forth from the heights
of prosperity to the depths of poverty, from health and
beauty to disfiguring illness, from safety and comfort to
hunger and humiliation. Pitting her wit and vitality
against misfortune, she becomes in the end an outcast,
because neither man nor woman can win in a world in
which God is silent and which is more surely of the Devil
than of God. But she survives and, like Simplicissimus,
lives forever.

Finally, by all ordinary standards of Christian morality,
which Grimmelshausen himself reasserts continuously, if
only in the interstices of his tale, Courage is corrupt and
wicked, whereas the heroines of the idealistic novel remain
of untarnished virtue, no matter how often and how cruelly
this virtue is put into thrilling jeopardy. Courage does not
want to be virtuous. She has wild, unsatiable appetites for
men and riches, but no conscience. Her moral character
owes nothing either to religious teaching or to Descartes's
theory of passion, but almost everything to Galen's views
of the human temperament. "I cannot take out my gall,"
she says, "as the butcher turns the pig's stomach inside out
to cleanse it." She is full of lust and avarice and envy, and
most easily aroused to fierce anger; she is evil, although it
should be stressed that she never inflicts pain on others
without provocation. But she is natural, and this cannot be
said of the heroines whose Christian conscience she in fact
denies with every fiber of her existence.

Like Defoe's Mrs. Flanders, Grimmelshausen's Courage
is a challenge to morality, but Moll Flanders belongs al-

ready to the age in which virtue began to be identified largely with chastity in women. She is a middle-class heroine. By contrast, Courage boldly calls virtue in the older, broader sense into question; in the account of her life she rocks even the Christian foundation of virtue. Moll Flanders has many children and finishes her dissolute life as a dowager, who has become respectable through remorse and wealth. Grimmelshausen created Courage barren, and he was aware of it. Childless, Courage is more of a man, as it were, without becoming any less desirable as a woman in the eyes of men. In the end, Courage prefers the life of a gypsy to that of a respectable widow, and so perhaps did Grimmelshausen. While Moll Flanders in her reckless life has only three principal sources of income—needlework, men as husbands and lovers, and theft—Courage adds to these booty in war, which she gains sword in hand. There is, of course, nothing manly about Mrs. Flanders, and the risks she takes lack grandeur.

The gulf separating Courage and Moll Flanders can perhaps best be shown by the involuntary, physical expression of their feelings. For all her wickedness Moll Flanders cries and blushes and faints hardly less often than her female, middle-class readers were prone to do. Her sickly femininity easily falls prey to lingering fevers when she receives adverse news. This woman, whom Defoe gives "that unmusical, harsh-sounding title of whore," weeps on every possible occasion, including the hour in which fear of being hanged overcomes her. Courage, too, weeps, especially in the early part of her career, but almost always in order to deceive men. She cries by design, her tears are a trick that never fails her. Only twice does Courage cry to express despair, the first time when she is among troops who are forced to surrender to the enemy and again after she has

[37]

been utterly debased, humiliated, beaten and cruelly abused many times by a mob of drunken, brutal officers and servants for several nights in succession. Courage never faints or blushes and yet, despite her vengefulness, her insatiable sexual appetite, and her excessive abandon, at the end of her enormous tale she appears to the reader as a radiantly beautiful woman of rare natural power, unquenchable zest for life, and inexhaustible vital resources. Courage is her just name in the extraordinary equivocation of meaning that Grimmelshausen in a master stroke of genius and humor bestowed upon it.

To the modern reader the name of Courage is most familiar from Bertolt Brecht's play, *Mother Courage and Her Children*. Anna Fierling is called Mother Courage because she meets all adversity and misfortune with ever new hope and resolution to make a miserable profit in her trade. She stands for all the downtrodden who believe that they have nothing but their own courage to lose.[51]

The meaning which Grimmelshausen attached to the name Courage is quite different. Courage is first introduced as a young girl under the name of Libuschka. While dressed like a boy to escape rape she is called Janco. As Janco she becomes a captain's servant and gets into a fight with another boy at the sutler's. "When we were in the thick of it," she says, "this fellow grabbed me between the legs, because he wanted to get hold of my tool that I did not have." She prevails over him. Later in his quarters the captain asks Janco, whom he still takes for a boy, why she had beaten up her opponent so terribly. She replies, "Because he tried to grasp my courage which no other man

---

[51] Bertolt Brecht, *Mother Courage and Her Children*: A Chronicle of the Thirty Years' War, English version by Eric Bentley, New York: Grove Press, Inc. (Evergreen Book no. 372), 1963, pp. 75-76.

has ever touched with his hand."[52] Then she confides in the young captain that she is a girl who disguised herself as a boy merely to escape abuse by the soldiers. She begs him to protect her honor, and he promises to do so but to her delight does not keep his word.

When the captain understands the meaning of the word "courage," with which the girl had "so colorfully described the emblem of her sex," he cannot help laughing at her and calls her Courage. Try as she will to rid herself of that name it clings to her forever. The name Courage, then, stands for what Grimmelshausen regarded as the physiological site of vitality, bravery, and godlessness.

Grimmelshausen's choice of Courage as a picaresque character for one of his main works invites some speculation. Today, it is considered unlikely that *Courage, the Adventuress* owes much to Francisco de Ubeda's *Picara Justina* (1603), although Grimmelshausen may have been familiar with the long-winded German translation of that work. Ubeda's novel was an avowed imitation of *The Celestina* (1449)[53] and other picaresque Spanish tales,

[52] *Courage*, chap. 3. All main characters in the first eight books of the Simplician cycle of novels have significant names. Both Simplicissimus and Courage have many names, each appropriate to the respective stage of their careers. The meaning of this practice in Grimmelshausen's work has been commented upon by many modern critics. See, for example, Werner Welzig, *Beispielhafte Figuren. Tor, Abenteurer und Einsiedler bei Grimmelshausen*, Graz-Köln, 1963, pp. 42 ff. On the question of significant names in general, see Franz Dornseiff. "Redende Namen," *Zeitschrift für Namenforschung*, 1940, Vol. xvi, pp. 24 ff. and 215 ff.

[53] An English edition of *Tragi-Comediade Calisto y Melibar*, popularly known as *The Celestina* (after the character of the procuress in the play), has been prepared by Lesley Byrd Simpson, Berkeley and Los Angeles: University of California Press, 1955, paperbound edition, 1959.

whereas Grimmelshausen's *Courage, the Adventuress*, like *The Celestina*, is a masterpiece in its own right. Even if Grimmelshausen's work depended closely on *Picara Justina*, however, the question would still remain why the author's imagination was captured by a female picaro. Why did Grimmelshausen despite all his ostensible contempt for love and women, create such an extraordinarily vivid picture of a manly woman whose beauty and vitality excelled the evil in her? No one who has read *Courage, the Adventuress* will escape the conclusion that he was fascinated by Courage. He admired her.[54] While condemning sex in all his writings, in this novel he succeeded in presenting at the same time the portrait of an irresistible woman, who reacts with lusty sexual abandon and revenge to terrible abuse by men and yet remains human and attractive to the reader.

It is striking that both Simplicius and Courage, the tomboy, have their first sexual experiences in homosexual situations. Later, Courage repeatedly mentions her burning desire to wear man's clothing and to be in every way like a man. Grimmelshausen himself had a keen interest in hermaphrodites and in the changing of sex. References to hermaphrodites occur in several of his works. In his tale which deals with the birth of a false Jewish messiah the child turns out to be a girl. When the gullible Jews in Amsterdam believe that God may change this girl into a young man at the age of maturity, Grimmelshausen points

[54] The point that Grimmelshausen admired Courage is also made by Siegfried Streller, *op.cit.*, p. 195. Streller speaks of Grimmelshausen's "unconfessed sympathies for this hated and loved character" and refers to the magnificent description of Courage (then already 66 years old) by the Swiss clerk in *Grimmelshausens Springinsfeld*, ed. J. H. Scholte, Halle, 1928 (hereafter cited as *Skipinthefield*), chap. 4.

[40]

out that it would be no miracle for a female child to develop male sex characteristics.[55]

It should also be noted that the only feelings of close attachment to another human being that Grimmelshausen ever describes are those prevailing between father and son and between two young men. In this respect, as a writer on friendships, Grimmelshausen is unique among the novelists of the 17th century. When he speaks of the friendship between Simplicissimus and Heartsbrother he finds words expressing deep emotion, but all his words on heterosexual love are detached or cynical and arouse either disgust or raucous laughter.

Finally, there is a most curious description of Skipinthefield in distress. Tortured by his love for Courage, Skipinthefield enters the woman's tent under the pretense of wanting a pot of wine. Grimmelshausen describes his appearance as seen through Courage's eyes as follows: "He looked so pale and disconsolate then as though he had just gotten a child without having or knowing its father, and without having either milk or meal-pap for it."[56] Along with everything else that has been said, this strangely ambiguous sentence might lend credence to the suggestion that Grimmelshausen had ambivalent feelings toward women and sex. Perhaps he felt even dimly anxious or uncertain about his own sexual wishes.

But these are speculations. There are few baroque au-

---

[55] *Bird's-nest II*, chap. 18. Cf. also the story of Aemilia who after twelve years of marriage changes her sex and becomes Aemilius (*Ewigwährender Kalender*, ed. Engelbert Hegaur, Munich, 1925, pp. 396-397).

[56] "Er sahe so bleich und trostlos aus, als wann er kürzlich ein Kind bekommen und keinen Vatter, Mehl noch Milch darzu gehabt oder gewüsst hätte" (*Die Landstörzerin Courasche*, ed. J. H. Scholte, Halle, 1923, chap. 15).

[41]

thors who do not invite similar speculations. In many conventional baroque novels as in comedy and farce, disguise and confusion of the sexes are common. Homosexual allusions are far more prominent in Callot's engravings than in Grimmelshausen's Simplician writings, and other writers of the period, like Harsdörffer, were intrigued by hermaphrodites.

Leaving these speculations aside, it certainly was not Grimmelshausen's main intention in *Courage, the Adventuress* to parody the conventional literary motif of the amazon. While he succeeded in doing that, he had a still more important purpose in mind. He stated his intention clearly through the mouth of Courage in the grand opening chapter of the novel. The old whore explains that the sole purpose of her confession is to avenge herself on Simplicissimus. At the same time she laughs derisively at the idea that her monstrous confession might be taken as an act of penitence: her vengefulness involves not only Simplicissimus, but God himself. She defies both. The intensity of her feeling is conveyed by Grimmelshausen by a whole series of rogueries in which revenge is the main motive and with startling force, by Courage's observation that her heart is like her body: when hurt, it takes a long time to heal.[57]

[57] In many of his works Grimmelshausen's interest in revenge is so intense that one cannot help wondering whether he was himself a resentful and vengeful man. He had red hair, which according to a very old and widespread superstition was a sign of evil character. Since superstition holds especially the lower classes in its grip, it is likely that he was exposed to the full force of this prejudice in the army camps and taverns, the villages and the countryside where he spent most of his life. It is known that a colleague of his in the employ of the Schauenburg family derisively called him "the red steward" (*"der rote Schaffner"*). Grimmelshausen wrote a humorous pamphlet in fierce de-

Courage's soul is entirely untroubled by the dissolute life she has led. If she confesses anything it is her godlessness. She fears God as little as men. She loves life and is not afraid of death. Thoughts of punishment and damnation, of divine justice and hellfire, never curb her worldly passion. She loves money, but not her neighbors, and she says so. Her life is exuberantly evil. Nature has made her so, and neither the magistrate nor the priests, neither man nor God, are able to change it. By telling her story in order to avenge herself, she makes a mockery of the act of confession in the Christian sense.

Grimmelshausen's novel is cruder and coarser than Defoe's but, paradoxically, less lascivious. In *Moll Flanders* the most shocking episode is the marriage of the heroine to a man who unbeknownst to her is her brother. One of Mrs. Flanders' many children is the fruit of this incestuous relationship. But in the end her brother conveniently dies, giving Mrs. Flanders a chance at social respectability which she presumably deserves by her riches, her enterprising

---

fense of red beards, "Der Bart-Krieg." Grimmelshausen's authorship of this pamphlet was proved only in 1940 by Manfred Koschlig, "Der Bart-Krieg—Ein Werk Grimmelshausen," *Neophilologus*, Vol. xxiv, pp. 42 ff. ("Der Bart Krieg" is included in *Simpliciana*, pp. 128-148). At least one perceptive literary historian, Walter Muschg (*Tragische Literaturgeschichte*, Bern, 1948, pp. 265-268) has suggested that Grimmelshausen must have regarded his red hair as a misfortune. Muschg mentions in this connection a number of writers who may have felt their physical deformity as a stigma; and he suggests that their work may have been influenced by the cripple's hatred of the healthy and by feelings fluctuating between "horror of themselves, extreme sensitivity and cynical conceit." He points out that "many great satirists and polemicists had such a stigma." Excluding from Muschg's list those writers who were repulsively ugly, there remain the cripples: Aesop, Thomas Murner, Scarron, Pope, Lichtenberg, Gottfried Keller, Kierkegaard. The name of Quevedo may be added: he was lame.

commercial talent, and by the confession and repentance of her sins in Newgate Prison. It is inconceivable that Grimmelshausen could have stooped to thrill his readers with the cheap pornography of inadvertent incest. For *The Enchanted Bird's-nest* Grimmelshausen borrowed from Bandello a shocking scatological story, in which a man takes revenge in the filthiest possible manner on his unfaithful wife, but the German author did not borrow from the Italian, as he could have, the story of an incestuous relationship, a tale that in plot and elegant execution far exceeds Defoe's prurient adventure.

The most shocking incidents in the life of Courage are not those in which refined tastes or affectations are offended, but those in which religious propriety is flaunted. The supreme instance is the extraordinary contract in which Courage makes a mockery of the sacrament of marriage. The musketeer who becomes her man under conditions stipulated in this contract must not only pledge submission to her in all affairs of the household, but also grant her the right to remain a whore, in order to get the phantom of a spouse. This perversion of Christian marriage results in the utter degradation of the musketeer to the status of a servant, thief, and mock husband. The woman whom he must treat as his wife insists on his own cuckoldom in the marriage contract. Moreover, Courage exercises her right to give him a name of her own choosing that marks him forever. The burlesque humor of this marriage arrangement cannot hide its fierce, shocking affront at the religious sanction of the relation between the sexes.

It is evident that Grimmelshausen was fully aware of the boldness of his conceit. He carefully prepared the reader for the incredible contract by dwelling first in detail upon the infatuation of the musketeer and the manner in which Courage cunningly exploits it for her purposes. In these passages of the book Grimmelshausen displays great power as a satirist of polite conversation. When the acceptance of the contract by the wretched musketeer is thus made credible, Grimmelshausen interrupts his narrative to issue a pious warning to "honest Christians" not to follow Courage's example!

Courage, the Adventuress, like all novels of the Simplician cycle, abounds with Christian warnings. They occur in prefaces and postscripts and as insertions in the main body of his tales. Since the use of such apologetic material is traditional among satirists[58] to justify their colorful depiction of that which is disapproved in society on moral, political, or religious grounds, Grimmelshausen's effort to dissociate himself by pious words from the evil he describes with so much gusto and humor should not distract the attention of the critical reader from the impious implications of his tales. In *Courage, the Adventuress* moral and religious protestations are made with particular insistence just prior to the description of the extraordinary marriage contract and in "The Author's Postscript" which concludes the novel. This Postscript is taken almost literally from *Piazza Universale* by Tomaso Garzoni and thus is written in borrowed prose like the sonorously Christian ending of the fifth book of *The Adventurous Simplicissimus,* which Grimmelshausen took verbatim from Guevara. As one critic put it, the curiosity of Grimmelshausen's reader "is legitimized by a moral superstructure which pacifies his conscience and thus leaves him free to enjoy pure adventure."[59] We may add that this superstructure protects the author from the wrath of censorious readers who lack his impious humor.

[58] Hans Ehrenzeller, *op.cit.*
[59] Hildegarde Wichert, *op.cit.,* p. 140.

THE FALSE MESSIAH[60]

The False Messiah takes up nine of the twenty-seven chapters in Grimmelshausen's last work, *The Enchanted Bird's-nest*, Part II (1675). It is an independent novella, which at least once, in 1920, was published separately under the title *Die Judennovelle*; for reasons that will become evident, the title *The False Messiah* is more appropriate. Literary historians have paid little attention to this story although it is a novella of great distinction, a tale of considerable interest to students of seventeenth century beliefs and superstitions, and an imaginative treatment of an ancient irreverent dream of man.

The subject of *The False Messiah* is a battle between nature and religion, or to put it more specifically, between unbridled sexual appetite and religious beliefs. This battle, which nature wins by resorting to an outrageous ruse, can be described also as a confrontation of two different kinds of folly. The folly of superstition consists in embracing false beliefs, which sustain false fears and vain hopes and thus stand in the way of good sense and true faith. To the consequences of unbridled appetites, all great fools bear witness: Rabelais' Panurge, Shakespeare's Falstaff, Grimmelshausen's Simplicissimus (in his youth), and many others. All of them enjoy food and wine and sleep.[61] So do, characteristically, all picaros; in Lazarillo de Tormes loaves of bread are the face of God and it is said that the dead are taken to the house "where they neither eat nor

[60] Grimmelshausen does not give any separate title to this story.

[61] Cf. Walter Kaiser, *Praisers of Folly: Erasmus, Rabelais, Shakespeare*, Cambridge: Harvard University Press, 1963.

[46]

drink."[62] Nor are fools in the habit of otherwise defying nature. Indeed, many of the great fools in literature boast of their amorous exploits, in contrast to Christian moralists who, particularly in the seventeenth century, found passionate love "to be nothing but folly."[63]

Like the first three novels of the Simplician cycle, the last two, parts I and II of *The Enchanted Bird's-nest*, consist in the main of a series of adventurous tales told by picaresque anti-heroes; but the two narrators of *The Bird's-nest*—a young halberdier in the first part and a merchant in the second—do not claim the same attention as do Simplicissimus, Courage, or Skipinthefield. Grimmelshausen attributed great importance to the significance of names.[64] The main characters in all his other Simplician novels carry names that signify their nature, or rather the specific roles in the human comedy which Grimmelshausen assigned to them. When these roles change, so do their names: Simplicissimus has at least four other names—boy, Simplicius or Simplex, the Hunter, Beau Alman; and Courage has two—Mistress Libuschka and Janco. In the light of these precedents, it is not unimportant that the young halberdier and the merchant remain

[62] "The Life and Adventures of Lazarillo de Tormes," in Mendoza, *Lazarillo de Tormes*, tr. Thomas Roscoe, and Mateo Aleman, *Guzman d'Alfarasche*, 2 vols.; London: J. C. Nimmo and Bain, n.d., vol. I, p. 59.

[63] Francisco de Quevedo, *Visions*, tr. Sir Roger L'Estrange and intro. J. M. Cohen, Fontwell, Sussex: The Centaur Press, 1963, p. 67. (These words are the conclusion of Vision IV, "Of Loving Fools.") Quevedo was born in Madrid in 1580. He wrote his powerful picaresque novel *La vida del Buscon* and his *Sueños* or *Visions* while still in his twenties, and was translated into German before he was translated into English. H. M. Moscherosch was the author of the German adaptation of the *Sueños*.

[64] Cf. above pp. 38-39.

nameless. The center of the last two books of the Simplician cycle is, as their title indicates, a bird's-nest rather
than a particular picaro or a picara. Before turning to the
story of *The False Messiah*, let us look at this magical
object, this bird's-nest.

In many different lands we encounter the beliefs that
certain plants, stones, and other objects, such as rings,
have the power to make their owner invisible. When
leaves or twigs of such plants or stones are carried by a
siskin, a raven, or some other bird into its nest, the nest
itself assumes magical potency and becomes invisible. Invisibility is always closely associated with the divine and
its opposite, the satanic, just as there is a close relationship
between soul and shadow, shadow and mirror, mirror
and truth. Casting no shadow is a sign of non-corporeal-
ity, a quality of God and in certain countries of the devil,
a characteristic of saints according to the Persians and of
Mohammed according to Arabic tales. Similarly, in the
folklore of many lands people who are allied to, or have
studied with, the Devil cast no shadow: they have lost
their souls.

While the magical object and the person who carries
it are invisible, their shadows and their reflections are
not. The mirror image of the magically invisible person
can be seen in water or in a looking-glass. This notion
may derive either from the belief in the purifying power
of water and its equivalent, the mirror, or from the
identification of the mirror image with the non-corporeal
soul of the subject. In various languages the word for
shadow also means mirror image. Often the mirror is
believed to show everything that is hidden and mysterious,
and to be itself a magical instrument for seeing what is

beyond the natural power of the eye to perceive.[65] Thus, in Rembrandt's famous etching, Dr. Faustus watches the appearance of the sign of the Holy Spirit in a looking-glass. It has been suggested that Rembrandt's inspiration for this etching may have come from I Corinthians 13:12 in which Paul compares man's knowledge with looking into a mirror.[66] What he sees is enigmatic, in need of interpretation: "*fidimus nunc per speculum in aenigmate*: for now we see through a glass, darkly."

Probably Grimmelshausen was in some regards a super-stitious man himself, but in any event he was too good a storyteller not to use for dramatic effect superstitions that could be counted on to keep his readers spellbound. In following this practice he gave voice to hopes and fears among the people of his time; even today his works can be studied with great benefit as source books of beliefs current in the second half of the seventeenth century, particularly in the lower and middle regions of society. In three books of the Simplician cycle various aspects of the belief in invisibility are preserved for students of folk-lore, and much of what is now known about the super-stition in Germany is derived from Grimmelshausen: the discovery of the nest through its reflection in the waters of a brook;[67] the protection of the hidden magic stone by folding the nest into a handkerchief;[68] the ap-pearance of the second invisible owner, the halberdier, as

---

[65] See Hanns Bächthold-Stäubli, "Spiegel," *Handwörterbuch des deutschen Aberglaubens*, vol. IX, Berlin, 1938-1941, pp. 547-577.

[66] Martin Bojanowski, "Der Spiegel in Rembrandts Faustradierung," *Deutsche Vierteljahrsschrift für Literaturwissenschaft*, vol. XVIII, 1940, pp. 467-469.

[67] *Skipinthefield*, chap. 13.

[68] *Bird's-nest I*, p. 4; *Bird's-nest II*, chap. 3.

a mirror image in the looking-glass of a lady;[69] and the final destruction of the nest by a priest who drops it from a bridge into the Rhine River.[70] Grimmelshausen, however, wrote neither for folklorists nor merely for readers wishing to be entertained. As we shall see, he used the fantastic notion of the invisibility of certain persons to convey his ideas on man's relation to nature and God. In his hands the miraculous nest turned into a device for exploring beliefs more momentous than the attribution of magical properties to stones, nests, and mirrors.

The first part of *The Enchanted Bird's-nest* consists of a series of incidents in which the young halberdier observes people from all walks of life. Invisible by virtue of the bird's-nest in his possession, he is able to see them when they think they are unobserved. A nobleman and a young lady, both of them impoverished, try to trick each other into marriage by pretending to be rich. An old grandmother instructs a young beggar how to profit from charity by pretending to share whatever faith prevails in the place where he happens to be: "Lutheran or Catholic or Calvinist." The young wife of an old steward laments the news that her sick husband will not recover just after she has confided to her mother that she wished him dead. A parson tries to seduce the wife of a parishioner. A monastery is riddled by evil intrigues.[71] Two students of theology and law, while disputing the beliefs of the Pre-Adamites are held up by a highwayman and found less well prepared to face death than they are to discuss heresy.

Folly, hypocrisy, and sin pass before the eyes of the

[69] *Bird's-nest I*, p. 63.

[70] *Bird's-nest II*, chap. 27.

[71] In *Bird's-nest I*, p. 111, Simplicissimus compares life at court and life in a monastery with life in prison.

halberdier. He is in the position of the dreamer in Francisco de Quevedo's fifth *Vision,* "Of the World," who is led by an old man called "The Undeceiver-General" to "the Hypocrites' Walk," there to behold the "difference between things themselves and their appearances."[72] It is important to note, however, that Grimmelshausen's social panorama, besides being more varied than Quevedo's, serves a more radical purpose than that of the Spanish satirist. The halberdier and the merchant do not merely have satirical dreams; both of them can make themselves invisible at will, and since invisibility is a divine-satanic quality, the two parts of *The Enchanted Bird's-nest* are books involving God and the Devil. Like God, the halberdier is omniscient about the human heart. He learns secrets kept from ordinary mortals by simulation and dissimulation. He is able to unmask the people who hide their true faces and sees them in their nakedness.

In the age of enlightenment, not many years after Grimmelshausen's death in 1676, concern with the practice of unmasking others became a fashionable subject. In 1692, Christian Thomasius offered to Frederick III, Elector of Brandenburg, "the new inventon of a science, well founded and highly necessary for the commonweal, of how to recognize in ordinary conversation the secrets hidden in the hearts of other people, even against their will."[73]

Thomasius explained that a single word inadvertently dropped in conversation at dinner or at the gambling

[72] Francisco de Quevedo, *Visions,* pp. 69ff.
[73] Christian Thomasius, "Erfindung einer Wissenschaft anderer Menschen Gemüt zu erkennen," in F. Brüggemann, ed., *Aus der Frühzeit der deutschen Aufklärung,* Weimar and Leipzig, 1928, pp. 60 ff.

[51]

table, a glance, a fleeting expression—any of these might be a clue to the true intention that a man tried to hide. Sometimes the dissembler was bound to be careless, and an astute observer would in the end distinguish the affected from the natural. Even the most careful dissembler would fail: he would not conceal minor excesses of his passion, either because he simply did not regard them as excessive or because most persons reputed to be sensible and wise did not bother to conceal them.[74] Thomasius pointed out that great statesmen like Richelieu and Mazarin had possessed the skill of unmasking others, and indeed without it no prince could ever choose his advisers wisely, no minister could recognize worthy clients, and no client succeed in dealing with his patron.

The techniques of unmasking were grounded in the belief that everyone hides his true self either defensively in fear of others who are more powerful than himself or aggressively in the endeavor to attain his own ends and satisfy his passions at the expense of others. Thomasius was careful to explain that his new science was of no avail when used against men who were "to a high degree true Christians," because in order to explore their hearts, "a supernatural and divine science was required."[75] He warned also that no knowledge of others could be attained without self-knowledge. He might have added that many older conduct books written for aspiring courtiers by clerics and disappointed men of affairs contained everything that could possibly be said about dissimulation. This literature flourished in the era of absolutism. The conduct

[74] This psychology of unmasking was elaborated in pedantic detail by Julius Bernhardt von Rohr in *Einleitung zu der Klugheit zu leben*, 3d ed., Leipzig, 1730.
[75] Christian Thomasius, *op.cit.*, p. 78.

books were founded on political experience at the courts where success and security depended on the favor of the prince. Such favor would not be predicted with confidence; many sought favor, but only one could grant it, and it was always granted to the disappointment of others who had sought the same favor. As Guevara said in his *Institutiones Vitae Aulicae*, "A courtier must fear everyone and be on guard against him. Is there anyone who loves another person at court so much as not to wish him dead or at least to try to become his equal, no matter how close he is to him through family bonds or confidence?"[76] In the serious novels of the Baroque era reserve and distrust between lovers, as well as rivals, are prominent and pervasive, and in conduct books like de Refuge's *Treatise on the Court* (1623) or *The Instructions of Cardinal Sermonetta to his Cousin Petro Caetano* (1633), reserve and distrust are recommended as "a counterpoison" against the secret malice and evil designs of others.

Grimmelshausen's Simplician writings are closer to the worldly spirit of this literature than is generally recognized. Dissimulation and distrust are as prominent in his writings as they are in the conventional novels of the period. Not only stark evil, but intense distrust and dissimulation pervade Grimmelshausen's world.[77] Thus it is not surprising that in a prefatory poem to *Dietwalt and Amelinde*, one of his conventional novels, Grimmelshausen pointed out that *The Adventurous Simplicissimus* could teach the reader when it was safe to speak, when it was neccessary to be silent, and how to be on one's guard in the company of the powerful in order not

[76] Antonio de Guevera, *Institutiones Vitae Aulicae Oder Hofschul*, German tr. Aegidius Albertinus, Munich, 1602, p. 4.

[77] Cf. *Simplicissimus*, pp. 55, 236, 414.

to become a laughing-stock like a fool.[78] This remark notwithstanding, Grimmelshausen did not write *The Adventurous Simplicissimus* merely for the practical purpose of teaching his readers how to guard against malice and evil and how to make use of prudent dissimulation in order to survive in this treacherous world. Nor does *The Enchanted Bird's-nest* instruct the reader in the techniques of detecting hidden malice and evil intent. Instead, the book presents a general view of life according to which appearances cannot be trusted, because behind the façade of reasonableness, politeness, and morally impeccable behavior lie boundless folly and evil.

Folly and evil are rooted in the passions: in lust and greed, in the desire to excel others and the will to dominate them, in envy and vengefulness, miserliness and sloth. Man is evil, and evil grows in the company of evil man. What rules should govern the conduct of a wise man? The moral precepts which the hermit gives shortly before his death to the child *Simplicius* are, interestingly enough, not specifically Christian in character, a fact to which critics of Grimmelshausen have paid no attention. The dying hermit says nothing about loving one's neighbor, turning one's cheek, or trusting in God's will. Instead, he urges the child to observe these three rules of conduct: know thyself, avoid bad company, and be steadfast.[79]

[78]   ". . . Simplicissimus kan zeigen
   Wann man füglich reden soll, und wann man soll
        wiederschweigen;
   Wie man bey grossen Herren müsse nemen wol in acht,
   Wann man nicht, wie andre Narren wolle werden ausgelacht."
Quoted by Manfred Koschlig, " 'Edler Herr von Grimmelshausen,' " *Jahrbuch der deutschen Schillergesellchaft*, IV, 1960, p. 217. Grimmelshausen wrote this dedicatory poem himself under one of his many pseudonyms.
[79] *Simplicissimus*, p. 35.

INVISIBILITY AND OMNIPOTENCE

In the first part of *The Enchanted Bird's-nest* the world is like a puppet show which only the halberdier understands, because with the help of the nest he observes both the play and the strings of passion that make man move on the stage of this world. Like God, however, the halberdier is not only omniscient, but also omnipotent: he pulls the strings whenever he disapproves of the play.

The halberdier helps the poor, throws the wanton parson onto a heap of manure, boxes the ears of Calvinist peasants in a tavern when they make fun of Catholic rites, saves the students from being robbed and slain, prevents a shepherd from committing sodomy, and acts in many other ways sometimes like an avenging angel and sometimes like a guardian angel. Is he an agent of the Almighty or does he do what God fails to do? Nothing in the novel suggests that Grimmelshausen regarded him as anything but an ordinary man who had magically acquired complete knowledge of man. The halberdier is a simple fellow with some charmingly mischievous traits. In particular, he does not do any work, but with the help of his nest steals food and wine to his heart's delight; and on one occasion, after a dedication festival of a church, he deflowers a willing young girl.

Twice the halberdier is indeed taken for an angel: by the shepherd whom he saves from committing sodomy and suicide, and by a poor laborer's family, whose abject misery he relieves without betraying his presence by giving stolen food to the starving children and two gold coins to their parents. The second incident, a very rare indication of Grimmelshausen's own feelings of compassion, occurs the day after the halberdier's reflection appears in the looking-glass of a vain, wealthy lady, striking her with fear that she is looking at the Devil himself.

Now comparing the lady's terror with the poor family's belief in angelic assistance, the halberdier becomes pensive. "Why are human judgments," he asks, "generally so false?"[80] He concludes that errors in opinion result from the emotions of the person who passes judgment. The lady in front of the mirror was told by her conscience that her vanity was sinful folly; and it is for this reason that she believed the mirror image to be that of the Devil. The poor family bewailed their misery and prayed to God for help. To whom were they to attribute the miraculous presents "but to the one to whom they had complained in their misery"?[81] Did Grimmelshausen want to suggest that God helped the poor as little as he did the sodomitic shepherd? He certainly suggests that the gratitude of the poor for God's charity was as misplaced as was the fear of Satan which gripped the rich lady in front of her mirror. Or as the halberdier puts it: "Although each party in his judgment about me had completely contradicted the other, both of them were equally deceived by opinion; and this taught me how little confidence we may have in our own notions."[82]

This is an extraordinary statement. It is the only passage in the Simplician cycle where Grimmelshausen applied

[80] *Bird's-nest I*, p. 73.

[81] *Ibid.*, p. 74.

[82] "Ob nun gleich beyde Theil von mir so unterschiedlich geurtheilt/ dass sie auch nicht unterschiedlicher hätten urthlen können/ so hat doch der Wahn alle beyde betrogen/ und mich gelernet/ wie wenig unserm eignen Beduncken zutrauen und zu glauben sey" (*Bird's-nest I*, p. 74).

the word *"Wahn"* (opinion or delusion)[83] to the belief in divine help as well as to the belief in the machinations of the Devil. The passage is also important because it is immediately followed by the halberdier's remark, "Small wonder, therefore, that old Simplicissimus put on all the engravings to be found in the story of his life: 'Opinions Deceive' [*'Der Wahn betreugt'*]"[84] Like so many other words and phrases in Grimmelshausen's work "Opinions Deceive," the famous Simplician adage, thus has various meanings. It certainly implies that appearances cannot be trusted, because of man's proneness to simulate and dissimulate. "The world is full of masks," reads one line of the poem that appears on the frontispiece of *The Enchanted Bird's-nest*. Only those who see through man's dissembling will not be deceived. "Opinion" or "delusion" in a more specific application, however, denotes man's notions about God and Satan, and these opinions or delusions seem to be a special kind of folly, influenced like all judgments by emotions.

The halberdier finally decides to part with the bird's-nest. It frightens him that he nearly caused a shepherd to commit suicide. Moreover, he becomes aware of his own sins: his sloth, his petty thefts, and the seduction of the girl. No longer does he want to "conceal misdeeds, whoring, and thieving through invisibility,"[85] like those who love darkness because they do evil. God alone "in

[83] The word *"Wahn"* is used by Grimmelshausen to denote either "blind judgment" (e.g., "das blinde Urtheil oder der Menschen Wahn"; *Bird's-nest I*, p. 73) or "opinion" (e.g., "Verbleibe dennoch bey meinem gefasten Wahn . . ." *Bird's-nest I*, p. 106). On the relation between Baroque *"Wahn"* and *"opinio"* according to the Stoics cf. Werner Welzig, *op.cit.*, pp. 170-175.

[84] *Bird's-nest I*, p. 74.

[85] *Ibid.*, p. 142.

his supreme wisdom has reserved for himself omniscience. . . ."[86]

The halberdier's exit is morally enigmatic. He finds the gold coins that an evil woman, the former owner of the nest, had stolen with its magical help. He considers how he can use his suddenly acquired fortune to bring joy and restore honor to "the friendly girl" whom he had "robbed and violated in her sleep, as it were."[87] The moral worth of this resolution is equivocal. A similar episode occurs in Grimmelshausen's main novel when neither Simplicissimus nor Heartsbrother, his pious friend, hesitates very much to spend the tainted money that Simplicissimus has taken from Olivier after the death of this villainous highwayman and murderer.[88] Perhaps the good ends to which the treasure is to be put are supposed in each case to nullify its immoral origin, in much the same manner in which King David was a great king despite his dissolute and immoral youth.[89] Perhaps the innocent way in which the halberdier acquired the gold coins implies that

[86] *Ibid.*, p. 143.

[87] *Ibid.*, p. 147.

[88] *Simplicissimus*, bk. v, chaps. I and III.

[89] In his *Ratio Status*, Grimmelshausen points out that David was "reprehensible" because he lied, robbed and murdered for which he would not be praised among Christians, even by clerics, but he was a legitimate king obliged to persecute the hereditary enemies of his nation; hence he could not be accused of any iniquity. ("Was nun dieses vor ein stück der Redlichkeit und eines Gottseeligen gewesen/ wurden auch unter uns Christen die Geistlichen kaum loben; Aber deme sey wie ihm wolle/ David war allbereit ein gesalbter König der Israeliten/ und dannenhero Ambtshalber verbunden seiner *Nation* Erbfeinde zu verfolgen/ und wie im Krieg erlaubt ist/ seine Feinde mit allerhand List/ Betrug/ Vortheln/ *Stratagematis* und was den anhängig zu schwächen; also ist diss Orts David keiner Unbilligkeit zu beschuldigen" [Grimmelshausen, *Simplicianischer Zweyköpffiger Ratio Status*, Nüremberg: Felszecker, 1670, p. 58]).

[58]

the money is no longer tainted: he found it knowing that its former owner, who had stolen it with the help of the Devil, suffered violent death in consequence of her sin. Perhaps Grimmelshausen agreed with some of his readers that finding something meant owning it: the treasure no longer belonged to anyone. Finally, there is the remote possibility that Grimmelshausen wrote the concluding passage in the first part of *The Enchanted Bird's-nest* with tongue in cheek, casting a last ironic glance at the young halberdier in his new role of a converted sinner proposing to make amends in a manner that entangles him anew in the evil he has just renounced.

MAN PLAYING GOD

In the second part of *The Enchanted Bird's-nest* the owner of the magical object is not a Simplicius-like simpleton, but a merchant who is full of enterprise. His projects are more ambitious than the mere theft of food and wine, which the halberdier, like any picaro, commits in order to avoid work. Nor does the merchant try to check the evildoers around him and help their victims. Instead, he himself does evil with perfect abandon. Since the nest gives him a measure of supernatural power denied to ordinary mortals he is capable of sinning in a grand manner. Comparing the halberdier with the merchant, we may say that the novel passes from a reflective phase to one of reckless and fantastic action.

The second part of the novel contains two main adventures. The first involves an act of brutal revenge that the merchant commits on his unfaithful wife and her helpers. The story can be traced to one of Bandello's novelle: Grimmelshausen took it from the German translation of

[59]

a later French version of the original tale. The second adventure is the story of *The False Messiah*. The Christian merchant falls in love with Esther, a Jewish maiden. With the help of his magic nest and other tricks he presents himself as Elijah, the prophet, who upon God's command has chosen Esther for his divine pleasure.

The story of the man who pretends to be a god or an angel in order to possess a woman can be found in the literature of many ages and many lands, including ancient Greece and India, ancient Rome, medieval Europe, Renaissance Italy, France, and Germany.[90] Often, though not invariably, the deception is enlarged by a fraudulent promise that a demigod, hero, or savior will be born of the scandalous union.

Probably Grimmelshausen did not use the classical sources, but modern derivations in which a fraudulent promise to a Jewish maiden contributes to the success of the deception. Today Grimmelshausen's sources are familiar to only a few specialists. For example, various details in *The False Messiah* may have been taken from a fifteenth century Fastnachtsspiel by Hans Folz, *Von der Juden Messias*.[91]

Probably more important to Grimmelshausen as a writer and as an observer of human folly than any literary antecedent in the long history of the theme was some extraordinary news that spread over Europe in the years immediately before *The Enchanted Bird's-nest*, Part II was written. This was the news of Sabbatai Zevi, a Sephardic Jew, born in 1626 who under the influence of the Lurian Cabbala and driven by self-delusion claimed to be

[90] Otto Weinreich, *Der Trug des Nektanebos*, Leipzig and Berlin, 1911.

[91] *Ibid.*, pp. 98-99.

the redeemer of the Jews. On his extensive travels he succeeded in gaining a large following of believers in his messianic mission. In the seventeenth century, apocalyptic fears and millennial frenzy were spurred by religious persecution, by the long and destructive Thirty Years War, and by such heavenly portents as the appearance of the comets of 1618 and 1652. There were many learned calculations to determine the year in which the world would come to an end: 1648, 1666, 1668, 1673 were all miracle years in the belief of some Jewish or Christian messianists. A contemporary, Friedrich Brekling, enumerated "one hundred and eighty visionaries of that century, men and women, who were millenarian dreamers and eschatologists."[92]

Grimmelshausen may have read an account of the enthusiastic delusions which news and rumors about Sabbatai Zevi aroused in many Jewish communities in Europe. For example, the *Theatrum Europaeum*, which Grimmelshausen is known to have consulted on various occasions, reported the following happenings in 1666:

> In their blind zeal the Jews residing in Amsterdam wanted to excel all others and could not contain their jubilation. . . . They held joyous, public celebrations in their synagogue. Candles were burned and psalms about the redemption of Israel were chanted, all in the presence of several hundred, if not a thousand, Christians. . . ."[93]

Sabbatai Zevi discarded his messianic role by eventually

[92] Abba Hillel Silver, *A History of Messianic Speculation in Israel*, with a new preface by the author, Boston: Beacon Press, 1958, p. 162.

[93] Cited from *Theatrum Europaeum*, X, by Arthur Bechthold, *J. J. Ch. v. Grimmelshausen*, Munich, 1919, p. 159.

choosing conversion to Islam in preference to martyrdom. He died ten years later, in 1676, but the faith he had inspired survived his conversion and death.

Even though Grimmelshausen may not have known classical stories about the amorous man who played God, for understanding the author's intention in *The False Messiah* it is useful to compare his treatment of the theme with its rendition in the classical sources and with the literary efforts of three eminent postclassical authors.

In certain tales about the birth of Alexander, the great magician and astrologer Nectanebo, the last king of Egypt, falls in love with Olympias, the wife of King Philip of Macedonia. He persuades the queen, who is more beautiful than the moon, that a god loves her and will visit her first as a snake, then as the horned Ammon, next as Herakles, then as Dionysos, and finally in the human form of Nectanebo himself. The queen does not resist, and Nectanebo, before leaving her room, announces to her that she has conceived by him an invincible son who will rule the world.[94]

In a story by Josephus,[95] the Roman knight Mundus declares his love to Paulina, the young and beautiful wife of Saturninus, and a woman of excellent character. He is rejected by her, but the priests of Isis intercede in the service of the lovesick Mundus, convincing Paulina that the god Anubis is enamored of her beauty and desires to lie with her in the temple. Mundus then enjoys her, pretending to be Anubis. After the adulterous act, he humiliates the woman by disclosing to her how he deceived her in order to conquer her virtue. The story is supposed to be founded on fact and the ensuing scandal is said to have led to the destruction of the temple of Isis by order of

[94] Otto Weinreich, *loc.cit.*

[95] Flavius Josephus *Antiquitates Judaicae*, lib. XVIII, chap. 3.

Emperor Tiberius in A.D. 19. Only in the Latin translation of *Josephus* does Mundus-Anubis announce that Paulina will give birth to a divine child.

According to the tenth letter of Aeschines, Cimon, an Athenian youth, observes a maiden named Callirrhoë *bathing in the river Scamandros in observance of a local* custom followed by prospectives brides. Cimon hides from the girl's sight in the bushes alongside the riverbank. When she addresses the river god with the words, "Scamandros, receive my virginity," Cimon emerges from his ambush with reeds in his hair, saying like a god, "I accept it with pleasure,"[96] and disappears with her from sight. Later he is reproached by a companion who has witnessed the incident and is in fact the narrator of the story, but Cimon makes light of his frivolity, saying that many other maidens have been deceived in the same manner.

These ancient stories reverberate with echoes of the mystery religions which promised man communion with God through sacred orgies. In spiritualized form such beliefs appear later in the notion of mystics that there is a special way to communion of the human soul with God. In addition, the stories suggest the most ruthless degradation of religion to a mere device for attaining the pleasures of love. The motif of the man who plays God in order to reach his aim in love, with its juxtaposition of the sacred and the sexual, the fraudulent, the cruel in the human heart, must have fascinated Grimmelshausen, just as he *was attracted by the closeness of madness to religious* zeal.[97]

[96] Eshine, *Discours*, texte etabli et traduit par Victor Martin et Guy de Budé, Paris, 1928, bk. II, p. 134.

[97] *Simplicissimus*, bk. III, chaps. 3-6 (the story of the madman who thinks that he is Jove), and V, chap. 2 (the first conversion of Simplicissimus following the outburst of a madman in a church).

The three principal postclassical authors who should be briefly considered at this point are Boccaccio, Bandello, and Pierre Bayle. The story of Frate Alberto[98] is inspired, like all tales in the *Decameron* by Boccaccio's desire to entertain educated Renaissance society with a basically anti-Christian view of love as man's natural right to pleasure. This view is implied rather than overtly stated. The direct attack is not on religious belief, but on the monk—an unreconstructed cheat, procurer, hypocrite, and murderer—and to a somewhat lesser extent, on Madonna Lisetta, his mistress, who is ludicrously stupid and vain, and boasts of being "paradisaically fair." Boccaccio's elegant story lacks the fierce sarcasm and vindictive scorn that is heaped upon superstition in the tale of *The False Messiah*. In Boccaccio's story, Madonna Lisetta's superstitious credulity receives no special attention. More than on religious superstition, the plot relies for plausibility on the stupid vanity of the lady and the hypocrisy of the voluptuous monk. The story ends with a scene in which Frate Alberto is exposed to public ridicule and shame on the Piazza San Marco in Venice.[99]

Bandello chose the adventure of Mundus and Paulina for the theme of one of his polished novelle. Since he followed the Greek version of Josephus, he did not mention the fraudulent promise that a divine child would be born of the union. In introducing his tale, Bandello distinguished between religion and "good usances," but he refrained from any comparisons of Roman and Christian religious beliefs. He said, "Now how much weight religion

[98] Boccaccio, *Decameron*, Fourth Day, Second Story.
[99] For a distinguished comment on the story of Frate Alberto cf. Erich Auerbach, *Mimesis*, Garden City, New York: Doubleday Anchor Books, 1957, pp. 177-202.

had with the Romans at a time when all good usances were marred, you shall hear out of hand. . . ."[100] A little further on, Bandello presented the ancient "superstition that the gods got women with child" as an explanation of Paulina's credulity: the Romans did not suspect such "wickedness" as that possessed by Mundus and the priests of Isis "to be hidden under the colour of religion."[101] Bandello made no comments in the novella on religion in general, and any possible inference concerning Christian beliefs is left to readers who are bold enough to disregard the difference between heathen superstition and Christian religion.

As we turn from the Renaissance novelists to Pierre Bayle, the picture changes. "When we consider that wit and learning never appeared with so much lustre, as in the age that Aeschines lived in," Bayle remarked, "we may the better apprehend the fatal power of a false religion. It destroys good sense, it extinguishes the light of nature, and in some sort degrades a man to the condition of a brute beast."[102] He then attributed the downfall of Callirrhoë to "the impertinences of poets, canonized by the heathen priests,"[103] who succeeded in making the maiden believe, her noble education notwithstanding, that "rivers were deities who crowned themselves with reeds, and

[100] *The Novels of Matteo Bandello, Bishop of Agen.* Now first done into English prose and verse by John Payne, London, 1890 (printed for the Villon Society for private circulation), Vol. v, Part iii, Story 15, p. 255.

[101] *Ibid.*, p. 257.

[102] Pierre Bayle, "Scamander," in *Dictionnaire*, English tr., London, 1734, Vol. v, p. 77.

[103] *Loc.cit.* The French text reads, more simply, "les impertinences des Poëtes canonisées par les Prêtres" (Pierre Bayle, "Scamander," *Dictionnaire historique et critique* 5ᵉ édition, Amsterdam, 1734, Vol. v, pp. 75-78.)

[65]

could enjoy a woman." Referring also to Josephus, Bayle said that in the age of Tiberius another illustrious lady became the victim of deception. Then Bayle contrasted these happenings among the ancients with Christian civilization. He denied that monks "who have played so many tricks chiefly to inveigle women" ever dared to tell them that a saint would want to lie with them: "The ideas of purity and immateriality have always been strictly joined in Christianity with those of beatification." Bayle stressed that, unlike the ancient stories, Boccaccio's tale is merely fiction. To this praise of Christianity, however, Bayle added one sentence that makes it clear that he spared the Christian monks in his comments in order to obscure his contention that true Christian religion as well as "false religion" can "destroy good sense and extinguish the light of nature." Immediately following the sentence on beatification that has been quoted, Bayle said, "But I have no doubt, if they [i.e., the monks,] would undertake such a thing, but they might bring such devout women, as there are, to believe that of which the Roman votary of Anubis suffered herself to be persuaded."[104]

Thus, Bayle contended that the Christian monks who have seduced so many women would never use the ruse of impersonating a saint or an angel in their amorous conquests. But were the monks to resort to such methods in the manner of the fictional Frate Alberto, the virtue of devout Christian women might falter because of their religion, just as Callirrhoë and Paulina succumbed for that reason. In other words, Bayle suggested that as a

[104] The original reads, ". . . mais je ne doute point que si on l'entreprenoit on ne vînt à bout de persuader à telles dévotes qu' il y a, ce que la Dame Romaine dévote d'Anubis se laissa persuader" (*loc.cit.*).

[66]

source of delusion about love true religion does not differ from false religion.[105]

IRONY

It is possible that Grimmelshausen in satirizing the superstitions of the Jews took a position somewhat resembling that of Bayle when the latter pointed to certain deplorable consequences of false religion among the Greeks and Romans. That Esther is not the target of Grimmelshausen's derisive humor is evident from the treatment of her character in the story. She lacks the vices of vanity, lust, greed, and the other qualities that Grimmelshausen often attributed to women. There is no suggestion of her being the least amorous. Compare Esther with the princess in the story of *The Panchatantra*. When the beautiful princess is visited by the weaver in the guise of god Vishnu, she is "gazing at the moon, her mind idly dallying with the thoughts of love."[106] When the queen, her mother, finally suspects her trespasses and hastens in great perturbation to the maiden's apartments, she finds "her daughter with lips sore from kissing and with telltale traces on her limbs."[107] Similar details suggesting the pleasures of love are included in Boccaccio's story of Frate Alberto. Grimmelshausen did not admit such erotic suggestions to his tale. The seduction in Esther's bedroom is told smilingly in dialect, as if Grimmelshausen were talking about the aftermath of a country dance. Esther

[105] The point is missed by Otto Weinreich, who wrote in his excellent monograph that "it is not worthwhile reporting Bayle's statements in detail; they are remarkably beside the point ["schief"] . . ." (*op.cit.*, p. 80).

[106] *The Panchatantra*, tr. from the Sanskrit by Arthur W. Ryder, Bombay and Calcutta: Jaico Publishing House, 1949, p. 82.

[107] *Ibid.*, p. 84.

[67]

has only those traits which are necessary for the plot to be credible: beauty, reserve, and religious faith. While she is credulous, she is not more gullible than any other member of her family and community.

Grimmelshausen's tale is centered on a religious superstition, the expectation of a second Messiah. This belief is described in considerable detail as the main prerequisite of the extraordinary deception perpetrated in Esther's chamber. When Grimmelshausen described the seduction he smiled, but when he talked about the religious beliefs of the Jews his humor grew fierce and profoundly ambiguous, as is illustrated by the following instances.

The merchant learns from Erasmus that the words, "I, the Lord, will hasten it in his time" are taken by the Jews "to mean that suddenly and in great haste God will send their Messiah, by post coach, as it were, and put them into the Promised Land as into an earthly paradise."[108] Again, the Jews "doubt these tales about their future Messiah as little as a good Christian doubts that the true Messiah has already come."[109] Note that this observation (made by the merchant after he has allegedly repented his sins) can be read to mean that the gullibility of the Jews equals the gullibility of the Christians!

When the merchant impersonating the angel Uriel appears in front of Eliezer's bed at night, he addresses Esther's father as follows:

> Let your heart not be frightened and let your soul banish all needless fear! For lo, I am the angel Uriel, who stands in the presence of God. I have been sent by the King of Kings and His prophet Elijah, whom

[108] *The False Messiah*, p. 247.
[109] *Ibid.*, p. 245.

you have served all your life in the fear of God, in order to bring you the glad tidings for which the house of Jacob has prayed for so long a time: The chosen people of Israel shall be redeemed.[110]

This is close, even in language, to the way in which, according to Luke, the angel Gabriel speaks to Zacharias, promising him the miraculous birth of a son, John the Baptist.

Fear not, Zacharias: for thy prayer is heard. . . . I am Gabriel, that stand in the presence of God; and am sent to speak unto thee, and to shew thee these glad tidings.[111]

In Grimmelshausen's tale, Eliezer at first doubts the angelic promise, since he thinks that God has chosen Sarah, his old wife, to become the mother of the Messiah: "True, everything is possible for the Lord, but how can this happen when my Sarah is old and unable to bear children?"[112] In the Scriptures as well the advanced age of the woman divinely chosen for miraculous childbirth is twice the cause of all too human doubt in the possibility of the miracle. Genesis speaks of Sarah's faithless laughter when Abraham entertains the three angels and is promised that his wife would bear a child:

Now Abraham and Sarah were old and well stricken in age; and it ceased to be with Sarah after the manner of women. . . . And the Lord said unto Abraham, Wherefore did Sarah laugh, saying, Shall I of a surety

[110] *Ibid.*, p. 252.
[111] *Luke* 1:13,19.
[112] "Dem Herrn ist zwar alles Möglich, aber wie wird dies geschehen können, dann meine Sara alt und zum Kinderzeugen untüchtig worden ist?" (*Bird's-nest II*, p. 402).

[69]

bear a child, which am old? Is there any thing too
hard for the Lord?[118]

And according to Luke, Zacharias, hearing the Elizabeth
shall bear him a son, replies to the angel Gabriel, "Where-
by shall I know this? for I am an old man and my wife
well stricken in years."[114]

The angel punishes Zacharias for his doubt with dumb-
ness during Elizabeth's pregnancy. Five months later,
when Gabriel announces to Mary, the Virgin, in Nazareth
that she shall give birth to the Son of God, Mary wonders
how this shall be "seeing I know not a man,"[115] but the
angel reminds her that Elizabeth conceived a son in her
old age, adding, "For with God nothing shall be impossible."[116] In Grimmelshausen's tale, Eliezer uses the same
argument to reinforce his doubt rather than to silence it,
when he says, "True, everything is possible for the Lord,
but . . . my Sarah is old. . . ." In order to deal with this
doubt the merchant, in the role of the pretending angel,
merely needs to enlighten Eliezer that his young and
beautiful daughter, and not his old wife, has been divinely
chosen to become a mother. The humor in this passage
is as subtle as it is daring. Nature prevails over religion
quite naturally—or employs it persuasively—so that at
the end of the conversation even skeptical old Eliezer need
no longer qualify his belief that with God nothing is impossible by "it is true . . . but . . . ." The merchant, however,
in his disguise might well have recited to himself at this
juncture the passage from *The Praise of Folly*, where
Stultitia says to her listeners:

[118] *Genesis* 18:11, 13-14.
[114] *Luke* 1:18.
[115] *Luke* 1:34.
[116] *Luke* 1:36-37.

But why not speak to you more openly, as I usually do? I ask whether the head, the face, the breast, the hand, or the ear—each an honorable part—creates gods and men? I think not, but instead the job is done by that foolish, even ridiculous part which cannot be named without laughter. This is the sacred fountain from which all things rise. . . .[117]

Subsequently, Grimmelshausen dryly refers to Eliezer twice as "grandfather of the Messiah."[118] Esther is promised a painless childbirth, but it is noted with a malicious chuckle that she suffers the same birth pangs as other women do. When the newborn Messiah is discovered to be a girl, the Jews firmly believe that God in his wisdom resolved to protect the child from Christian persecution, from "another Herodian play."[119] Grimmelshausen (through the mouth of Erasmus) the merchant's friend, ridiculed the expectation that the girl-child will be turned into a young man later, but added that if this expectation were really fulfilled it would be "nothing novel and hence no miracle."[120] In the meantime, he designated the child with outrageous scorn and daring, as "the slit Messiah."[121] Later, when the girl is baptized she receives the name Eugenia, for a reason which, the narrator says, he cannot fathom: he does not mention that Eugenia means "the well-born child." Finally, Esther is given an additional

[117] Erasmus, *The Praise of Folly*, tr. Leonard F. Dean, New York: Hendricks House, Farrar, Straus, 1946, p. 49. It is not known whether or not Grimmelshausen read Erasmus' famous book. Nor is it easy to make a plausible conjecture regarding the use of his name in *The False Messiah*.

[118] *The False Messiah*, p. 254.

[119] *Ibid.*, p. 262.

[120] *Ibid.*, p. 280.

[121] *Ibid.*, p. 267.

[71]

Christian name at the time of her baptism, and this name is—Mary; she becomes Mary Esther.

THE SUGAR-COATED PILL

Overtly, Grimmelshausen's tale is that of a Christian sinner who is punished and reformed at the end of the novel, and of Jewish superstition, which is ridiculed. The merchant repeatedly scorns the folly of the Jews and in particular their belief in the coming of the Messiah. Does not every Christian know that God sent the Messiah a long time ago? In addition, there are lengthy passages in which Erasmus, the somewhat fickle convert to the Christian faith, admonishes the sinful merchant to reform. To be sure, this zealous and learned new Christian later lets himself be bought by the merchant and lies to his beloved that he is the father of her child. Then, in numerous other passages, the merchant as narrator interrupts his comic tale to remind the reader what a terrible sinner he used to be. Even these pious passages, however, contain certain phrases which suggest that the merchant's contrition is hardly more than a conventional act of hasty compliance with Christian rules. For example, when Erasmus senses the merchant's rekindled passion for Mary Esther—"oh horrible ungodliness!"—the merchant remarks, "Meanwhile, the good Lord who, as I have said, watches his flock, opened Erasmus' eyes."[122] Does the clause, "as I have said," reinforce the statement that the Lord watches his flock? Or does it rather resemble Eliezer's equivocal addition, "It is true," to the biblical quotation "with God nothing shall be impossible?"

Grimmelshausen's Christian outlook has never been seriously doubted by any literary critic of his work. In

[122] *Ibid.*, p. 292.

particular, *The Enchanted Bird's-nest* has uniformly been considered to depict the world from the viewpoint of a Christian moralist. The humorous aspect of the tales contained in this novel are considered to be the sugar-coating of the pill of Christian truth that Grimmelshausen wanted his readers to swallow. The ancient image of the sugar-coated pill is traditional among satirists through the ages and is associated with two different ideas, one concerning laughter as a medicine for un-Christian melancholy, and the other concerning truth as being unpalatable because of its bitterness.

Grimmelshausen, too, often used the image of the sugar-coated pill, among other places in the Second Preface to *The Enchanted Bird's-nest*, Part II.[128] In this preface Grimmelshausen explained that he did not write his novel for entertainment but for instruction and that it would be understood correctly only by very few readers. At the same time he explained what the novel is meant to teach the reader: that he is being watched by God and should not believe that his sins will go unpunished. A literal understanding of this message must ignore the difficulty that only the first, passive, part of the novel can be said to show how man dissembles and does evil in the belief that he is not being watched, whereas the second part, presenting a more active use of the bird's-nest, shows man doing great mischief and evil not because he believes that he is unobserved but because invisibility gives him added power to do so. And invisibility is a divine as well as a satanic property.

Let us disregard this difficulty, however, and assume that Grimmelshausen did intend to tell his readers to be

[128] For the text of this Preface, cf. below, p. 227.

[73]

mindful of God, who takes account of whatever man is doing, and metes out rewards and punishments justly. Then the question arises how this can possibly be the kernel of truth that "perhaps only one in every seventeen readers will understand." Precisely this interpretation of the Preface and, more generally, of Grimmelshausen's intention in all his Simplician writings, governs the critical literature.

"Seventeen" was one of Grimmelshausen's favorite numbers.[124] He employed this number often to convey the meaning of "very many." Today, we might colloquially say "one in a thousand" in lieu of "hardly anyone," where Grimmelshausen said "only one in seventeen." Now Grimmelshausen saw to it that hardly anyone—in fact, no one —could miss the Christian teaching of *The False Messiah* and of his other Simplician tales, for the reader is lavishly treated to sermonizing in the Prefaces, at the end of the novels, and many times in between. By no stretch of the imagination can this Christian teaching be considered to be hidden or in the least difficult to grasp. The Preface to *The Enchanted Bird's-nest*, Part II, is therefore more puzzling than appears at first glance.

On the basis of a comprehensive inspection of the prefatory material appearing in old books, one critic has recently come to the conclusion that "the more daring the content [that an author offers in his writings to the reader] the more assiduously is the work morally fortified and buttressed in the Preface."[125] In licentious and sensational literature, pious tricks are sometimes played in the Preface in order "to bestow absolution and an honorable

[124] Manfred Koschlig, "Der Bart-Krieg—Ein Werk Grimmelshausens," *loc.cit.*
[125] Hans Ehrenzeller, *op.cit.*, p. 78.

character on even the most ambiguous products."[126] The same critic called this phenomenon "the dialectic of the comic novel" and referred for illustration to *Moll Flanders*, the autobiography of a thief and prostitute, which Defoe presented in the Preface as an edifying book. These observations are sensible, but do they apply, as the critic believes, to *The Enchanted Bird's-nest?* Recognizing that no other book in Grimmelshausen's work is morally and religiously justified in "such insistent, almost pleading manner" as is the second part of the *Bird's-nest*, he exclaims, "No wonder, for nowhere is the 'style' so 'comic' as in '*Bird's-nest, II*' with its gross, erotic Messiah-scenes in Amsterdam."[127] This explanation is not convincing. There are very many scenes in Grimmelshausen's works which are more comic and more erotic than is that of the seduction of Esther. The sexual activities overheard by the innocent young Simplicius in the goosebin, Simplicius in girls' clothing arousing homosexual desires in his mistress, the adventures of Simplicissimus as a male prostitute in Paris, the seduction of Courage as a young girl after she reveals her true sex to her master, the sadistic scene of the rape of Courage by many men in quick succession— all this is far more daringly erotic than anything to be found in *The False Messiah*. What is extraordinarily "comic" in this tale is the treatment of religious beliefs, and it is very likely indeed that it is the discussion of this topic, rather than the erotic passages, that needed moral support and buttressing in the Preface.

Unless we assume that Grimmelshausen grossly exaggerated, for rhetorical effect, the difficulty of understand-

[126] *Ibid.*, p. 133.
[127] *Ibid.*, p. 78.

[75]

ing the plain, traditional, and frequent Christian pleas made in the Preface and many times elsewhere in the novel we are thus obliged to consider the possibility that his treatment of religious belief itself may point to the answer. To put it differently, unless we make the absurd assumption that *The False Messiah* is written for readers of devotional tracts and sermons, we must put ourselves in the position of readers with different interests. Grimmelshausen's treatment of Jewish beliefs is ambiguous enough to hoodwink those readers who attribute conventional anti-Jewish views to the author. While the joke in the story is not only on Esther, it does not seem to be exclusively on the Jews. In the seventeenth century no writer could dare to tell the story of the Divine Pretender in a Christian setting and ridicule Christian beliefs in the manner in which Grimmelshausen made fun of Jewish beliefs. Among the numerous works dealing with the ancient motif throughout the ages, there is only one in which the author, Morlini, had the poor taste to show the seducer in the assumed role of Christ, but this shocking adventure was turned into comedy in the last instant. Before the pretender reaches his goal, a companion of the villain in the mask of Peter beats the false Christ with clubs.[128] Thus Morlini brought the story to a tolerable ending, barely managing to turn blasphemy into farce.

Grimmelshausen wrote neither in the period of the Italian Renaissance nor in a literary climate of enlightenment. He was a man of the Baroque age, formed by war, the Counter-Reformation, and religious conflict in Germany. He wrote for an audience from whose memory the

---

[128] Morlini, *Novellae*, Paris, 1855, No. 69 (first ed. Naples, 1526) Cf. Otto Weinreich, *op.cit.*, pp. 121-132.

extraordinary story of Sabbatai Zevi had not yet faded, so that he could safely and, as it were, naturally, put his tale of the divine pretender into a Jewish setting. Moreover, he was familiar with literary precedents which, though less distinguished in the world of letters than his own story, had done the same. Everything considered, it is unlikely that *The False Messiah* is merely a humorous tale about Jewish beliefs. Perhaps a parallel to Grimmelshausen's prefatory remarks that "only one in seventeen readers" will understand him is to be found in Rabelais rather than in Defoe. Rabelais wished for himself a reader who like a dog would break open the bones of his book in order to suck its marrow.

Like the ambiguous treatment of omniscience and omnipotence in *The Enchanted Bird's-nest* and of the birth of a Messiah, several stories in his *Everlasting Almanac*[129] throw doubt on the contention, made by almost all critics, that Grimmelshausen was a deeply religious man.[130] This contention must be regarded as controversial, whereas the author's rare gifts as a storyteller, his irony, his delight in portraying human follies, his insistence on giving nature its due, his grim humor—all these are indisputable. Close reading of *The Adventurous Simplicissimus*, including the accounts of the hero's three conversions, raises many further questions about the depth of Grimmelshausen's religious faith; so does a careful perusal of *Courage, the Adventuress*. It is true, Grimmelshausen's discussion of the question as to whether man is made to laugh at his follies or to weep at his sins makes it clear

[129] Grimmelshausen, *Ewigwährender Kalender,* ed. Engelbert Hegaur, Munich, 1925, pp. 202, 204, 213.
[130] An important exception is Paul Gutzwiller, *Der Narr bei Grimmelshausen,* Bern: Francke Verlag, 1959.

[77]

that the author refused to declare himself a jester.[181] Christ, Simplicissimus remarks, was serious: the Scriptures do not say that he ever laughed. Even this discussion is full of ambiguities, however, and it should be remembered that in *The Adventurous Simplicissimus* the mad character who thinks he is Jove does not like to be laughed at. He, too, is very serious. Indeed, this man, described as "the son of the great numen" is the only character in Grimmelshausen's novels of whom it is said explicitly that he has an aversion to laughter. So Simplicissimus, if not the author, courteously refrains from laughing at him and hears him out on the subject of how the world will be saved.

At the very least, it seems certain that Grimmelshausen was deeply troubled by the government of God whom Simplicissimus addresses at one point as "a dark light."[182] It is for this dark light that the halberdier gives up the nest and renounces a career of thwarting or punishing

---

[181] *Springinsfield*, chaps. 2 and 3. For a fuller treatment of this discussion cf. Hans Speier, "Grimmelshausen's Laughter," *loc.cit.*

[182] "Ach allerhöchstes Gut! du wohnest so im Finstern Liecht!
      Dass man vor Klarheit gross
      den grossen Glantz kan schen nicht"
(*Continuatio des abentheurlichen Simplicissimi*, p. 107). Scholte, "Das finstere Licht," in his *Der Simplicissimus und sein Dichter*, pp. 81-106, has shown that this verse was taken from a poem by Vittorio Colonna. Grimmelshausen found it in the German translation (1619) by Aegidius Albertinus of Tomaso Garzoni's *Piazza Universale*, a compendium from which he often borrowed material for his writings. Scholte has pointed out that Grimmelshausen changed the words in Albertinus "unerforschliches Licht" (*inaccessibil luce*) in the original to "finsteres Licht." Scholte regards this interesting change as proof of Grimmelshausen's closeness to medieval Christian doctrines, Neoplatonism, and Cusanus (*op.cit.*, p. 103). More convincingly, Gutzwiller has interpreted this stanza as "Schauer vor der Unerreichbarkeit Gottes," and as a substitute for true love of God (Paul Gutzwiller, *op.cit.*, p. 69).

evil and helping the needy; it is in this dark light that, converted, he decides to do penance for his sins and to use for this purpose tainted money magically stolen by an evil woman. It is in this dark light that the merchant makes amends for having used the nest in playing God and enjoying love. He bribes Erasmus to marry the girl who has been defrauded of her virginity, and Erasmus, the pious Christian who, shocked by the impiety of the merchant, preached repentance to him, wins his bride by a lie that is as convenient as it is big. This lie also serves to bring about Esther's conversion, at which time she acquires her Christian name Mary!

At one point when Simplicissimus talks about religious subjects he is referred to as "a natural person" (*ein natürlicher Mensch*). Grimmelshausen said in respect to his main novel that he gave nature its due in his description of the world.[188] He described it laughingly but with defiant insistence on the horrors of natural life, its inconstancy, its filth, its violence.[184] Perhaps Grimmelshausen's clear perception of human folly and evil made it possible for him to accept God as a dark light. Perhaps his grim laughter at the victory of nature over "good usances" and religious dogmas gave meaning to his work and some comfort to him, as it gave pleasure to his readers and something more to "one out of every seventeen" of them.

[188] The reference to Simplicissimus as "a natural man" occurs in his talk with Jove (*Simplicissimus*, p. 210). Grimmelshausen's claim that he gave nature its due in *The Adventurous Simplicissimus* appears in the dedicatory poem he wrote to *Dietwalt und Amelinde*: "Er beschreibt so Naturäl diese Welt und ihre Sachen" (Manfred Koschlig, " 'Edler Herr von Grimmelshausen,' " *op.cit.*, p. 217).

[184] "Die Gottferne des menschlichen Daseins lässt sich in jedem seiner Werke nachweisen" (Paul Gutzwiller, *op.cit.*, p. 89).

COURAGE,

THE ADVENTURESS

THE TRUE ORIGIN AND CONTENT
OF THIS LITTLE BOOK

When Courage, the gypsy, learns from the story of Simplicissimus' life, book v, chapter 6, that he holds her up for derision, she becomes so bitter that she reveals the whole course of her dissolute life—to his disgrace and her own shame—but having forsaken honor and virtue among the gypsies, she cares little about her shame—all this in order to rub in well her own cunning and masterly revenge and to ruin the said Simplicissimus in the eyes of the whole world for not having feared to soil himself with so loose a slut, as she really is and admits to be, and for having in addition been boastful about his wantonness and malice; from all of which it may be concluded that the bolt is not better than the nut, nor the whoremonger by a hair's breadth better than the whore.

BRIEF BUT SUFFICIENTLY DETAILED CONSPECTUS OF
THE MOST CURIOUS HAPPENINGS TO BE FOUND IN EACH
CHAPTER OF THIS ENTERTAINING AND INSTRUCTIVE
STORY OF COURAGE, THE ADVENTURESS AND GYPSY

CHAPTER I

Thorough and necessary preface dealing with the question for whose sake and pleasure and for what pressing reasons Courage, the old master cheat, vagrant, and gypsy, relates her wondrous and very strange life and displays it before the eyes of the whole world.

CHAPTER II

Mistress Libuschka, later called Courage, gets into the war, calls herself Janco, and for a while acts as a servant. Item: an account of her behavior and of the strange things which happened to her.

CHAPTER III

Janco loses his fine little virgin wreath in the quarters of a resolute cavalry captain, receiving in return the name Courage.

CHAPTER IV

Courage becomes the wife of the cavalry captain because it was certain that she would be a widow soon thereafter, but first she is single in the wedded state.

CHAPTER V

The honest and virtuous as well as evil and godless ways of Courage, the cavalry captain's wife: how she yields to the will of a count, gets the pistoles of an ambassador, and submits willingly to others in order to snap up a rich booty.

CHAPTER VI

By a miraculous fate Courage enters her second wedlock, marrying a captain with whom she lives in joy and happiness.

[83]

CHAPTER VII

Courage enters her third marriage, thereby becoming the wife of a lieutenant instead of a captain, and fares not as well as before; fights with her lieutenant with cudgels for the pants of the family and wins them through brave resolution and valor; whereupon her husband jilts her and takes off.

CHAPTER VIII

Courage stays fresh and healthy in an encounter, cuts a soldier's head off, captures a major, and learns that her lieutenant was caught and hanged as a deserter who had broken his oath.

CHAPTER IX

Courage quits the war when her lucky star fades and almost everyone makes fun of her.

CHAPTER X

After a long period of longing, wishing and craving Courage learns who her parents were and gets another captain.

CHAPTER XI

Courage, newly wed to a captain, again joins the war and by heroic bravery in a bloody encounter captures a cavalry captain, a quartermaster and an ordinary trooper. Thereafter she loses her husband, and this makes her an unhappy widow.

CHAPTER XII

The major whom she had captured in an earlier encounter makes Courage pay a high price for her high courage: she is forced to be everyone's whore and, stripped naked, to perform a vile task, but the cavalry captain, whom she had also taken prisoner some time in the past, comes to her rescue, saving her from the worst fate, and takes her to his castle.

[84]

CHAPTER XIII

Courage is maintained like a little princess in a castle where the cavalry captain visits her very often. He serves her well until finally his parents learn of his love and have two servants cunningly abduct Courage from the castle to the city of Hamburg, where she is abandoned in her misery.

CHAPTER XIV

Courage casts her loving eyes on a young trooper who so violently strikes down a corporal for trying to give horns to him that the man forgets to get up. In consequence Courage's lover is shot by a firing squad and she is driven from the regiment by the floggers. She makes two troopers fare badly in their attempt to violate her and a musketeer comes to her help.

CHAPTER XV

Courage lodges with a sutler. A musketeer falls deeply in love with her. She stipulates the various conditions under which she promises to live with him in the wedded state singly. Then she becomes a sutler woman.

CHAPTER XVI

Courage gives the name Skipinthefield to her musketeer lover, when an ensign on the sly, upon her instigation and with the loyal help of the woman who passes for Courage's mother, gives a pair of big horns to that musketeer. In short, she leads him by the nose and he does not mind at all.

CHAPTER XVII

Incited by an Italian courtesan a furrier's wife plays a practical joke on Courage while she sups with a nobleman, but Courage gets even with both the courtesan and the furrier's wife and invents a marvelous trick to play on an apothecary.

CHAPTER XVIII

Unscrupulous Courage buys a spiritum familiarem *from a musketeer and thinks that she is in great luck since her every wish comes true.*

CHAPTER XIX

Courage teaches many tricks to Skipinthefield. He dupes a distinguished lady by pretending to be a treasure-digger, is admitted to the cellar of her house, gets hold of several precious gems, and at night is hoisted from the cellar by Courage.

CHAPTER XX

Courage and Skipinthefield rob two Milanese in an unheard of manner, squirting sharp vinegar into the eyes of the one who put his head through a peephole to see what was causing the noise in their hut, and putting a truss of sharp thorns into the way of the other.

CHAPTER XXI

Courage is boxed on the ear and maltreated by Skipinthefield in his sleep; when he wakes up, he humbly asks for her pardon and forgiveness, but to no avail.

CHAPTER XXII

Skipinthefield in his sleep lifts Courage from her bed and runs with her, clad only in her shirt, to the colonel's watch-fire. When she awakens she screams miserably so that all the officers come running and laugh at the farce. Thereupon Courage gets rid of Skipinthefield, giving him her best horse, a hundred ducats, and the spiritum familiarem.

CHAPTER XXIII

Courage again marries a captain but is deprived of her husband before he gets warm at her side. Then she settles down on the estate of her first captain in Swabia to resume her former trade as a whore, but she is careful in her dealings with the soldiers billeted in her home.

CHAPTER XXIV

Courage contracts a vile disease and journeys to a watering place, where she gets to know Simplicius. When he betrays her she, in turn, betrays him, ordering the newborn child of her maidservant to be left on his doorstep along with a written statement to the effect that the child is his and begotten with Courage.

CHAPTER XXV

In her garden Courage transacts improper business with an old adulterer, while two musketeers are stealing fruit in a pear tree and one of them carelessly drops all the stolen pears. Courage and her old lover run away; she is finally found out and banished from the city.

CHAPTER XXVI

Courage becomes the wife of a musketeer and carries on a low trade in tobacco and brandy. Her husband is sent away, finds on his way a dead soldier whom he strips bare and whose legs he cuts off since he can't get his trousers off. Having packed up his loot, he stays in a peasant's house overnight, leaves the legs there and runs away—all of which leads to a hilarious farce.

CHAPTER XXVII

After her husband is killed in an engagement, Courage escapes on her mule. She meets a band of gypsies, whose lieutenant takes her as his wife. She tells the fortune of a young lady in love, purloining from her in the process all her jewels without being able to hold on to them for long; she gets a good beating, and is forced to return them.

CHAPTER XXVIII

Courage and her company arrive in a village where the annual festival of the dedication of the church is being held. She incites a young gypsy to shoot a chicken; her husband pretends he is going to hang him and when everyone leaves the village to watch the spectacle, the gypsy women steal all the food they can find, and with cunning and dispatch the whole band takes off.

CHAPTER I

THOROUGH AND NECESSARY PREFACE DEALING WITH
THE QUESTION FOR WHOSE SAKE AND PLEASURE AND
FOR WHAT PRESSING REASONS COURAGE, THE OLD
MASTER CHEAT, VAGRANT, AND GYPSY, RELATES HER
WONDROUS AND VERY STRANGE LIFE AND DISPLAYS IT
BEFORE THE EYES OF THE WHOLE WORLD.*

YES (you will say, gentlemen), who would have thought the old hag would ever attempt to escape the wrath of God? But what else could she do? She had to, for the gay times of her youth had come to an end. Now, her sauciness and wantonness have subsided, her stricken conscience is anxiously awake, and the listless old age she has reached makes her feel ashamed of keeping on with her excessive follies. She loathes having her past rogueries locked up in her heart. The old gallows-bird knows full well that soon inevitable Death will knock at her door for the last handshake, forcing her to depart irrevocably to another world and give an exact account of her actions. For this reason, she now is about to unload the heavy burdens of her old self in the hope that she can yet ease herself sufficiently and obtain heavenly mercy after all.

Yes, dear gentlemen! This you will say. Others, however, will wonder whether Courage really believes that she can restore smoothness to her old wrinkled skin after having smeared it so much in her girlhood with French ointment for scabs, later with various Italian and French

---

* Grimmelshausen's descriptive chapter headings do not always follow consistently, in wording and length, the summaries in his *Conspectus*.

rouges, and in the end with Egyptian salves for lice, and with much goose-drippings. Does she really believe that her skin will become white again after she has blackened it in the smoke of many fires and changed its color ever so often? Does she really think that it is possible to efface the deep wrinkles of her wicked brow and give it the smoothness of her original innocence merely by unburdening her heart and telling the tale of her vices and of her knavish tricks? Should this old hag, now that she stands with both feet in the grave—if she be deserving of any burial at all—should this jade, you will say, who has wallowed in shame and vice all her life and is burdened with more crimes than years, more roguish tricks than months, more thieveries than weeks, more common sins than days; should she, who never once in her life thought of repentance, now be brazen enough to try to make her peace with God? Does she still believe that things can be straightened out, now that her conscience is suffering hellish tortures and pains more numerous than all the pleasures of life she has indulged in and enjoyed in her youth? Yes, there might be some hope for mercy, if this useless, exhausted creature had not wallowed in many other rank vices in addition to such lusts; indeed she went down to the deepest abyss of evil and liked it.

Yes, gentlemen, this you will say; this you will think; and in this manner you will be amazed if the news of the complete confession I am about to make comes to your knowledge. But when I hear you, I shall forget my age and laugh and laugh until I split my sides or get young again.

Why, Courage? Why would you laugh like that?

I will tell you why. You believe that an old woman, who has lived for so long a time, and imagines her soul to be almost a part of her body, now thinks of her death; that a person like me, such as you have known me all my life, now thinks of repentance; that she who has led her whole life, as the priests have continually reminded her, on the road to hell, now thinks of heaven. I confess frankly that I cannot make up my mind to prepare myself for such a journey, as the priests have tried to persuade me to do. Nor can I completely give up that which, they also say, hinders such a resolution. To make that resolution I lack one thing, while of two other things, I have too much.

What I am lacking is repentance, and what I ought to be lacking are avarice and envy. I have collected a heap of gold at the risk of my life and, as I have been told, at the price of my salvation. Now if I hated my gold as much as I envy my neighbor, and loved my neighbor as much as my money, then perhaps I would also have the heavenly gift of repentance.

I know about the different ages every woman goes through, and my example confirms that it is difficult to teach an old dog new tricks. With the years, I have become more choleric, and I cannot take out my gall, as the butcher turns the pig's stomach inside out to cleanse it. How then should I control my anger? Who will rid me of my phlegm and thereby cure my indolence? Who will banish the melancholy humors and with them my inclination to envy? Who can persuade me to hate ducats since I know from long experience and only too well that they can save me in distress and will be the only consolation of my old age? Listen, you priests, there was a time, there was a time when you could have shown me the way which you now urge me to take. But that time was long ago, when in the flower of my girlhood, I lived in a state of innocence. For although I ran quickly into the dangers of an itching temptation, it would then have been easier to control my sanguine disposition than it now is for me to combat the strong pressure of the three worst humors combined. Turn to the young, therefore, whose hearts are not yet soiled with other images; teach, admonish, beg them, yes, plead with them that they should never stray as far in their thoughtlessness as poor Courage has done.

But listen, Courage, if you don't intend to repent, why do you want to tell the story of your life as in a confession and disclose your vices to the whole world?

This I will do to spite Simplicissimus† because I have no other way of taking revenge on him. For after this scoundrel made me pregnant at the spa§—or so he thought —and got rid of me by a cheap trick, he proceeded in the story he himself told of his fine life to broadcast his and my shame to the whole world. But now I will tell him what honorable sort of strumpet he consorted with. Then he will know what he has boasted about and probably wish that he had kept his mouth shut. From all this the whole world will learn that goose and gander, whore and whoremonger are of the same lot, and neither of them is a jot better than the other. "Birds of a feather flock together," said the Devil to the collier, and sins and sinners are usually punished by sins and sinners.

† Simplicissimus: the main character in Grimmelshausen's novel *The Adventurous Simplicissimus,* published in 1669. He is mentioned often in *Courage, the Adventuress,* sometimes by the name Simplex, sometimes by that of Simplicius. On the relationship between the two novels, see above, Introduction, pp. 6ff.

§ The spa, mentioned many times in the novel, is Griesbach, a watering place in the Black Forest.

CHAPTER II

MISTRESS LIBUSCHKA, LATER CALLED COURAGE, GETS
INTO THE WAR, CALLS HERSELF JANCO, AND FOR A
WHILE ACTS AS A SERVANT. ITEM : AN ACCOUNT OF HER
BEHAVIOR AND OF THE STRANGE THINGS WHICH HAP-
PEN TO HER.

THOSE who know how the Slavonic nations treat
their serfs might easily be led to believe that I
was begot by a Bohemian nobleman and born of
a peasant's daughter. But believing and knowing are two
different things. I, too, believe many things and yet have
no knowledge of them. If I said that I knew who my
parents were, I would lie; and it would not be the first
time either. But I do know that I was brought up nicely
enough at Bragoditz, went to school there, and was instructed better than an ordinary girl in sewing, cooking,
embroidery, and other such womanly skills. The money
for my board came regularly from my father, but I did
not know where he lived; and my mother often sent me
greetings, yet I have never talked to her.

When the Prince of Bavaria went to Bohemia with
Bucquoy, in order to drive out the new King,* I was thirteen years old, a pert little thing that was beginning to
wonder where it had come from. And this question both-
ered me greatly because I was not permitted to inquire
and could not find any answer to it by myself. I was
guarded against company like a fine painting against dust.

* The Prince of Bavaria: Duke Maximilian Emanuel of Bavaria (1573-
1651). Bucquoy: Karl Bonaventura of Longueval, Count of Bucquoy
(1571-1621), a general of Emperor Ferdinand. The new King: Frederick V, Elector of the Palatinate, who became the "Winterking" and
was defeated in the battle of the White Mountain, November 8, 1620.

My guardian constantly kept her eyes on me, and since I was not permitted to play with other girls of my age, my mind was full of whims and follies and cared for nothing else.

The Duke of Bavaria parted from Bucquoy, the former marching against Budweis, the latter against Bragoditz. Budweis was wise enough to surrender in time, Bragoditz did not, and experienced the full force of the Imperial troops, who repaid the obstinacy of the city with great cruelty. When my guardian saw what was coming she said to me in good time, "Libuschka, my girl, if you want to remain a virgin, you must cut your hair and put on man's clothes; if you don't, I will not give a farthing for your honor, which I have been ordered to protect." She got a pair of scissors and cut away the golden hair on my right-hand side, arranging it on my left side in the way the most distinguished men wore their hair at that time.

"There, my daughter," she said, "If you escape from this turmoil with your honor, you will have enough hair left to show and within a year the rest will be grown again."

I was easily consoled, because ever since my girlhood I have liked to do wild things—the crazier the better. Then she dressed me in hose and a jerkin, and taught me to take bigger steps and use other manly gestures. In this way we waited for the town to be taken by the Imperial nations, my guardian in fear and trembling, I in great eagerness to see what kind of new and unusual fun-fair was going to follow. I was soon to learn. But I will not dwell on tales of how the men in the conquered town were slaughtered by the captors, the women ravished, and the town itself plundered. All this became so widely known during the past long war that everyone can tell a tale about it. But if I am to tell my whole story, I am obliged to report that I was taken along as a boy by a German trooper to attend to his horses and to go foraging, that is to say, to help him steal.

I called myself Janco. Although for a Bohemian I could talk German well enough, I did not let on to it. I was delicate, handsome, and distinguished in manners; whoever, knowing me the way I am now, does not believe that should have seen me fifty years ago. He would have agreed with me.

Now when my first master brought me to his company, his captain, who was truly a handsome and gallant young cavalier, asked him what he intended to do with me. The trooper replied: "Just what all other troopers do with their boys, use him for stealing and tending the horses, which, I am told, the Bohemians are especially good at. They say that when a Bohemian has rifled a house a German won't even find a nail left."

"What happens, however," said the captain, "if he takes to using his Bohemian craft on you, riding off with your horse, just to keep in practice?"

"As long as we are in his homeland," said the trooper, "I will watch him closely."

"Peasant boys," answered the captain, "brought up with horses, make better helpers for troopers than do burgher's sons who do not learn in the town how to tend a horse. Besides, it seems to me that this boy comes from respectable parents and has been brought up too delicately to tend the horse of a trooper."

I pricked up my ears, without betraying to the company that I understood their talk in German. My greatest worry was that they might get rid of me and take me back to the plundered town of Bragoditz. The sound of drums and fifes, of guns and trumpets, made my heart leap for joy; I could not hear enough of them. In the end it turned out—and I don't know whether this was my luck or misfortune—that the captain himself kept me to wait on him personally as a page and servant. To the trooper who insisted upon a boy of my nationality for a thief, he gave another Bohemian, a coarse fellow.

I made every effort to play the game right. I wheedled the captain so skillfully, kept his clothes so clean, prepared his linens so properly, and in every regard took such good care of him that he considered me a model servant. And since I was much taken by his weapons I attended to them so well that master and servant could safely rely on them. Thus it happened that the captain gave me a sword and with a box on the ear† declared me worthy of bearing arms. Everyone was amazed that I did so well. I was held to be unusually bright because I learned to talk German so quickly, for none knew that I had learned it in my early childhood. I was careful to suppress my girlish habits and to adopt manly ones instead. I assiduously learned how to swear like a trooper and to drink like a tinker. I drank the pledge of brotherhood with my presumed equals, and whenever I had anything to confess it had to do with theft or roguery. All this I did lest anyone notice what I had been lacking at birth and had not acquired since.

† A box on the ear: mock substitute for knighting.

CHAPTER III

JANCO LOSES HIS FINE LITTLE VIRGIN WREATH IN THE
QUARTERS OF THE RESOLUTE CAVALRY CAPTAIN, RE-
CEIVING IN RETURN THE NAME COURAGE.

AS I have said, my captain was a handsome young
cavalier, a good rider, a good fencer, a good dancer,
a daredevil; and he had a special passion for the
hunt, his great pleasure being to hunt hares with greyhounds. He had as much of a beard as I had, and had he
worn women's clothes, everyone would have thought him
a beautiful young lady. But I am losing the thread of
my story.

After Budweis and Bragoditz had fallen, both armies
went to Pilsen, which defended itself valiantly, but later
on received its punishment in the form of miserable stran-
gulations and hangings. From there the army went on
toward Rakonitz, where I saw my first encounter in the
field. At that time I wished I were a man and could take
to war all my life. For there was so much fun that my
heart leaped for joy. And my desire grew at the battle of
the White Mountain near Prague because we scored a
great victory, and suffered few losses. My captain got
plenty of booty then. As for me, I was employed not as a
page or servant, let alone as a girl, but as a soldier who
is sworn to meet the enemy and gets paid for it.

After this encounter, the Duke of Bavaria marched
into Austria, the Elector of Saxony to Lusitia, and our
General Bucquoy to Moravia in order to subdue the rebels
against the Emperor. While he was being treated for the
injury he had suffered at Rakonitz—and for this reason
we were living through a period of calm—I received a

mortal wound myself, which the charm of my captain inflicted on me. For I looked only at those of his qualities which I have mentioned and disregarded altogether that he could neither read nor write and was a coarse man who, I swear by all that is holy, never once thought of praying. But even if the wise King Alphonsus himself had called him nothing but a beautiful animal, the fire of my love would not have been extinguished. Yet I intended to keep all this a secret because of a sense of shame which sprang from my hard-pressed virginity.

Nevertheless, although I was still too young for any man, I was so impatient that I often wished I could take the place of those girls whom I and others procured for the captain. Besides, at the beginning I was kept from an impetuous and dangerous show of love by the fact that my sweetheart came from a noble and distinguished family: I thought such a man could not possibly marry someone ignorant of her parents. And I could not make up my mind to become his mistress, because every day I saw so many whores surrender themselves in the camp.

Although I was in terrible torment because of the battle that raged in my heart I was rank and wild and so full of life that neither the unrest of war nor work could subdue me. It is true that I had nothing to do but serve my captain, but love taught me to attend to that so zealously and assiduously that my master would swear that nowhere on earth was there a servant more loyal than I. Come what may, I was at his side and stayed near him whether he needed me or not; at all times I was eager to do something that would please him. If he had not been deceived by my clothes he could easily have seen from my face that I was devoted to him and adored him in a way no ordinary servant does. Meanwhile my bosom was growing more and more and so was my distress, so that I believed I could no longer hide my breasts outside nor the fire of my heart inside.

We stormed Iglau, subdued Trebitz, and forced our terms upon Znaim, put Brünn and Olmütz under the yoke and compelled many other towns to obey us. In all these enterprises I gained a lot of booty through my captain who rewarded me for my loyal service. Thus I fared well; I got myself a good horse, filled my purse, and often joined the other fellows to drink my quart of wine at the sutler's.

Once in such company, some of my companions were driven by spite to provoke me. Especially one of them, a malicious fellow, talked with contempt about the Bohemian people. The fool told me that some Bohemians had confused the decayed carcass of a dog, full of maggots, with a stinking cheese and eaten it, and he dared me by saying that I had myself been present when that happened. Soon both of us were using abusive language, from words we proceeded to blows, and from blows to an all-out fight. While we were in the thick of it, this fellow grabbed me between the legs because he wanted to get hold of the tool that I did not have. And this futile but murderous grip annoyed me more than it would have done had he not come away empty-handed. I became furious and indeed half mad. Defending myself with all my strength and agility, I scratched and bit my opponent. I struck and kicked him so hard that he fell, and in the end his face was so battered that it looked more like a devil's mask than human. I would have choked him to death, if others had not intervened and torn me away. I got off with a black eye, but I could not imagine that the scoundrel had failed to notice my true sex. I believe he would

not have hesitated to disclose it, had he not been afraid
that he would either have received still more blows or
been laughed at for letting himself be beaten by a girl.
Since I was afraid that in the end he might talk, I left
the canteen.

When I returned to our lodgings my captain was not
at home but in the gay company of other officers. That's
where he learned of the fight I had been in, before I saw
him. Now he liked me as a resolute youngster and, for
this reason, did not scold me much, although he did not
fail to give me a warning. When he reached the climax
of his sermon and asked why I had beaten up my opponent so terribly, I answered, "because he tried to grasp
my courage which no other man has ever touched with
his hand." (I did not want to express myself clearly or as
coarsely as the Swabians do when they talk of "scabbards"
and if I were a master in their country I would not suffer
their obscene talk but speak only of "lewd scabbards."*)
My virginity was nearing its end in any event, especially
since I was in danger of my opponent betraying me after
all. So I uncovered my snow white bosom and showed
the captain my budding, firm breasts. "Look, sir," I said,
"here you see a virgin who disguised herself in Bragoditz
in order to save her honor from the soldiers. And since
God and good fortune have delivered her into your hands,
she begs and prays that as a sincere cavalier you will protect her honor." As I said this I began to cry so miserably
that anyone could have put his hand into the fire to take
his oath that I was serious about it all.

* Scabbard: Grimmelshausen has "Fündli-Messer" (the Swabian word
for knives), which is related to the popular word for *female* organ.
For the literal translation I have substituted "scabbard" to avoid the
misinterpretation that Grimmelshausen wanted to suggest an association with the *male* organ.

The captain was much astonished and yet could not help laughing at the word courage, the new name with which I had so colorfully described the emblem of my sex. He consoled me in all kindness and promised in polite words to guard my honor like his own life. His deeds, however, revealed him at once as the first to go after my little wreath. I liked the touch of his lascivious hands much better than his fine promises, but I resisted gallantly, not in order to get away from him or to escape his desire, but in order to arouse and excite him to even more fervent efforts. I succeeded so well in this game that he swore on oath against the Devil that he would marry me, but I could well imagine that he intended to do that about as much as to hang himself.

And now, my dear Simplex!† At the spa you thought perhaps that you were the first to skim the sweet cream off the milk. But no, you fool, you were deceived. It was all gone. And because you got up too late, you were not worthy of more than what was left, and that's what you got. All this was mere child's play, however, compared with the way I have otherwise fooled and deceived you. Nor will I fail to tell it to you in full.

† Simplex: See Note † to Chapter 1.

CHAPTER IV

THUS I lived with my captain in secret love serving him both as wife and valet. I pressed him often to keep his promise and lead me to church, but he always found some excuse for postponing the matter. He was never more moved than when I showed myself madly in love with him and wept at the same time for my virginity, like Jephtha's daughter. Actually I could not have cared less about its loss and was even glad that I had been relieved of this unbearable burden and with it of my curiosity. By charming and importuning my captain I succeeded, however, in getting him to have made for me in Vienna a dazzling, stylish dress of the kind then worn by ladies of the Italian nobility. This success aroused my highest hopes and made me willing to stay with him: now I lacked nothing but a marriage ceremony and public recognition as the captain's wife. It is true, I could as yet neither wear my dress nor present myself as a woman, let alone as his spouse, but this annoyed me less than the fact that he no longer called me "Janco" or "Libuschka" but "Courage." Others imitated him and called me by the same name in ignorance of its origin, thinking that my master addressed me so because of the single-minded resolution and incomparable ardor with which I met the enemy. Thus I had to swallow what was hard for me to digest.

Therefore, let me warn you, my dear girls, you who have kept your honor and virtue still intact, not to let yourselves be carelessly robbed of them, because with them you lose your freedom in exchange for nothing but torture and slavery which are more difficult to endure than death itself. I speak from experience and can tell you a tale about it. I did not mind the loss of my treasure, for I had never been eager to buy a lock for it, but it vexed me that I had to take my captain's taunting about it and yet smile and be kind to him for fear that he would betray my secret and let me be jeered at and shamed by everyone.

You fellows, too, who like highwaymen are always thinking of robbery, beware of just retribution for your wantonness. Remember what happened to the cavalier in Paris who betrayed one lady and wanted to marry another; he was invited to sleep again with his first lady but was murdered at night, miserably cut to pieces, and thrown out of the window into the open street. I must confess that had my captain not given me such good proof of his ardent love and continued to keep me hoping that he would surely marry me in the end, sooner or later I would have shot him at some moment when he least expected it.

In the meantime we marched under Bucquoy's command into Hungary. In Pressburg, which we conquered first, we deposited most of our baggage and our best things because my captain anticipated that we would have to fight a pitched battle with Bethlen Gabor.* From there we went to St. Georgen, Bösing, Modern, and other places, which we plundered first and then burned down. We captured Tirnau, Altenberg, and almost the whole island

* Bethlen Gabor (1580-1628), Prince of Siebenbürgen, an ally of the Winter King.

of Schütt in the Danube†, but at Neusohl we suffered a reverse. Not only was my captain mortally wounded there, but our general, Duke Bucquoy, was himself slain. Because of his death we took to flight and did not stop until we reached Pressburg.

I nursed my captain with all my devotion, but the physician predicted that he would die since his lung was pierced. Because of his condition people continually told him that he ought to make his peace with God. Our regimental chaplain was such a zealous minister of souls that he gave my captain no rest until he confessed and partook of the Lord's Supper. After that both his father confessor and his own conscience spurred and drove him, bedridden as he was, to marry me, an act which was held to be good for his soul rather than his body. This he did all the more readily since I had persuaded him that he had made me pregnant.

How topsy-turvy this world is! Some men take women to live with them in wedlock; but this one wedded me because he knew that he was about to die. After these developments people believed, of course, it was not as a servant but as a mistress that I was devoted to him and shed tears for his misfortune. The dress he had ordered for me came in handy for the marriage ceremonies, but I could not wear it for long. Now I needed a black one instead, because he made me a widow a few days later. I, too, was like the woman who, at her husband's funeral, replied to a commiserating friend, "What you love most, the Devil takes away first."

I arranged for a magnificent burial suitable to his condition, for he left me not only beautiful horses, weapons,

† The words "of Schütt in the Danube" are not in the German text but have been added for the sake of clarity.

[104]

and clothes, but also a handsome sum of money; I asked the priest to certify all arrangements in writing, hoping thereby to snatch something of his parents' estate. Despite my diligent search, however, all I discovered was that he had been of noble birth but poor as a church mouse; indeed, had the Bohemians not arranged a war for him, he would have had to shift for himself quite miserably.

Not only did I lose my sweetheart in Pressburg, but I was also besieged by Bethlen Gabor in that city. However, ten companies on horseback and two regiments on foot from Moravia relieved the town by means of a stratagem so that Bethlen Gabor, despairing of conquest, abandoned the siege. At an auspicious moment I departed with my horses, servants, and all my baggage for Vienna in order to return from there to Bohemia. I wanted to see whether by any chance my guardian at Bragoditz was still alive and could perhaps tell me who my parents had been. At the time, I was tickled by the idea of being highly esteemed and honored when I returned home with so many horses and servants, all of them proved by my documents to have been gained fairly and honestly in the war.

CHAPTER V

THE HONEST AND VIRTUOUS AS WELL AS EVIL AND GOD-
LESS WAYS OF COURAGE, THE CAVALRY CAPTAIN'S
WIFE: HOW SHE YIELDS TO THE WILL OF A COUNT,
ACQUIRES THE PISTOLES OF AN AMBASSADOR, AND SUB-
MITS WILLINGLY TO OTHERS IN ORDER TO SNAP UP A
RICH BOOTY.

I DID not dare to undertake my journey from Vienna to Bragoditz right away because the roads were unsafe and lodging in the inns was terribly expensive. So I sold my horses, dismissed all my servants, engaging a maid instead, and rented from a widow a sitting room, bedchamber, and a kitchen for my household while awaiting opportunity for a safe return home. This widow was a real ace of trumps; there are not many like her. She had two daughters who introduced me to the courtiers and officers, in whose circles they were well known, and before long these robbers began to praise the great beauty of the captain's widow in their midst. Even as my black mourning clothes lent me a special appearance, a grave dignity which added to the radiance of my beauty, so I conducted myself at the beginning with studied reserve. My maid had to spin, while I saw to it that the people took notice of my sewing, weaving, and other womanly work to which I had turned.

Secretly, however, I paraded my beauty for hours in front of my mirror in order to study the effects of laughter and tears, sighs and similar fleeting changes of expression. This foolishness should have revealed to me my frivolity and indicated clearly enough that I was well on the way to imitating my landlady's daughters. They and

[106]

the old woman began soon enough to seek my company to promote this very end. Often, they visited me in my room to while away my time and then turned to the kind of talk which undermines the modesty of young girls, especially those of my inclinations. My landlady had a clever way of first approaching my maid and suggesting to her how to dress me and how to do my hair according to the latest fashion. Then she told me how to make my fair complexion even fairer and how to heighten the luster of my golden hair. When she had prettied me up like that, she said that it was a pity for a noble creature like me to be always hidden in a black sack and to live like a turtledove. All this I liked only too well; it was oil for the lively fire of my desires. She also lent me *Amadis** to occupy my leisure and to acquaint me with the use of polite compliments. Nothing that she could think of to excite the lusts of love did she leave undone.

Meanwhile, my former servants had broadcast among the townspeople what kind of captain's wife I had really been and how I had arrived at that estate. Since they *knew of no other name for me, I was still called Courage.* As for myself, with the passage of time I forgot my captain, since he no longer kept me warm; and as I noticed that my landlady's daughters were much sought after,

* *Amadis*: This famous novel was much admired by the nobility of Europe in the baroque era. It was introduced into Germany from Spain via France in the second half of the sixteenth century, and ever new continuations appeared until no fewer than twenty-four volumes were available in 1595. In Grimmelshausen's time *Amadis*, because of the amorous adventures of its knights and ladies, had become a favorite of the lower classes as well. Middle-class theologians and moralists like Moscherosch criticized the immoral character of the work. So did Grimmelshausen, not only in *Courage, the Adventuress* but also in the dedicatory poem to *Proximus und Lympida* (1672) and in the conclusion of *The Enchanted Bird's-nest*, Part I.

my mouth began to water for fresh fare, which more than anything else my landlady, too, wanted me to have. But as long as I did not doff my mourning she could not impose such things on me openly, especially since she noticed that I remained quite cold to all suggestions of this kind. Nevertheless, not a single day passed without several gentlemen approaching her, swarming about the house like wasps about the beekeeper's sugar trough.

Among them was a young count who had seen me in church and fallen deeply in love with me. He spent a considerable amount of money to meet me, but when my landlady whom he often asked for help did not dare simply to introduce him to me, he made inquiries of one of my former servants about everything concerning my captain's regiment. Then, having learned the names of all the officers he humbled himself and called on me in person in order to inquire about his old acquaintances whom he had never seen in his life. This led him to speak of my captain. In his youth, said the count, he had studied with him and ever since had been his good and close friend. The count deplored his early death, lamenting at the same time that I had become a widow in my tender youth and offering me, should I be in need of any assistance, that . . . etc. In such and similar fashion the young gentleman sought to make my acquaintance. He succeeded.

Although it was clear to me that his story was full of holes—for my captain had never studied anything—the count pleased me well enough because he apparently wanted to take the place of my late captain. I pretended to be reserved and cool, however, and replied only briefly, shedding a few pretty tears. I thanked him for his sympathy and his gracious offer with a few compliments, intimating that he should be satisfied with the good beginning of his affair and take leave.

Next day he dispatched his footman to inquire if a visit would put me to any inconvenience. I replied that it would cause me no inconvenience and I would welcome his presence, but since there were strange people in this world who were ready to suggest anything I begged him to desist and not to become the cause of evil gossip about me. This discourteous reply† did not arouse the count's anger, but on the contrary increased his love. He passed by my house in drooping melancholy,§ hoping to catch at least a glimpse of me at the window, but in vain: I wanted to sell my goods at a good price and did not show myself.

When this man was nearly dying of his love, I doffed my mourning and made a show of myself in my other dress, which was quite something to behold. I neglected nothing that would add to my elegance and thus attracted the eyes and hearts of many noblemen. But this happened only when I went to church, because I did not go anywhere else. Every day I had to listen to greetings and messages from various men who had all come down with the count's disease. Yet I remained firm as a rock until all of Vienna was filled not only with the praise of my incomparable beauty but also with the glory of my chastity and other rare virtues. When I had succeeded to the point where everybody regarded me almost as a saint I thought that the time had come to give full rein to my passions

† It seems that Grimmelshausen characterized Courage's refusal to receive the count as "discourteous" mainly because he was a count; and this explanation allows for Grimmelshausen's unlimited capacity for irony.

§ The German is *maulhenkolisch*, a play on the words *melancholisch* and *maulhängerisch* (hangdog).

which I had controlled until then and undeceive the people who thought so highly of me.

The count was the first to receive and enjoy my favor, because he had spared neither trouble nor expense to obtain it. It is true, he was charming, loved me dearly, and I considered him the most suitable of the whole lot for satisfying my desires, and yet he would not have got so far had he not sent me, immediately after I abandoned mourning, a piece of dove-colored satin with all the trimmings for a new dress and, above all, had he not presented me with a hundred ducats for my household in order to console me for the loss of my husband.

After him came the ambassador of a great potentate who let me earn sixty pistoles the first night. Others followed him—all of them capable of spending a good deal. For whoever was poor, or rather not rich and noble enough, either had to stay outside or be satisfied with my landlady's daughters. In this way I arranged everything so that my mill was never idle. I did so well that within a month I amassed more than a thousand ducats in cash, not counting gifts in the form of jewels, rings, chains, bracelets, velvet, silk, and linen (nobody dared to show up merely with stockings or gloves), and also food, wine, and other things. In this way I put my mind to making use of my youth, because I was aware of the saying,

> Your beauty fades a bit each day
> 'Till to the grave you go away.

At this very moment I would still regret it had I done otherwise. But in the end I went pretty far and hardly refused anyone at all so that people began to point their fingers at me and I began to think that in the long run things might not turn out too well.

My landlady was of great help to me and made a handsome profit herself in the bargain. She taught me various neat tricks, not only such as are useful to loose women but also others which are practiced by shady men, including the arts of making oneself invulnerable and of stopping up gun barrels at will.** I believe that if I had remained with her any longer I would have learned even witchcraft. I received warning, however, that the authorities were about to search out our nest and destroy it, and so I bought myself a coach and two horses, hired a servant, and took to my heels as soon as I had a chance of getting safely to Prague.

** As has been pointed out above (cf. Introduction, pp. 14 ff.), Grimmelshausen's works contain many references to "the art of making oneself invulnerable and of stopping up gun barrels at will." In *The Adventurous Simplicissimus* it is the villains who are invulnerable. In *The False Messiah*, the hero, a merchant, learns the art of making himself invulnerable in the pursuit of "evil" designs and disregards Christian teachings. Later (in *Bird's-nest II*, chaps. 25-26), a Catholic priest exposes the sinfulness of invulnerability and other magic qualities. Thus "invulnerability" of a person suggests that the Devil has a grip on his soul, although Grimmelshausen also says through Simplicissimus (*Simplicissimus*, bk. VI, chap. 13) that the skill of "freezing" a man is a "natural art" and not witchcraft; in other words, it is not "black magic." For the influence of pansophy on 17th century interest in "freezing and other arts associated with "vulnerability" see W. Peukert, "Festmachen," *Handwörterbuch zur deutschen Volkskunde. Abteilung I: Aberglaube*, Vol. II, pp. 1353 ff. Cf. also Karl Amersbach, *Aberglaube, Sage und Märchen bei Grimmelshausen*. Beilage zum Program des Grossherzoglichen Gymnasiums zu Baden-Baden, Part I, 1891, p. 28 and Part II, pp. 35-42.

CHAPTER VI

IN Prague I had many fine opportunities to continue in my profession, but my desire to see my guardian and find out about my parents spurred me on to Bragoditz. Since the country was at peace, I thought it safe to do so, but lo and behold, one evening when I could already see the settlement spread out in front of me, eleven horsemen from Mansfeld's army suddenly came upon me. Because of their sash and emblems I took them, as everyone else would have done, for friendly men of the Emperor's, but they grabbed me and went off with me and my carriage toward the Bohemian Forest as if the Devil himself were chasing them. I screamed, it is true, as if hung up for torture, but they silenced me soon enough. Around midnight they reached a lonely dairy farm at the rim of the forest. There they fed the horses and then they began to treat me according to custom. I felt badly enough about that, but they were rewarded for it as dogs are for eating grass. For while the brutes were satisfying their desires, a captain with thirty dragoons who had escorted a convoy to Pilsen attacked and slaughtered them all, because by carrying false colors they had denied their true master.

Mansfeld's men had not yet divided my possessions among themselves; since I had an Imperial passport and had been in enemy hands for less than twenty-four hours, I protested to the captain that he could not seize and keep me and my baggage as fair booty. Although he had to admit that I was right, he said that nevertheless I was obligated to him for my liberation and would surely understand that he did not intend to let go a treasure such as this, which he had captured from the enemy. If, as my passport claimed, I was a captain's widow, he in his turn was a widower and a captain. With my consent the booty could soon be divided, otherwise he would take me along anyway and be ready afterward to dispute with anyone whether or not the booty was rightfully his. Thus he made it clear enough that he was already smitten by me. In order to divert the brook toward his mill, he added that he would let me have the privilege of electing either that the booty be distributed among all his men or else that I and all my possessions remained his through marriage. In the latter case, I could be sure he would persuade his men that I was not fair booty but had become his alone through marriage.

I replied that had I free choice I would not want either but would ask permission to continue on to my home. And at that point I began to cry as though I were quite serious about it all, following the old ditty:

> When women seem to cry from smart
> Their tears do not reveal their heart.
> They can cry at any time
> For a reason or a rhyme.

I thought that I would give him an opportunity to console me and to fall more deeply in love, since I knew that the hearts of men open most readily to women who are sad and cry. My trick worked. He comforted me, and when he assured me of his most sincere love, I consented to marry him under the explicit condition and with the proviso that he was not to touch me at all prior to the wedding. He gave me this promise and kept it until we reached Mansfeld's fortifications at Weidhausen, which at that time had been turned over to the Duke of Bavaria by an agreement between him and Mansfeld. Then my suitor's ardent love would not suffer any further delay just because there was no wedding feast. So, before he had learned in what way Courage had earned her money —and no pittance at that—he quickly arranged for us to be married.

I had been with the army less than a month, when several high officers turned up who not only had known me but had been on quite familiar terms with me in Vienna, yet they were discreet enough not to cast any public aspersion on my honor or theirs. There was some gossip, it is true, but it gave me little concern except that I had to suffer once again being called Courage.

Otherwise, I had a good and patient husband who enjoyed my gold as much as my beauty. He was more miserly than I liked, but since I put up with him in this regard, he let me be all the more free toward everyone in speech and manner. Whenever he was teased that in time he would surely grow horns, he replied jokingly that he was not concerned about that, for if someone should get on top of his wife he would not let matters stand at that but take time out to do the stranger's work over again.

At all times, he kept a horse for me equipped with a fine saddle and harness. Unlike the other officers' wives I did not ride on a saddle for ladies but on a man's saddle, and although I sat sideways like a woman, I had a stirrup hanging on the other side at all times and kept pistols and a Turkish saber under my thigh. Underneath my little skirt of thin taffeta I wore breeches so that I could sit up like a man at any moment and conduct myself like a young soldier on horseback. Whenever there was an encounter with the enemy it was impossible for me not to be in it. I used to say that a lady unable to defend herself against a man on horseback ought not to wear plumes on her hat like a man. And since in a few skirmishes I managed to capture some men who did not consider themselves poor soldiers, I became even bolder. I hung a carbine—or as it is sometimes called, a dragon—on my saddle and took on two men, away from the main fight, pressing them all the more relentlessly since through the art of my memorable landlady I and my horse were made so invulnerable that no bullet could as much as give us a scratch.

Such was my life at that time. I gained more booty than many a sworn soldier, which annoyed men and women alike; but that did not bother me as long as I was fattening my soup all the while. For a woman with my appetites my husband was virtually impotent, but I stuck with him even though officers higher in rank than captain called on me to take his place and be his lieu-tenant.* He always let me have my way. Nevertheless, I was gay at parties, forward in conversation, but also as dashing as a man against the enemy, as domestic and thrifty as any wife in the field, better than a good groom in tending the horses, and so solicitous in our quarters that my captain had no reason to wish for anything better. When he had cause to contradict me he did not mind that I talked back to him and that I insisted on having my way, for he knew that I made our coins multiply so quickly that we deposited a good part of them in a large town for safekeeping.

Thus, I lived happily and in joy. If only my husband had been, at night, a better horseman, I could not have asked for a different arrangement. But fortune or fate did not long favor my condition; my captain was shot dead at Wisloch, and I became once more, after so short a time, a widow.

* Lieu-tenant: play on the original meaning of the word "lieutenant."

[115]

CHAPTER VII

COURAGE ENTERS HER THIRD MARRIAGE, THEREBY BE-
COMING THE WIFE OF A LIEUTENANT INSTEAD OF A
CAPTAIN, AND FARES NOT AS WELL AS BEFORE; SHE
FIGHTS WITH HER LIEUTENANT WITH CUDGELS FOR
THE PANTS OF THE FAMILY AND WINS THEM THROUGH
BRAVE RESOLUTION AND VALOR; WHEREUPON HER HUS-
BAND JILTS HER AND TAKES OFF.

MY husband was hardly cold and buried when I already had a full dozen of new suitors and could choose among them. For not only was I young and beautiful but I also had fine horses and stacks of lovely coins. And although I made it known that I wanted to mourn for half a year in honor of my late captain, I could not drive away the importunate bumblebees which swarmed about me as though I were a pot full of honey without a lid. The colonel promised me room and board until I decided what to do. In exchange I let two of my men do service for him. As for myself, whenever there was an opportunity to snatch something from the enemy, I risked my skin as much as did any soldier. In the pleasant, almost joyous encounter at Wimpfen I took a lieutenant prisoner and in addition during the pursuit not far from Heilbrunn a cornet with his standard. When the wagons were plundered my two servants got considerable booty in cash, which they divided with me according to our agreement.

After this battle, I had more lovers than before. I had had more good days than good nights with my previous husband and since, after his death, I had fasted against my inclination, I planned to make up for all this neglect through a wise choice. I promised myself to a lieutenant who, I thought, excelled all his rivals in beauty, youth, intelligence, and courage. He was an Italian by birth, with black hair and white skin, and he appeared to my eyes to be so handsome that no painter could have painted him more so. Until I yielded to his wooing he conducted himself toward me almost with doglike humility, and when I said Yes he was as jubilant as if God had robbed the whole world in order to make him alone happy. We were married in the Palatinate and were honored at the wedding by the presence of the colonel and most of the high officers in our regiment. All of them wished us much happiness and a long lasting marriage—in vain.

For this is what happened. After our first night, we were lying side by side when the sun was rising, idly engaged in friendly and amiable conversation. Just when I was about to get up, my lieutenant called his boy to his bedside and ordered him to fetch two big cudgels. He obeyed, and since I imagined that they would at once be tried out on the poor fellow, I did not fail to ask mercy for the boy until he returned bringing the two cudgels and putting them, as he was ordered to, on the table next to our night things.

When the boy had left, my bridegroom said to me, "Now, my darling, as you know, everybody was convinced that you wore the pants when your former husband was alive, and when people began to talk about that in honest company, it redounded not a little to his shame. I cannot help thinking that you might still want to keep to your old habit and wear my pants, which I would find difficult to put up with; in fact, it would be quite intolerable. Take a good look at them, therefore, on the table over there, and at the two cudgels lying right next to them. We will be able to have it out right away with those cudgels, should you be inclined to take the pants and put them on as you did before. I am sure you agree with me, my precious, that it is better that they go to the one or the other right now at the beginning than that we have a daily war about them in our marriage.

"My darling," I replied, giving him a long kiss, "I thought that the battle between us had already taken place. I have never had in mind to put on your pants. Just as I am fully aware of the fact that woman was not taken from man's head but from his side, so I have hoped that this would be known to you, my sweetheart, as well. I have trusted that, remembering my origin, you would consider me your spouse and not a rag, as if I had been taken off the soles of your feet. Please notice that I did not presume to sit on your head but that I am lying at your side. I humbly request that you dismiss the bizarre idea of giving me a fencing lesson."

"Fiddlesticks," he said, "those are the very tricks of a woman who wants to get hold of the reins before one knows it. But no, first there will have to be a fight so that it be established once and for all which one is to obey the other."

Thereupon like a fool he tore himself from my arms. But I, too, jumped out of bed. Quickly putting on my chemise and pants and grabbing the shortest yet heaviest cudgel, I cried, "Since you insist on commanding me to fight and want to give to the victor supreme lordship over the vanquished (a position which I have not coveted) I would be a fool indeed if I let slip through my hands an opportunity of getting what I would otherwise never have dreamed of."

Nor was he idle in the meantime. I waited for him to

put on his pants and then he got hold of the other cudgel intending to grab me by my hair and let me have it in good measure on my back. But I was too quick for him. Before he knew what was happening I hit him over the head so that he was dazed like a clubbed ox. I took the two cudgels to throw them out of the room, but when I opened the door there standing in front of it were several officers who had listened to our quarrel and watched us through an opening. I let them laugh as much as they cared to, banged the door shut again in their faces, put on my skirt and brought my stupid wretch, that is to say my bridegroom, to his senses with water from the basin. When I had seated him at the table and dressed myself a little, I let the officers who were still standing in front of the door enter our room.

You can imagine how we all looked at each other. I had not failed to notice that my bridegroom had invited these officers to be outside the room at that time so that they might witness his folly. For when they had jeered at the bully, telling him that he would have to let me wear the pants, he had boasted that he knew of a special way of teaching me docility the very first morning; afterward I would tremble whenever he gave me as much as an angry look. But the good man should have tried that with someone other than Courage. By taking me on he became everybody's laughingstock.

I would not have shared a room with him had I not been enjoined and ordered to do so by our superiors. You can easily imagine just how we lived together, namely like cat and dog. When he realized that he could not get his revenge and when he was no longer able to bear being everyone's laughingstock, he got all my cash together one fine day and went over to the enemy with three of my best horses and a servant.

CHAPTER VIII

THUS I became a half-widow, which is a condition much worse than that of a woman without a
man. Some people suspected that I had planned
the escape with my husband and would follow him. But
when I asked the colonel to advise me as to what I ought
to do, and to give me his orders, he told me to stay with
the regiment and promised me a widow's ration as long
as I remained honest. In this way I allayed everyone's
suspicions.

It was difficult for me to make ends meet, because my
money was gone out of the window and I had lost my
beautiful army horses with which I had captured so much
fine booty. But I concealed my poverty to avoid contempt.
I still had my two menservants, a boy, and a few sorry
jades or baggage horses. Anything of value I turned into
cash, including some stuff in the baggage of my men, and
so got myself well mounted again. It is true, as a woman
I was not allowed to take part in any raids, but among the
foragers none excelled me. Often, I wished for another
battle like that at Wimpfen, but what could I do? I had
to bide my time, because it was not possible to arrange a
battle just to please me. In order nonetheless to get hold of
some money again, which was hard to do on the marauding expeditions, and at the same time repay my fugitive
for his infidelity, I made myself available to various spend-

thrifts. In this way I managed, and was able to hire another strong fellow to help out when I went looting; the other two men I used to keep watch for us.

This was my way of life until we chased Brunswick across the river Main and drowned many of his men, on which occasion I joined our men and conducted myself in the colonel's presence with a courage he had never thought possible even in a man. For in the melee I captured an enemy major under the eyes of his own troops just when he was about to renew his charge. And when one of his men tried to save him and fired his pistol at my head, so that my plumes and hat went sailing in the wind, I repaid him with my saber: for a few steps he kept riding at my side, but without his head—a sight both miraculous and gruesome to behold. His squadron was isolated and turned to flight.

When the major had given me a handsome sum in gold, a gold chain, and a precious ring in payment for his life, I let him change horses with my boy and then turned him over to our troops where he was safe. Then I rode once more to the destroyed bridge. There was no end to the miserable drowning in the water and to the cruel slaughter on land. Although all of us were still supposed to remain with our unit, I seized a carriage with six beautiful horses. It contained neither man nor money, but in it I found two boxes with fine clothes and white linen, and with my boy's help I took it to the rear where I had left the major. He was nearly dying of shame at having been captured by a young woman. But when he saw the pistols in the pockets of my breeches and in my holster, and noticed that I made them ready again along with my carbine, and heard what I had done at Wimpfen, he calmed down a little and said, "She is of the Devil, I wash my hands of this witch."

I returned to the scene of battle with my boy, whom I had made as invulnerable as myself and my horse, only to find the lieutenant-colonel of our regiment lying beneath his horse. When he recognized me he cried for help. So I loaded him onto my boy's horse and took him back to the captured carriage to keep my captured major company.

It is unbelievable how much my enemies as well as my friends praised me after this battle. Everyone said that I was the Devil Himself. At that time my fondest wish was not to be a woman. But what could I do about that? All my wishing was vain and futile. Often I thought that I might pretend to be a hermaphrodite so that I could wear breeches in public and pass for a young fellow. But my excessive desires had given so many men an opportunity for first-hand knowledge of what I really was that I did not have the heart to do what I wanted to ever so much. Too many witnesses would have gainsaid me and caused me to be looked over by physicians and midwives. Therefore, I managed as best I could, telling those who reproved me that in the old times the Amazons had fought their enemies as boldly as had the men.

To gain the colonel's favor and his protection against those who begrudged my success, I presented to him my carriage and the horses, for which he made me a gift of two hundred Imperial taler. This money, together with my booty and earnings, I deposited in a large town for safekeeping.

When we had occupied Mannheim and were still besieging Frankenthal, playing lord and master of the Palatinate, Corduba and Anhalt defeated once more the Duke of Brunswick and Mansfeld at Fleury. In this battle, my fugitive husband, the lieutenant, was recognized by our men and, as a deserter who had broken his oath, was

hanged from a tree with a rope around his fine neck—
which freed me from my husband and made me a widow
again. But the number of my enemies grew thereafter.
They said, "That infernal witch has taken the poor devil's
life. She could have been patient with him for a little while
and let him live a little longer until he was done in some
other way and came to an honest end."

CHAPTER IX

FROM day to day I was ever more vexed. My servants became disaffected, because so often they heard it said, "The deuce! How can you work for such a slut." While I was still hoping to get another man, everyone said, "You take her, I don't want her." Honest people raised their eyebrows at us and, so, too, did almost all the officers. As for ordinary folk, men without means and power, I did not allow them to come near me; I was not in the habit of giving them as much as a glance anyway. Thus, although I did not, like my husband, feel the rope that our foolish quarrels had put around his neck, I suffered the consequences a longer time than it had taken him to put up with the hanging. I would have liked to change my ways, but neither habit nor the company I kept would let me better my lot. That's how it goes in times of war: most people become worse rather than better.

Again, I made myself pretty and set various snares and traps, hoping for a good catch. But it was all in vain, because I was already too deep in disrepute and the whole army was well informed about Courage. When I was riding by a regiment, a thousand voices publicly decried my honor so that, like a night owl, I had to avoid the light of day. When we were on the march, honest women shunned me, the riffraff of the baggage train pushed me about, and unmarried officers who might have protected me for the sake of their nocturnal hunting had to stay with their regiments, where I was scalded in a brew of shameful gossip. It seemed to me that in the end things would not turn out well for me.

A few officers still befriended me but they sought their own welfare rather than mine. Some of them wanted to satisfy their lust, others were after my money, still others after my horses. All of them were parasites, and this annoyed me greatly. No one wanted to marry me, either because they were ashamed of me or attributed to me an evil quality that harmed all who consorted with me, or because, for some other reason unknown to me, I scared them off.

I decided therefore to quit not only my regiment but the army, nay, the whole war as well. Nor was it hard for me to do this, because the high-ranking officers were glad to get rid of me anyway. Indeed, I don't think that there were any honest folk who shed many tears at my departure, except perhaps a few officers of middle rank, young unmarried lovers of sweetmeats whose nightshirts I had washed at some time. The colonel did not cherish the idea that his beautiful carriage had been captured from the enemy and presented to him by Courage. Nor did he respect me at all for having saved the wounded lieutenant-colonel from death on the battlefield. In fact, he cursed me for the trouble I had taken and got hot under the collar whenever he saw me. You can imagine the kind of happiness and good health he wished to bring down on my head. As to the women and the officers' wives, they hated me, because I was the most beautiful woman in the whole regiment and many of their men preferred me to them. Finally, the soldiers of high and low rank were my enemies because I had shown heart for enterprises that would have made most of them tremble in their boots, for

[125]

they lacked the reckless courage required for such ventures and shunned the grave hazards involved.

Knowing that I had more enemies than friends I was well aware that many people were only waiting for a chance to do me harm, each in his own special way. So I said to myself, "Courage, how will you escape from so many enemies who are all planning your ruin? You have enough enemies who could hire some fellow to kill you secretly if only for your beautiful horses, your beautiful dresses, or for the money that they believe you have stacked away. What if such a fellow were to murder you or do away with you in battle? Who would care a brass farthing about it? Who would avenge your death? Why, can you still trust even your own servants?" With such worries I tormented myself and I had no one but myself to turn to for good advice. So I did just that and made up my own mind.

I asked the colonel for a passport to the nearest Imperial city, which was well located to serve as a haven from the armies. I got not only the passport without much effort but also in lieu of a discharge a document certifying that whereas I had been legally married to a captain (for I was not eager to claim any association with my last husband); and whereas after losing him on the battlefield I had spent some time with the regiment deporting myself with such propriety, honesty, and reserve as befits a lady of virtue and honor, I was highly recommended to whom it might concern for my irreproachable and virtuous conduct. These fat lies were declared under hand and seal. No one need be surprised at all that. For the worse a person behaves and the more people want to get rid of him, the finer will be the testimonial with which he will be sent on his way, especially if that is all the wages he receives.

To show my gratitude to the colonel, I presented to him, for his company, a horse and one of my servants who, although no officer, was well equipped. I succeeded in getting away with another servant, a boy, a maid, six horses (each worth a hundred ducats) and a well-stocked coach. And I cannot tell for all my conscience (some call it a rather free conscience) in what manner I had captured and amassed all these things.

When I reached the town in safety with my possessions, I turned my horses into cash and got money for everything else of value that I did not immediately need. I also dismissed all my servants in order to reduce my expenses. But in one particular respect I fared in this town as I had in Vienna: again I could not escape the name Courage, although there was nothing that I would have more readily parted with than it. The reason the name stuck to me was simply that my old customers—that is, rather, my young ones—rode into town to see me and asked after me by that name so that even the street urchins learned it more quickly than their paternoster. I showed the fig to these gallants but when they told the townspeople what an ace I really was, I in turn declared under my hand and seal that the officers spread such gossip about me only because I was not one of the sort they wanted me to be. In this way, I got myself somehow out of trouble and on the strength of my favorable written testimonials persuaded the town to take me under its protection for a small fee, until I had an opportunity to move on. Thus, against my will, I led an honest, pious, quiet, and reserved life, devoting myself to my appearance, which became ever more beautiful, and hoping to get another good man in due time.

CHAPTER X

BUT it would have been a long wait for a bite worth anything. The patrician families stuck together and whoever else was well off could get married to a rich, beautiful, and honest girl—honesty still had some value at that time—so that there was no need for such a man to hang on to an abandoned soldier's whore. Those who either had gone bankrupt or were about to do so, wanted my money of course, but this was no reason for me to want them; artisans were in any event not good enough for me. So I stayed single for a whole year, a state that became harder and harder for me to endure and seemed ever more unnatural, especially since the good life I could afford whetted my appetite and made me quite restless.

By putting the money I had in various large cities into the hands of merchants or bankers, I made a nice profit so that I was able to live comfortably without depleting my capital. But I suffered from want in another spot and my weak nature could not endure this good life. That's why I sent my money by draft to Prague and, joining the company of some merchants, went there myself. I sought refuge with my guardian in Bragoditz to see if I would have better luck there.

I found my guardian as poor as I had left her. Even before the war she had lived off me rather than I off her, and now the war had ruined her. She was very happy to see me, above all because she noticed that I had not come empty-handed. Yet her first welcome consisted of nothing but tears. She kissed me and called me an unhappy young lady, who could not lead a life appropriate to her station. She added that in the future she would no longer be able to help, advise, and guide me, because my closest friends and relations had been driven away or were dead. Furthermore, I must not show my face to the Imperial forces because of my origin. Meanwhile she wept continually so that I was completely unable to make any sense whatever of what she said. Noticing that the poor fool was miserable and hungry I gave her something to eat and drink. This calmed her down and even seemed to make her a little tipsy. Then she candidly told me the true story of my origin.

My father, she said, was a count. Only a few years ago, he was the most powerful personage in the whole kingdom but had been driven out of the country because he had rebelled against the Emperor. He was reported to be living now at the Ottoman Porte, having changed from the Christian to the Turkish religion. My mother, she said, had come from an honest family, but had been as poor as she was beautiful. She had been a lady in waiting to the count's wife. While she attended the countess the count had become her subject and rendered her such services that finally he had to take her to a country house where she had given birth to me. At that time my guardian was herself weaning a little son begotten by a nobleman of that castle. So she was chosen to become my wet nurse and to educate me at Bragoditz as a nobly born child. Both my father and mother had provided ample means for my support. "It is true, my dear young lady, that your father promised your hand to a brave cavalier, but he was captured when Pilsen was taken by the Imperial troops and, together with others, hanged as a deserter."

[129]

Thus I learned what I had so much wanted to know, but now wished I had never learned, since I could not hope to put my noble birth to good use. I was unable to think of anything better than reaching an agreement with my wet nurse that henceforth she should be my mother and I her daughter.

She was much craftier than I, and on her advice we left Bragoditz for Prague, not only to get away from a place where many people knew us but also to try our luck elsewhere. Incidentally, we were made for each other, not because she could act the procuress and I the whore, but because she needed a provider and I someone loyal like her to whom I could entrust my honor and my possessions. Not counting my dresses and jewelry I had three thousand Imperial taler in ready money and hence I had no reason at that time to earn my living shamefully. I dressed my mother like an honest old matron, and showed great honor and respect to her in the presence of others. We pretended to be people who had lost their home in the war and earned our livelihood by doing needlework and embroidery in gold, silver, and silk. For the rest, we lived quietly and withdrawn, carefully husbanding our money, since money is wasted before you know it and one cannot regain it just by wanting to do so.

Ours would have been a life as fine, so to speak, as in any cloister, if only we had not been lacking in constancy. Soon I had lovers. Some of them went after me as they would after any girl in a brothel. Other fools, who did not dare to pay for my honor, talked a great deal about marriage and tried to persuade me that it was nothing but the torments of their love for me which had roused their desires. Had I had a trace of modesty, I would not have listened to them. But everything went in accordance with the old proverb, "birds of a feather flock together." And just as the saying goes that "a straw in a shoe, a spindle in a bag, and a harlot in a house cannot be hidden," so I soon became famous for my beauty.

We were given a lot of embroidery work to do, including a shoulder belt for a captain who claimed that he was about to die of his love for me. But I made so much of my purity that I almost drove him to despair. For I judged the quality and wealth of my customers after the rule of the tavern keeper at "The Golden Lion" in N. He always used to say, "When a guest enters extending very many polite compliments to me, I take it for a sure sign that he either hasn't got much or doesn't want to spend much. But if somebody enters boldly and gives his orders like a master as though he had every right to do so, then I say to myself, 'Holla, here is someone with a fat purse, I must drain it.' Therefore I counter courtesies with courtesies, so that my inn be praised elsewhere, while I treat the braggarts to everything they demand and then plunder their money-bags." I viewed my captain in just the same way the courteous innkeeper looked at his various guests, while the captain regarded me if not as someone close to an angel then at least a model and image of chastity, nay, of piety incarnate. In short, he finally began to babble something about marriage, and did not cease until I had said Yes.

The marriage contract contained the following items. I was to bring him 1,000 Imperial taler in cash, while he was to hold an equal amount in surety for me at his home town in Germany, so that they would revert to me should he die without heirs before me. My remaining 2,000 Imperial taler were to be invested at a certain place to bear interest, this interest to be used for the duration of the marriage by my captain, the capital to remain untouched until we had heirs. Furthermore, in the event I died childless, I reserved the right to dispose in my testament of all my property, including the 1,000 Imperial taler, freely and in any way I wanted.

Thus we got married, and just when we thought that we would be able to live for the duration of the war in the garrison at Prague as if in peace time, we received orders to march to Holstein to participate in the Danish War.

CHAPTER XI

WHEN COURAGE TRIES TO BEHAVE LIKE A DECENT
WOMAN, SHE UNEXPECTEDLY BECOMES A WIDOW
AGAIN.

I PREPARED myself well, for better than my captain I realized what it took to go on a campaign. For fear that I might find myself again in a place where Courage was only too well known, I told my husband the whole story of my life save for my various adventures as a whore and my relations with the cavalry captain. As for the name Courage, I convinced him of what everyone else thought, namely that it had clung to me because of my bravery. With this tale I intended to forestall the effects of evil gossip that he might hear from people who tried to get me into trouble by making him think that there is no smoke without fire. He thought it incredible that I had stood up against the enemy in open battle, until subsequently others in the army testified to my veracity, and because of this he later did not believe others who treated him to stories about my loose behavior, simply because I had denied that such tales were true.

Otherwise, he was a man circumspect and sensible in all his actions, fine looking in appearance and intrepid, so that I often wondered why he had taken me of all people when he so fairly deserved someone honest and good. My mother did not want to stay behind, so I took her along as a housekeeper and cook. I filled our baggage wagon with everything that could conceivably be useful on the campaign, and made all the arrangements for service, sparing my husband any concern about it and making it unnecessary for him to get a steward. As for myself, I had once again a horse with saddle, harness, and weapons as well. With such equipment we joined Tilly's army at the Gleichen.* There I was recognized before long, and all the scoffers cried, "Cheer up, oh brothers, here comes a happy omen of another victory!"—"Why?"—"Because Courage has returned to us." Nor can it be said that these scoundrels were so stupid, for the troops with which I arrived, made up a reinforcement of no less than three mounted and two foot regiments, which is not to be despised; they would have given courage to the whole army, even if I had not been with them.

As far as I can recall, it was on the second day after this happy conjunction that we picked a quarrel with the King of Denmark at Lutter.† At that encounter, I could not for the life of me stay with the baggage train; so when the enemy's first heat had abated and we had bravely renewed the fighting, I joined the scrimmage where it was thickest. I was determined not to capture just anybody but to prove to my husband right at the beginning that mine was a fitting surname which he need never be ashamed of. So I made room with my sword for my noble stallion, the like of which could not be found anywhere in Prague, and finally got my hands on a cavalry captain of noble Danish descent, whom I took out of the fighting and back to the baggage wagon. It is true, both I and my horse received some hard blows, but we did not lose a drop of blood on the field of battle and carried away only some marks and bruises.

When I saw that everything was turning out so well, I galloped back, arms ready, and rounded up two more men,

---

* The Gleichen: a place southeast of Göttingen.

† Lutter: in the battle of Lutter in the Duchy of Brunswick, Tilly defeated the King of Denmark on August 27, 1626.

a quartermaster and an ordinary trooper, neither of whom noticed that I was a woman until we reached the captain and my men. All three freely surrendered their money and valuables so that I did not need to have a talk with them; but I saw to it that the captain especially was treated civilly, and not touched, let alone stripped. When I was not looking, however, my servants exchanged clothes with the other two men, who were well dressed in their jerkins. I would have dared a third time to strike the iron while it was hot, but I did not want to be too hard on my good horse.

In the meantime, my husband, too, had taken some booty from those who had withdrawn to the castle of Lutter and surrendered without terms. In and after the battle, the two of us had captured from the enemy booty to the value of a thousand guilders all told. As soon as the fighting was over we secured it all and dispatched it without delay to Prague, where I had already my 2,000 Imperial taler. In the field we had no need of the money, living every day as we did, in the hope of getting still more booty.

I and my husband grew ever more fond of each other and each of us considered himself very fortunate in having the other as a spouse. If it had not been for a sense of shame that both of us felt, I don't think I would ever have left his side by day or night, whether in the trenches, on guard, or in an encounter. We willed each to the other all our possessions, so that the survivor—regardless of whether we had heirs or not—was to inherit all from the deceased with the obligation to provide for my mother or wet nurse as long as she lived, for she had proved to be a hard-working, faithful woman. Our testament was made out in duplicate; we deposited one copy with the senate in Prague, the other in South Germany, my husband's home country, which at that time was still flourishing and had not yet suffered in the least from the war.

After the encounter at Lutter, we occupied Steinbruck, Verden, Langenwedel, Rotenburg, Ottersberg, and Hoya.§ My husband had orders to make his quarters with some other troops, but without baggage, in the last mentioned castle of Hoya. Just as no peril of any kind could keep me away from my husband, so I did not want to leave him alone in that castle; I feared that he might be eaten up for me by lice, since there were no women to keep the soldiers clean. Our baggage, however, remained with the regiment which marched on toward enjoyable winter quarters.

I, too, would have been better advised to take my pleasure there. For as soon as all this had happened at the beginning of winter and Tilly had divided his troops in this manner, lo, the King of Denmark approached with an army to regain in winter that which he had lost in summer. At first, he endeavored to take Verden, but because this turned out to be too hard a nut for him to crack, he left that town alone and took out his wrath on the castle of Hoya. Within seven days he put more than a thousand holes in it by means of cannon shots, of which one hit my dear husband and made me an unhappy widow.

§ Steinbruck: north of Hildesheim; Verden: at the river Aller; Langwedel, Rotenburg: towns near Verden; Hoya: at the river Weser.

CHAPTER XII

FOR fear that the castle might collapse and bury all of us alive, we finally surrendered to the King and came out into the open. Downcast and in tears, I marched along with the others. To complete my misfortune, I was discovered by the same major whom I had taken prisoner among the troops of the Duke of Brunswick at the river Main some time ago. He confirmed my identity by inquiries, and when he learned that I had just become a widow, he seized his opportunity and dragged me away from the troops without more ado.

"You bloody witch," he said, "now I will repay you for the disgrace you brought on me at Höchst a few years ago. I will teach you not to run about armed to the teeth and without scruples to capture cavaliers."

He looked so horrible that his mere appearance terrified me. Had I sat on my black horse and met him in the field, I would have taught him different manners, you may be sure; but he took me into the midst of a band of troopers and entrusted me to the ensign. The latter inquired about every detail of my relationship with the lieutenant-colonel (for in the meantime the major had advanced to this rank). In his turn, the ensign told me that the major's capture by a woman in front of his brigade had caused disorder among his troops and their complete dispersal and that in consequence he would have paid with his head or at least with the loss of his rank, had he not made the excuse that he had been the victim of sorcery. Nevertheless, in the end shame had compelled him to resign and take service with the Danes.

The next night we stayed in quarters where nothing went well. Avenging his disgrace—to use his words—the lieutenant-colonel forced me to satisfy his animal desires, but although I did not resist him much, he banished all delight and joy by giving me instead of kisses only boxes on my ear; fie upon his wretched folly! Next day, he and his troops took to flight like hares that are chased by greyhounds, so that I was sure that they were being pursued by Tilly, albeit they fled only for fear of being pursued. The second night they found quarters where some peasants laid out a feast for them. My brave hero invited other officers of his ilk to be his guests, urging them to become his in-laws through me, so that in the end, my insatiable desires notwithstanding, I was sufficiently contented for once.

The third night, after they had been on the run once more all day long, as though the Devil himself were chasing them, I did not fare any better but indeed much worse. When I had endured them all in my misery and all these stallions were tired out—fie, I would be too ashamed to speak of it, if it were not for your benefit and in your honor, Simplicissimus—then I had to take on the manservants as well, while their masters looked on. Until then I had suffered everything in patience, thinking that I had somehow deserved it, but when it came to this I felt the abomination and the horror and cried and cursed them and called for God's help and revenge. But there was no mercy in these inhuman beasts. Forgetful of shame and Christian honor, they first undressed me so that I was as naked as I had come to this world. Then they spilled a few handfuls of dried peas on the ground and hitting me with their switches forced me to pick them up again. Yes, they salted and peppered me so well that I jumped about like a donkey with thorns and thistles fastened underneath its tail. Had it not been winter time, I believe they would have whipped me with stinging nettle.

Then they held counsel to consider whether they should deliver me over to the stable boys or have me tried by the hangman as a witch. The latter course, they decided, would redound to their dishonor, since they had possessed my body. Furthermore, the most sensible among them argued (if any of these beasts may be said to have had a spark of human sense left) that if such a procedure had been intended for me the lieutenant-colonel should not have touched me in the first place and should have delivered me at once into the hands of Justice. Thus they arrived at the judgment that I should be handed over to the stable boys in the afternoon. (Feeling secure on this day they had not moved on.)

When they had their fill of the miserable spectacle and had looked enough at me as I picked up the dried peas, they allowed me to get dressed again. Just when I had finished, the lieutenant-colonel was approached by a cavalier who asked to speak to him. He was no other than the same cavalry captain whom I had taken prisoner at Lutter; news of my capture had reached him. When he inquired of the lieutenant-colonel about me and declared that he wanted to see me because I had taken him prisoner at Lutter, the lieutenant-colonel led him to the room at once, saying, "There she sits, the low jade; I am about to turn her over to the stable boys." He thought, of course, that like himself the captain wanted to take cruel revenge on me. But this honest cavalier had something entirely different in mind. As he saw me sitting there in my misery, he sighed, shaking his head. Sensing that he pitied me, I fell on my knees and implored him in the name of all his noble virtues that he show mercy to me, a lady in distress, and protect me from further abuse. He lifted me up by the hand and said to the lieutenant-colonel and his comrades, "Oh, my good brothers, what have you done to this lady?"

The lieutenant-colonel who had drunk himself nearly into a stupor, grabbed his arm saying, "What? She is a witch!"

"Sir, excuse me," replied the captain, "everything that I know about her suggests to me that she is the true daughter of the brave old Count of T., a true hero, who has given to the common cause his body and soul, his possessions and men. Such treatment of his children will not find the approval of my most gracious King, even though she has made prisoners of a few officers on the Imperial side. Indeed, I venture to say that her distinguished father accomplishes at this very moment in Hungary more against the Emperor than a man in command of a swiftly moving army."

"Well," replied the churlish lieutenant-colonel, "how could I know that? Why didn't she open her mouth?"

The other officers, who were well acquainted with the captain and knew he was descended from a noble Danish family and was held in very high esteem by the King, implored him most humbly to overlook the facts that could not after all be changed and to use his influence to keep them out of trouble. They pledged their lives and property to him and fell on their knees to ask my pardon also, but I could forgive them only with my tears.

Thus, though terribly ravished I escaped from the clutches of these animals into the captain's hands. He treated me indeed most courteously. Without touching me even once he ordered a manservant and a soldier from his company to take me to a noble mansion in Denmark that he had inherited from his mother. There I was treated like a princess. I owed my sudden deliverance to my beauty and to my wet nurse who, unbeknownst to me, had told the captain in confidence the story of my origin.

CHAPTER XIII

I ATTENDED to my health and warmed myself like someone who comes out of the cold water half-frozen and reaches a stove or a fire. For at that time I had nothing else to do in the world but be lazy and get strong and plump like a war horse in its winter quarters, in order to reappear next summer all the more rested, fresh, and ready for any possible use in the field. Before long, I felt fine again, my hair was soft, and I began to yearn for my cavalier. And sure enough, he called on me before the nights grew shorter, since like myself he lacked the patience to await the lovely time of spring.

He came to visit me with four servants, but only one of them was permitted to see me, namely, the one who had brought me to the castle. My cavalier's eloquence was incredibly heart-rending. He told me how much my wretched state of widowhood grieved him; he assured me with boundless promises of his loyal service; he declared with great courtesy that he had become body and soul my prisoner at Lutter.

"My most honored fair lady," he said, "as far as my body is concerned, destiny had made me single once again, and yet left me otherwise entirely your slave who now has come here desiring only to hear from your mouth his sentence of life or death: life, if you feel compassion for your miserable prisoner and console him in his dire prison of love with the consolation of pity and save him from death; or death if you should withhold your mercy and love, deeming me unworthy of such love. I regard myself very happy indeed that you, like another valiant Penthesilea, made me a prisoner in the midst of battle; and although external freedom was restored to me, or so it appeared, my true misery commenced at that very moment because no longer was I able to behold her who kept my heart in captivity. Nor dared I hope ever to meet her face to face again, what with arms pitted against arms. Witnesses to this wretched misery of mine are the many thousand sighs that I have sent up to my charming enemy ever since. But, alas, all of them have sailed the winds in vain; I have fallen slowly into despair and would have. . . ."

These and similar things were advanced to me by the master of the castle, to persuade me to do that which I longed for anyway as much as he did. But since I had had my schooling in such matters and knew only too well that one thinks but little of easy gains, I feigned not to understand his meaning; I bewailed the fact that I was *his* prisoner, since I had no physical freedom but was being held in his power. I had to admit, I told him, that I was bound to him more than to any other cavalier in the whole world because he had saved me from my ravishers; I also acknowledged that, for the great and praiseworthy help he had rendered me, I owed him the highest gratitude.

If the real purpose of bringing me to this place was that, under the cloak of love, my debt might be paid with the loss of my honor, then I expected him to earn neither honor in the eyes of honest people nor thanks from me for my glorious deliverance. I begged him humbly not to put a blemish on himself by committing a deed that would perhaps soon give him cause for remorse, nor to mar the music of high repute that he, an honorable cavalier, enjoyed by an echo whispering of a poor, helpless woman

[143]

whom he had held against her wish in his house, etc. At that point I began to cry, as if I meant all this most earnestly and sincerely, in accordance with the old verse:

> When women wail and cry from smart
> Their tears do not reveal their heart.
> They can cry most any time
> Without reason, without rhyme.

Indeed, in order to make him think of me even more highly, I offered him 1,000 Imperial taler as a ransom, if only he would leave me untouched and allow me to travel home. But he replied that his love for me was such that he would not exchange me for the whole Kingdom of Bohemia; moreover, in origin and rank, he said, he was not inferior to me so that a marriage of the two of us would not give rise to any difficulties.

In short, we behaved just like a couple of pigeons, locked up together by a pigeon-breeder for pairing: they wear themselves out until they finally get down to business. We did, too. When I felt that I had resisted long enough, I became tame and pliable toward this young lover who was not yet over two and twenty years of age. Upon his golden promises I granted him everything he desired, and I was so good to him that he stayed with me for a whole month. But nobody knew about all that save for the servant and an old head-stewardess in whose care I had been placed and who was required to address me as "Your Grace." So I fared according to the old proverb:

> A whore in your house,
> On a sore a big louse,
> A tailor on his horse—
> All serve without remorse.

My lover visited me often that winter. He would have gladly put his sword away forever, had he not felt ashamed to do so. But he was afraid of his father and of the King as well who was deeply, though with little luck, engaged in the war. My young lover was so careless in his visits and came so often that eventually his old father and mother got wind of it. Through careful inquiries they discovered what sort of magnet, hidden in his castle, drew his weapons so often away from the war. They tried to find out what sort of person I was, for they were afraid that he might get caught in the toils of someone who would bring dishonor on their distinguished family. They wanted to forestall such a marriage in good time and yet not without due caution. They did not want to lay violent hands upon me nor affront my kin, for fear that their son had already promised to marry me or that I might belong to a distinguished noble family, as the head-stewardess had indeed told them I did.

The first attack occurred in the form of a warning from the head-stewardess. My lover's parents had learned, she told me in confidence, that their son secretly kept a mistress, whom he intended to marry against their will. They could not allow this, since they had already promised his hand to a most distinguished family. She said that they planned to seize and abduct me, but she claimed ignorance of what they had resolved to do with me thereafter.

The old woman frightened me with this tale, but I did not let on to my fear. Instead I pretended to be overjoyed as though the Grand Mogul of India would protect or at the very least revenge me. I relied entirely on the great love and ardent vows of my lover, especially since almost every week he sent me a love letter and fine presents as well. I wrote to him complaining about the news that the head-stewardess had given me. I begged him to protect me from this peril and prevent myself and my family from being treated with contempt.

This correspondence finally resulted in the arrival of two servants dressed in the livery of my lover. They presented a note from him saying that I should entrust myself to them; they would take me to Hamburg, where my lover would lead me publicly to church, whether his parents liked it or not. After that both his father and mother would have to say Yes and make the best of an accomplished fact.

Like a good old flintlock, I was ready at once. Traveling day and night, I let the servants take me first to Wismar and then to Hamburg. There my two servants disappeared, letting me search as long as I cared for a Danish cavalier intent on marrying me. Now I realized that lightning had struck and the deceiver had been deceived. Yes, I was told, I should put up with it in silent patience and thank God that the noble bride had not during her travels been drowned in the sea; otherwise, the bridegroom's party was powerful enough even in the middle of town, should I entertain false notions of my safety, to teach a person of my reputation how to jump.

What was I to do? My wedding, my hope, my fancies, and everything I had so keenly expected—all had gone, vanished into the air. The secret love letters that I had from time to time sent to my lover had fallen into the hands of his parents, and they had written his replies in order to get me to where I now found myself. Soon I began to be on short rations and Hunger had no trouble persuading me to gain my daily bread by my nightly handiwork.

CHAPTER XIV

I DO not know how my lover felt about his empty castle; he may have laughed or cried when next he came and did not find me there. I was certainly sorry that I could no longer enjoy him and I believe he, too, would have been content with me for a while longer had his parents not taken the morsel out of his mouth so suddenly.

At that time, the Emperor's troops under Wallenstein, Tilly, and Count Schlick* flowed like a deluge into the whole of Holstein and the other Danish lands, and the people of Hamburg and of various other towns were forced to help out with victuals and ammunition. This caused a great hustle of traffic to and fro in town and much work with clients in my lodgings.

One day, I learned that my adopted mother was still with the army, but she had lost all my belongings save for a few horses, and this jolted my compass badly. It is true, things went well with me in Hamburg, and I could not possibly have wished for more business, but I knew that my good fortune would last only as long as the army remained in the country and that I had better think of how to steer a different course if need be.

A young trooper paid me a visit, and since he seemed to be lovable, resolute, and in cash, I used every trick I knew in laying my nets until he was caught. He became

* Schlick: Count Heinrich of Passau and Weisskirchen, General Field Marshal who participated in Wallenstein's campaign to Jutland, Sleswig, and Holstein.

so infatuated with me that I believe he would have gladly eaten raw cabbage out of my hand. The young man swore by the Devil that he wanted to marry me, and I am sure he would have led me to church right away in Hamburg, had he not been obliged to ask his captain's permission first. He took me to his regiment, where he had no trouble getting the required consent. While he was awaiting the right time and occasion for us to take the marriage vows, his comrades expressed their great astonishment at the good fortune that had brought him such a beautiful young mistress. Indeed, many of them were wondering how they might become his relations through marriage. For at that time the men in this victorious army had been in a healthy and lively condition for a long while. They had been living off their booty, everything they needed was available in superabundance, and they were so well fed and padded that they had given up going out for more loot or searching for bread and forage. Instead most of them were driven by carnal appetite and given to debauchery.

My bridegroom's corporal happened to be a rascal of this sort who more than anyone else was fond of dainties. Having made it his profession to give horns to other men he felt thwarted whenever he missed an opportunity to do so or failed in his ventures.

We were stationed in Stormaren,† which had not been touched at all by the war and was therefore well stocked with food and had everything else in abundance. All of this we regarded as our own, and used the country folk as servants, cooks, and waiters. There was no end to the banquets day and night to which the troopers invited each other to dine and wine together at their host's expense.

† Stormaren: Southern Holstein.

Such was also my bridegroom's practice, and the corporal tried to take advantage of it and lay his hands on me. My lover was having a good time in his quarters with two of his comrades, who unknown to him were actually the corporal's creatures, when the latter suddenly appeared and ordered my bridegroom to the colors to stand guard. In this way the corporal hoped to get him out of the way and enjoy himself with me while my lover was absent. But my lover suspected trickery and had no intention of letting the corporal take his place or, putting it more plainly, of being made a cuckold by him. So my sweetheart replied that there were other men who could do the guard duty. The corporal told him not to argue but to obey orders, or else he would show him how to make speed. The corporal, of course, was loath to let such a fine opportunity to get hold of me slip through his fingers, but my lover did not intend to give him that opportunity and continued to resist the corporal until the fellow drew his sword to enforce his order or else, empowered by his authority, to make such an example of my lover that thereafter no subordinate would ever forget the obedience he owed to superiors.

Unfortunately, however, my darling took the whole business in bad part; he drew his own sword and wounded the corporal in the head, which rid the man of his lewd and heated feelings and calmed his inordinate passion: I was now quite safe. Upon the corporal's cries the other two guests came to his help and attacked my bridegroom with their swords, whereupon he gored one of them and chased the other out of the house. But the latter quickly returned bringing with him the army surgeon to attend the wounded men. He also brought some other fellows along who took me and my lover to the provost. My lover was put in chains.

Next day, he got only a summary proceeding. He was tried according to military law, and although it became as clear as daylight that the corporal had ordered him to guard duty for the sole purpose of taking his place in bed that same night, sentence was passed nonetheless in the interest of maintaining obedience to the officers. My bridegroom was to be hanged and I—the cause of everything—to be flogged. In response to our pleas, my groom was shot instead and I was driven from the regiment by the flogger, all of which vexed me greatly.

Bitter as my journey was, two troopers wanted to sweeten it for me and themselves. I had been on my way less than an hour when I came upon them lying in ambush to welcome me. To be truthful, I have never been hard on a good fellow in distress who wanted to take a joy ride with me, but these two rascals were about to use force in order to get from me in my misery precisely that because of which I had been chased away and for which my lover had been shot dead. So I met force with force.

In order to frighten me and to make me yield to them they shamelessly advanced with their swords drawn as though I was an enemy. I saw by their faces that after they had got what they wanted they would rob me of everything I had. Since I knew, however, that their two sharp blades could no more cut my skin than two switches, I met them armed with my two knives, one in each hand. In the twinkling of an eye the first fellow had a knife in his heart, but the other was stronger and more cautious so that I could not get at him any more than he at me. Both of us yelled wildly while we were fighting. He called me a whore, a slut, a witch, even a devil, while I addressed him in return as rascal, thief of honor, and whatever other titles of that sort came to my mind.

All this fracas attracted a musketeer. He came out of the woods and stood for a long while watching us as we leapt at each other. Apparently, he could not make up his mind which side to take and whom to help. When we noticed him, each of us urged him to come to the rescue against the other. You can imagine that in the end Mars preferred to assist Venus rather than Vulcan, principally because I promised him a potful of gold and because my extraordinary beauty blinded him and prevailed in the end. He looked at the trooper and threateningly pointed a gun at him so that the fellow turned and took to his heels as though he was running on coals, leaving his lifeless comrade behind in a pool of blood.

With the trooper gone, the young musketeer found himself alone with me. He was struck dumb, as it were, by my beauty and hardly dared to ask me through what misfortune I had come upon the troopers. I told him everything to a hair: first, what had happened to my former bridegroom, to the corporal, and to me; then, that the two troopers, the dead one and the one who had fled, wanted to use force in order to ravish me, a poor, forsaken woman; and finally, that I had staunchly resisted them, as he had seen himself. I asked him, now that he had helped me and saved my honor, to protect me further until I could reach safety with some honest folk. For such aid and assistance I assured him that I would not fail to give him a goodly reward. Thereupon he looked the dead man over and got an adequate reward for his trouble by taking everything of value that he found.

After that we went on our way. Since we did not favor

our feet, we passed through the woods all the sooner and that same evening reached the musketeer's regiment, which was about to march into Italy with Colalto, Altrinniger, and Gallas.§

§ Colalto: Rambold III, Count of Collalto (1579-1630), General of the Army that was sent to Italy. Altrinniger: Johann Altrinniger (died 1634), a colonel who advanced to this rank from the position of page. Gallas: Count Matthias of Gallas (1589-1647), led the advance guard of the army that went to Italy in May 1629.

CHAPTER XV

HAD there been a shred of decency left in me at that time, I could have arranged my affairs differently and chosen a more decent way of life. For when my adopted mother, who had managed to hold on to two of my horses and some of my cash, found out where I lived, she advised me to quit the war and live modestly and quietly in peace, either in Prague where I had money enough or on my captain's estate. But my heedless youth would not listen to wisdom or reason: the more intoxicating the brew, the better it tasted to me.

I and my mother lodged with a sutler of the same regiment in which my husband—the one who had perished at Hoya—had been a captain. Because of him I was treated with respect, and I believe that had the troops been quietly encamped I would have found another good officer for a husband. But our forces, which consisted of three armies, 20,000 men strong in all, were on a quick march toward Italy and broke through Graubünden which offered much resistance. In these circumstances hardly anyone in his right senses had a mind for wooing, and I remained a widow. Moreover, some lacked the heart and others had scruples about proposing marriage to me or trying to win me by more devious means; they thought that I was too respectable for that, because with my previous husband I had led such a life that most people held me to be more respectable than I had actually been.

But, just as I lacked the stomach for long fasting, so the

musketeer who had come to my rescue against the two troopers was so smitten and infatuated with me that he had no rest by day or night. He trotted over to see me whenever he could get away. I saw what was the matter with him and where the shoe pinched him, but since he lacked the courage to disclose his desire to Courage, my disdain for him was as great as my pity.

But gradually my proud intention to take only an officer for a husband weakened. As I watched the sutler's craft and trade and saw every day what profits he made while many a good officer was on short rations, I began to consider ways and means to establish a sutlery of my own. Adding up in my mind the value of the possessions I had with me, including a goodly number of gold pieces sewed up in my breastpiece, I found that I had quite enough. The only obstacle in my way was the dishonor or shame of changing from a captain's wife to a sutler woman. When I reminded myself, however, that I no longer was the wife of a captain and might never become one again, the die seemed already cast; in my mind, I already began to tap the barrels, sell wine and beer at double their price, and to chaffer and higgle worse than an old Jew.

Just at that time, when our tripartite army had crossed over the Alps into Italy, my gallant had reached the highest pitch of his love without ever having said as much as a word about it. One day he entered the sutler's tent under the pretext of wanting a pot of wine. He looked as pale and disconsolate then as though he had just given birth to a child without knowing its father and without having either milk or meal-pap for it.* He spoke to me only with sad eyes and longing sighs, but when I asked him what

* For comment on this sentence see the Introduction, p. 41.

[154]

he had on his mind, he finally dared to reply: "Oh, my dearest Madame Captain—for he was not permitted to address me as Courage—were I to tell you what is on my mind, I would either provoke you into depriving me of your lovely presence and never considering me worthy of another glance or else you would rebuke me for the outrage I committed; either one would suffice for me to die." Following which he fell stock still again.

I answered, "If both of these can cost you your life, you can equally well be revived by them. I am obliged to you for having saved me from the ravishers of my honor in Vierlanden between Hamburg and Lübeck, and you are therefore most assuredly welcome to look at me to your heart's and health's content."

"Oh, most honored lady," he replied, "you have put your finger on the real source of my trouble; my illness began the very moment I saw you the first time, and now it will bring me death, should I no longer be able to see you. What a wonderful and strange state of mind to be inflicted on me in compensation for having rescued my most honored lady from her peril!"

I said, "Am I guilty of an act of crass ungratefulness by having returned evil for good?"

"I do not mean that," my musketeer answered.

I replied, "What then is the cause of your complaint?"

"Myself, my misery," he answered, "and my destiny, or perhaps my forwardness, my imagination, or I don't know what. I cannot say that Madame Captain is ungrateful. For the little effort of chasing away the surviving trooper who wanted to affront her honor I was amply repaid from the estate of the other trooper whose life my most honored lady had gloriously taken lest he shamefully deprive her of her honor."

"Mistress of my life," he continued, "I am in such a state of confusion, which confuses me so much that I can clarify neither this confusion nor my desire, neither my reproach nor yours, and least of all my innocence or anything else that would help me. The truth is, most beauteous lady, that I am dying because destiny and my lowly station do not permit me to prove how happy I would be if I were your humblest servant."

I stood there like a fool as I listened to this lowly and very young musketeer whose speech was full of contradictions and admittedly born of confusion. Nevertheless, I had the impression that he was of an agile spirit and had sense enough to be worthy of my love and quite serviceable in the sutlery with which my mind was so pregnant. Thus, I was quite direct with the wretch and said to him: "My friend, first you call me mistress of your life, next you call yourself ready to be my servant, third you complain that without me you must die. I recognize in all this a sign of great love toward me. Now you must tell me how I can requite your love. For I will not be found ungrateful toward someone who has saved me from losing my honor."

"With your own love," my gallant cried, "and if I am worthy of it I will regard myself as the happiest man in the whole world."

I replied, "You yourself have admitted that your station is too low to become for me what you would like to be or anything else that your long-winded speech has given me to understand. The question is, what can be done now so that you will be helped and rid of your suffering and I escape any reproach of ungratefulness or disloyalty."

He replied that he would leave this to my discretion, since he held me to be a divine rather than an earthly creature. He would accept at any time a sentence of death or life, slavery or liberty, anything I was pleased to command. He reinforced all this with such gestures as to make perfectly clear to me that I had a fool on the rope who would be choked in servitude for my sake rather than live in freedom without me.

I pursued what I had begun, well knowing how to fish in troubled waters. And why shouldn't I have done it, since the Devil himself can get anyone in the condition of my suitor to take his bait? I do not say this in order that honest Christians, led astray by the works of their evil archenemy, may take their bearings from me who imitated him, but that Simplicius, to whom alone I have dedicated this story of my life, may see what sort of lady I was when he made love to me. And if you will listen, Simplex, you will learn that I repaid you for the trick you played on me at the spa by giving you a hundred-weight in return for a pound.

I got my gallant to the point where he accepted and promised to observe the following conditions:

First, he was to leave his regiment, because otherwise he could not be my servant and I did not want to be the wife of a musketeer.

Next, he was to live with me and show me the love and devotion that a husband owes his wife, as I would owe him mine.

Third, this marriage was not to be confirmed before the Christian church unless I were to find myself with child by him.

Fourth, until then I was to be and remain in full measure and form mistress not only of the household but also of my body, and of my servant himself, just as a man would have dominion over his wife.

[157]

Fifth and in consequence, he was not to have power to hinder or obstruct me, or to resent any relations I might have with other men or any other ventures of the kind which usually anger husbands.

Sixth, I planned to establish a sutlery, and he was to be the head of this enterprise and take good care of all business day and night like an honest and diligent master of the house, but leave nonetheless the supreme command over money and over himself to me, obediently suffering any reproof for negligence, and altering and improving himself accordingly.

In sum, he was to be generally regarded as the master and indeed have that name and honor, but yet always pay heed to his obligations toward me stipulated above. All this both of us were to pledge each to the other.

Seventh, in order never to forget his obligations he was to suffer me to call him by a strange name, this name to be formed of the first words of the first command I gave him.

When he had accepted all these points and had sworn to observe them, I confirmed the agreement with a kiss, but did not allow him more than that for the time being. He promptly resigned his service, while I applied myself to getting together everything that a sutler needed and began to do business like a Jew at another regiment of foot soldiers as though I had been in this trade all my life.†

† Do business like a Jew: *"mit dem Judenspiess laufen"* (literally "running about with the Jewish pike"), a proverbial phrase to be found in many 16th century writings and frequently in Grimmelshausen's works. Its connotation was "demanding an excessively high rent, interest or price." Hans Heinrich Borcherdt in the Notes to his edition of *Grimmelshausens Werke*, Part IV, p. 366, makes the following comment: "Originally, the expression was not applied to Jews, since they were not permitted to carry arms, but it was used only for

Christians with a Jewish disposition (sic)." He then refers to one of Martin Luther's *Table Talks* (chap. 20), in which Luther speaks of a sculpture in the cathedral of Speyer showing the Jews all carrying halberds. According to Luther, somebody asked why the Jews carried nothing but halberds. "Whereupon a witty man answered, 'They have loaned the pikes to our burghers,' thereby indicating that they were running about with the Jewish pike as usurers."

It may be worth noting in this connection that Grimmelshausen had no anti-Jewish prejudices. In *The Council Chamber of Pluto*, which of all of Grimmelshausen's works affords the most valuable insight into his views of the social order, a Jew named Aron is one of the participants in the conversation on wealth, frugality, and wastefulness. Aron says, "We are reputed to use dishonesty to deceive the Christians, but no one talks about the fact that the same practice is common enough among them; whoever trades with us tries hard to become rich like a nobleman in the bargain. And he who tricks a Jew believes that he has done the greatest thing on earth, laughs about it secretly and in public and cannot boast of it enough. Now if one of us poor wretches were to come and try to make a big noise about it—the way we are being treated when the roles are reversed—complaining and crying, 'He has cheated me, the rascal, the thief!' why, would not everyone scorn him and laugh at him? Would he not be given a beating or even be punished by the authorities?" (Grimmelshausen's *Simpliciana*, ed. J. H. Scholte, Halle, 1943, pp. 109-110.)

CHAPTER XVI

MY young man proved himself capable in all matters I had had in mind when I took him on and in which I used him. He observed the articles of our contract so nicely and minded me so well that I had not the slightest reason for complaint. No sooner did he guess my wishes than he was ready to fulfill them, for he was drowning in his love so that his good ears failed to hear and his sharp eyes to see what I was to him and he to me. Indeed, he believed that his was the most modest, the most faithful, the most sensible and the chastest sweetheart on earth, and my adopted mother, whom he honored greatly for my sake, mightily helped me in forming this delusion. She was more cunning than a fox, more avaricious than a wolf, and it is hard for me to say whether she excelled more in the art of the money-maker or in that of the procuress. Whenever I had any such venture in mind yet hesitated a little (for I liked to be considered modest and retiring), I had only to confide in her to be fully assured that my desire would be satisfied. Truly, her large conscience encompassed a wider span than the two thighs of the colossus of Rhodes which allow the biggest ships to pass through without striking sail.*

One day my appetite was strongly aroused by a young nobleman, then still an ensign, who had given me to understand that he loved me. At the time I took a fancy to him, we happened to be encamped near a little country

---

* Colossus of Rhodes: the ancient statue at the entrance of the harbor of Rhodes. Grimmelshausen's reference to the enormous "span of the two thighs" follows tradition rather than fact.

town to which my servants and other folk had gone to fetch firewood and water. My sutler had just put up my tent, turned our horse out to grass with the others, and was busy at the wagon. Since I had revealed my desire to my mother, she got the ensign to visit me, though at the wrong time.

The first thing I asked him, in the presence of my man, was whether he had any money. He answered yes, since he thought I was already asking (by your leave) for the whore's wages, and then I said to my sutler, "Skip in the field and catch our piebald horse! The ensign wants to ride it and if he buys it he will pay for it right away in cash." So my good sutler obediently went to carry out my order and the old woman stood guard, while the ensign and I agreed on the purchase and also paid each other gallantly.† But since the sutler could not catch the horse as easily as the ensign caught the sutler's woman, he returned to the tent as tired and impatient as the ensign feigned to be at having been left waiting so long. Later, this ensign wrote a song about the whole thing, entitled, "The Piebald Horse," which began, "Oh, my unspeakable pain," and for many years thereafter it was sung all over Germany, although nobody knew its origin.

By force of our marriage contract my sutler acquired the name "Skipinthefield,"§ and this is no other than the Skipinthefield whom you, Simplicissimus, praised in the story of your life as a good fellow. You should know, too, that all the various tricks that you and he played in Westphalia

† The ensign and I paid each other gallantly: Grimmelshausen has *ritterlich* (for gallantly), which contains an obscene allusion to *Ritt* (ride) that cannot be rendered in English.

§ The name is formed of the first three words of the order that Courage gave to her servant: *"spring ins Feld"* (skip in the field).

and Phillipsburg, and many more besides, he had learned from no one but me and my old mother. For at the time I teamed up with him, he was more stupid than a goose, although later, by the time he left us, he was more cunning than a lynx or any arch-rascal.

But to tell the truth, he did not learn these arts gratis but had to pay dearly for them. At one time, when he was still in his state of original simplicity, he and my mother had a discussion on the deceit and ill nature of women, on which occasion he did not blush to affirm that no woman could ever deceive him, no matter how sly she might be. Therewith he sufficiently exposed his simplicity to the broad light of day, and yet I felt that he had spoken too freely and too adversely about my skill and that of all women. I told him therefore in all candor that I could easily deceive him nine times before he ate his next morning soup. He in turn presumed to reply that should I succeed in so doing, he would be my serf and slave for life; nay, he challenged me to go ahead and try, but only under the condition that should I fail to deceive him even once before the following morning, I must let myself be taken to church for an honest wedding with him. We agreed on this wager.

Early next morning when I took his soup bowl and bread to him, I held in my other hand a knife and a whetstone. I asked him to sharpen the knife a little for me so that I could use it. When he took the knife and stone out of my hand, he saw that he had no water, so he licked the stone with his tongue to moisten it. Thereupon I said, "Amen. Twice already." This astonished him and he asked what I meant. Had he forgotten, I asked in turn, all about yesterday's bet? "No." And he questioned me if and how I had already deceived him. I replied, "First, I blunted the knife, so that you would have to sharpen it again. Secondly, I pulled the stone through you can imagine what and then gave it to you to lick with your tongue." "Oh, stop and keep quiet," he said. "I concede that you have won and I don't want to hear about the other seven times."

So I had my Skipinthefield as my knave. At night, when I had nothing better, he was my husband, and in daytime my servant or, when someone was watching us, my lord and master. He accepted the situation and my moods so well that I could not for the life of me have wished for a better husband. In fact, I would have gladly married him had I not thought that without the bridle of obedience and with the supreme power that would then be rightfully his, he would make me suffer a hundred fold for everything that I had done to him before we were married and that had doubtless vexed and pained him greatly many times. But we lived together in the harmony, if not the holiness, of the dear angels. My mother took my place as a sutler and I that of a handsome cook or maid whom the innkeeper has sleep in to attract more customers. So my Skipinthefield was master and servant and anything else I wanted him to be. He had to obey my orders and be at my mother's beck and call. Otherwise, all my servants had to mind him as their master.

I kept more servants than did many a captain. We had some slovenly army butchers with our regiment who were given to spending their money on drink rather than to making it. I bribed my way into this profession and kept two young butchers for every army butcher. So I made all the profit and gradually ruined the others, since I could offer to any wayfaring stranger a piece of flesh whichever way he wanted it: raw, broiled, fried, or alive.

When it came to theft, robbery, and plunder—and Italy was crammed to the hilt with booty—not only Skipinthefield and my servants had to risk their necks in grabbing things, but also Courage resumed the kind of life she had led in Germany. Since I fought in this manner against the enemy with my firearms and against the friends in our camp and lodgings with my kitchen knife, and since I was always ready to counter an attack, even one by friendly opponents, my purse grew so fat that I sent 1,000 crowns to Prague almost every month. Nor did I and my people suffer any want for that. Even had it meant that I myself would have to go hungry or naked and shift day and night under the open sky, I would have seen to it that my mother, my Skipinthefield, my other servants, and my horses had at all times enough food, drink, clothing, and fodder. In return they had to apply themselves night and day without rest to looting, even though it meant that they risked losing life and limb in their work.

CHAPTER XVII

HOW COURAGE BECOMES THE BUTT OF A PRACTICAL
JOKE AND HOW SHE TAKES HER REVENGE.

YOU see, my dear Simplicius, that I was the mistress of your comrade Skipinthefield at a time when you were tending the pigs for your papa and long before you were smart enough to become the fool of other people. And yet you imagined that you deceived me at the spa.

After the first siege of Mantua,* we took winter quarters in a lively little town, where I had many customers. There was no feast or banquet without Courage, and wherever she appeared the Italian courtesans counted for little. For I was fresh game and something novel to the Italians; I could speak with the Germans in their own tongue, and to the men of both nations I was very friendly indeed and beautiful besides. Nor was I too haughty or expensive; no one had to fear from me the deceit which the Italian girls were full of. Owing to these qualities I succeeded in unyoking from the foreign whores many a good fellow. Of course, when the men left them in order to visit me, that made for bad blood.

One day I was invited to sup with a nobleman who had served the most famous of the Italian courtesans but had abandoned her for me. She planned to take this morsel out of my mouth. With the help of a furrier's wife she managed to put something into my supper that puffed up my belly until it was ready to burst. Yea, the winds pressed me so hard that they finally opened the exit by force sing-

* The siege of Mantua took place in the winter of 1629-1630.

ing with such a lovely voice across the table that I felt terribly ashamed. And as soon as they had found the open door, they passed through it one after the other so impetuously that they produced a thunder, as though several regiments had fired a salvo. In my distress I got up from the table to leave, but the movement of my body only set things into real motion. With every step another ten winds escaped, albeit so swiftly that nobody could keep count; I believe that had I been able to control and time them properly, I would have been able to compete with the best drummer and beat the tattoo for two full hours. But it lasted for only about a half hour, during which time the host as well as the other guests suffered greater pain from laughing than I did from the continued trumpeting.

I considered this prank a great outrage and wanted to run away for shame and anger. My host, who had invited me for something other than such fine music, was as offended as I was. He swore solemnly that he would avenge this affront, if only he could find the peppercorn-and-ant's-eggs-cook† who had brought these harmonies to pass. I was still wondering, however, whether it was not he himself who had instigated the whole affair, so I sat down in defiance as though I was about to kill everyone

---

† Peppercorn and ant's-eggs: Grimmelshausen mentions the same recipe in his *Ewigwährender Kalender*. The adventure told in this chapter is one of the coarsest in the whole work, but what may appear to modern readers as an instance of Grimmelshausen's poor taste is a common humorous trait in the "realistic novel" of the time. In the 16th century *Contes d'Eutrapel* by Noël du Fail, an apothecary gives his wife a laxative drug which takes effect while she dances. In the *Histoire comique de Francion* by Charles Sorel (1623), the hero puts a purgative into the soup of some peasants with most deplorable effects. (See Antoine Adam, "Le Roman Français au XVIIe siècle," the Introduction to *Romanciers du XVIIe Siècle*. Bibliothèque de la Pléiade, Paris, 1958, p. 28.) See also above, Introduction, pp. 24ff.

with the fierce glances of my furious eyes; but eventually I learned from one of the men of the party that the wife of the furrier knew all about the peppercorn and ant's-eggs recipe. He had seen her downstairs in the nobleman's house and thought that she had been hired by a jealous lady to give some cavalier a distaste for me; besides, she was known to have once played just such a trick on a wealthy merchant who had lost the favor of his sweetheart by producing the same kind of music in her presence and that of other honest people. This explanation made sense to me and I thought of only one thing, swift revenge. But I could not avenge myself too openly and brutally, since we were all obliged to keep peace and order in our quarters despite the fact that we had taken the country from the enemy.

When I learned that what my companion had suspected was only too true, I sought out every detail I possibly could about the life and circumstances of the lady who had embarrassed me. Among other things, I learned of a window where she was accustomed to give audience at night to those who wanted to visit her. I then revealed my grudge to two officers. Under the threat of never having me again for pleasure, they promised to execute my revenge in the exact manner that I prescribed. I thought it only fair to repay for the vapors that had vexed me with the dung itself. This happened as follows.

I had an ox bladder filled with the worst ordure to be found at the bottom of what you might call the reversed chimney of clean Mr. Assmust.§ This bladder was fastened to a long stick or pole ordinarily used for shaking nuts down from trees or for cleaning chimneys. Then, on a

§ Clean Mr. Assmust: Grimmelshausen has *M. Assmussen, deren Säuberern*, an obscene allusion.

[167]

dark night, while the first officer played the gallant to the courtesan, who as usual was leaning over her window sill, the second whipped the contraption into her face with such force that the bladder burst and the filth besmirched her nose, eyes, mouth, and bosom, and all her jewels and gems as well. Then both the gallant and the other officer ran off, leaving the bawd at her window to lament as much as she wanted.

As for the furrier's wife, I paid her back thusly. Her husband used to collect all kinds of hair, even if it was only that of a cat, as if it had been shorn from a golden ram's skin on the isle of Colchis. Never did he discard or throw on the dung heap as much as a shred of skin whether it came from a beaver, a hare, or a lamb, without first picking it clean of all hair or wool. Whenever he collected a few pounds, he sold it to a hatter, and this helped the furrier to put bread into his soup; while all this took a long time and brought in little, it was always so much to the good. I learned the whole story from another furrier, who had lined my fur coat for me that winter. From that occasion I had a lot of wool and hair left over that could be used as shearing tools.** When these were ready, or to speak more plainly, after they had been used in this manner and were full of "pomade" like the little pots of a quack, I had one of my boys drop them into the furrier's privy, which was scarcely a privy place. When the pea-counting master of the household discovered all these clods of hair and wool, he thought they were his and fancied that his wife had disrespected and wasted them. Thereupon he flew into a rage at her, as though she had abandoned and was responsible for the loss of Mantua and

** Shearing-tool: euphemism for toilet paper.

Casale.‡ But since she stubbornly denied everything like a witch and amply talked back at him, he beat her up so hard that she got as soft as one of his prepared hides of a wild and vicious animal, not to mention the sloughed skin of a house cat. All this gave me so much satisfaction that I would not have exchanged it for a dozen crowns.

This left the apothecary whom I suspected of having filled the prescription that had made me raise my voice from deep down, for he kept some singing birds which were fed the stuff capable of producing the noise I have told you about. But the man was on good terms with officers of all ranks, for we needed him every day to help the sick who did not take well to the Italian air;§§ and I was concerned myself that I might need his cure any day. For all these reasons I did not dare to rub him the wrong way. Nevertheless I could not and would not stomach so many winds that had recently gone with the wind without some kind of retribution, although they had already been given a resounding distribution in good company after being in my stomach.

The apothecary had a small vaulted cellar underneath his house where he stored various goods to keep them fresh. Not far from it, on the town square, there was a running fountain whose water I diverted into the cellar by fastening one end of a long ox gut to the fountain and dropping the other end through the cellar opening. Throughout the whole long winter night the water kept running in so that next morning the cellar was full to overflowing. A few kegs of malmsey and of Spanish wine as well as other buoyant stuff were swimming on the surface; whatever could not swim was lying six feet deep be-

‡ Casale: fortress at the river Po.
§§ Italian air: allusion to syphilis.

low the surface to spoil. Since I had the gut removed before daybreak, everyone thought that either a spring had opened in the cellar or that the apothecary had been the victim of sorcery. But I knew what had happened and since everything had turned out so well I laughed up my sleeve when the apothecary lamented that all his goods were spoiled.

And at that time, it was a lucky thing that the name Courage was so firmly mine, since otherwise the mockers would no doubt have called me Madam General Fart, because I had done just that so much better than anyone else.

CHAPTER XVIII

THE gains I made in my various enterprises pleased me so much that I wanted more and more. Earlier I had never cared whether my ventures were honorable or dishonorable, and so now I began, in pursuing them, to disregard the difference between the help of God and that of Mammon. In my business I took advantage of others, I used trickery, I was without conscience—it was all the same to me, if only I grew richer. My Skipinthefield became a horse-trader; whatever he did not know, he learned from me, and in this profession I used a thousand different kinds of roguery, of thievish cunning and fraud.

No merchandise was too precious or too petty for me to acquire: gold, silver, gems, not to mention pewter, copper, linen, clothes, and many other things; and what did I care whether it was a piece of rightful booty, loot, or stolen goods. Anyone who did not know where else to chaffer away something, however he had gained possession of it, felt safe in coming to see me as if I were a Jew that cared more about the thief and his protection than about the authorities and his punishment. In consequence, my two wagons resembled a pawn shop more than a store of valuable victuals, and for the same reason I was in a position to lend money to soldiers of all ranks, whenever they needed any. But to protect myself and my trade I also had to be lavish with gifts and bribes: the provost was "my father," his old mother—I meant to say, his old wife—"my mother," the colonel's wife "my gracious lady," the colonel himself, "my honored sir"; all of them shielded me and my ménage, and their good will was my insurance against losing my trade.

One day, an old chicken thief, that is to say an old soldier, who had carried his musket long before all the trouble began in Bohemia, brought me, enclosed in glass, something that looked almost like a spider or a scorpion. But I did not think it was an insect or any other living creature, because there was no air in the glass which a living thing could have used to sustain its life. Since nonetheless it moved and wiggled incessantly, I decided that it was the work of an excellent master who had built an artful model of perpetual motion. I thought it very valuable, and asked the old man who offered to sell it to me how much he wanted for it. He was willing to let me have the bauble for two crowns which I paid him at once. But when I wanted to give him a pot of wine in addition, he said that he had already received sufficient payment. Coming from such an old drunkard, this answer astonished me, and I asked him why he refused a drink that I was in the habit of giving in the bargain to anyone who sold even the smallest thing to me.

"Oh, Madame Courage," he replied, "this treasure is not like other wares: it has a certain definite price and when you in your turn part with it you will have a hard time selling it for more than what you paid."

I said that then I would gain little from it.

"That's your affair," he replied. "As for me, I have had it in my possession more than thirty years, and I have suffered no loss, although I bought it for three crowns and have now given it away for two."

I was unable to make head or tail out of his chatter, nor did I care a great deal whether I did or not. Since I was

quite drunk and, besides, had to get ready to accommo-
date some ambassadors of Venus—or whatever else, gracious reader, you may want to call them—I simply did not
know what to do about the old fogy. He certainly did not
look the man who would try to cheat Courage; in my experience better men than he had often sold to me for a
ducat something worth a hundred times more, and this
made me feel so secure that I simply stored away the
treasure that I had bought.

In the morning, when I had slept myself sober, I found
my treasured purchase in the pocket of my pants; (you
should know that I always wore pants as well as a skirt).
I recalled at once the circumstances of the deal and put the
thing with my most precious possessions—rings, gems,
and so on—to keep it there until I met a connoisseur who
could tell me what it was really worth. During the day,
when by chance I put my hand in my pocket there was the
thing again! I was more astonished than frightened at the
discovery that it was not in the place where I had put it.
Curious to find out what it really was, I searched for the
man who had sold it to me and when I finally met him,
I inquired just what it was that he had sold to me. I told
him what strange things had happened and asked him not
to conceal from me its nature, power, effects, and qualities.

"Madame Courage," he replied, "it is a ministering spirit
that brings great luck to the person who has bought it
and carries it with him. It will tell you where things
are hidden; in every kind of business it arranges for a
goodly number of buyers and it augments prosperity; it
causes friends to love and enemies to fear its owner. Whoever has it and relies on it will be as strong and invulnerable as steel and safe from imprisonment; against enemies

[173]

it works good fortune, victory, and conquest and it brings to pass that the owner is loved by almost everyone."

In sum, the old rascal talked so big that I considered myself happier than Fortunatus with his wishing hat.* But since I did not imagine that the so-called ministering spirit would give all these gifts gratis, I asked the old man what I would have to do in turn to please the thing. For I had heard it said that the sorcerers who rob other people by means of a mandrake root or so-called little gallow's man, have to tend and revere that little gallow's man in certain weekly bathing rites and in other ways.†

The old man replied that such practices were unnecessary: the thing I had bought from him was different from the gallow's man. I repeated that no doubt it would not want to be a servant and fool of mine for naught; he should not hesitate to reveal to me in confidence whether or not I could own it without hazard and enjoy its considerable services without giving anything in return.

"Madame Courage," replied the old man, "you know already everything there is to know, namely that you must

* Fortunatus: the hero and title of a chap book, first published in 1509 and reprinted many times. Grimmelshausen often mentions it in his works. The "bag" of Fortunatus was inexhaustible: it refilled itself as the owner emptied it. His "hat" enabled Fortunatus to be instantly at any place where he wished to be.

† The "little gallow's man" is the mandrake root which was thought to resemble the human form. For its magical properties to be effective it had to be dug up under a gallows where it had grown from the semen of a hanged man. In a little treatise on the mandrake root, *Simplicissimi Galgenmännlin*, Grimmelshausen describes in detail various superstitions, practices, and beliefs associated with the mandrake root, including the washing or bathing of the root and the belief, also mentioned by Shakespeare, that it shrieked when torn from the ground. See also Harsdörffer, "Der Alraun," *Grosser Schauplatz jämmerlicher Mordgeschichten*, 1693, pp. 150-53; and Grimm, *Deutsche Sagen*, Vol. I, Berlin, 1891, no. 84, pp. 69-70.

sell it—when you are tired of its services—at a price lower than you bought it for, a fact that I did not withhold from you when you bought it from me. But the reason for that Madam may learn from others." And therewith the old man was on his way.

At that time my Bohemian mother was my confidante, father confessor, favorite, best friend, and my Sabud Salomonis:§ I confided everything in her and told her also what had happened to me with my purchase.

"Oh," she replied, "it is a *stirpitus flammiliarum*,** it will do everything that the seller said it would do. But I have heard that he who keeps it until he dies must travel with it to the other world, which to judge by the name of the thing will no doubt be the fire and flames of hell. For this reason the thing must be sold more and more cheaply as time passes until, when its price can no longer be reduced, it finally reaches its last buyer. And you, my dear daughter, are in great danger that you will be the last one to try to chaffer it away; for what fool will buy it from you, when he fears that he won't be able to resell it and that in this case he would get eternal damnation from you in the bargain?"

I realized that I was very badly off, but I did not care about that, because of my lightheartedness, the greenness of my youth, the hope I had of a long life, and because of the general godlessness of the world. I said to myself, "You might as well enjoy this help and assistance and exploit

§ Sabud Salomonis: Sabud, son of the priest Nathan, was the principal officer and friend of King Solomon (1 Kings: 4, 5).

** *Stirpitus flammiliarum*: a play on the words *spiritus familiarem*. As the context makes clear, "flammiliarum" is an allusion to hell fire and thus to the satanic properties of the *spiritus familiaris*, a ministering "spirit of the house" in German folk belief. See Grimm, *Deutsche Sagen*, Vol. 1, Berlin, 1891, no. 85, pp. 70-72.

this lucky chance as long as you possibly can. Sooner or later, you will surely find on this earth a fellow careless enough to accept the thing from you at its right price, for any one of many possible reasons: he may be drunk, poor, desperate, blindly hoping for a great fortune—or he may be prompted by miserliness, lewdness, anger, hatred, vengefulness, or the like."

After that I availed myself of the helpful thing in every possible way, according to the prescriptions that the old seller and my nurse and adopted Bohemian mother had given me. Every day I noticed its effects. In the time that it took other sutlers to get rid of one barrel of wine, I sold three or four. Once a guest had tried my food and drink, he was soon back again. Whomever I looked at with the desire to enjoy him, he was at once good and ready to serve me in most respectful devotion and to honor me like a goddess. When I came to quarters where the master of the house had fled, or to some inn or abandoned lodging where no one else would live—sutlers and regimental butchers were usually not put up in a palace—I discovered at once anything of value that had been left behind, including, by some kind of inspiration, treasures that had not seen the light of day for a hundred years.

But I cannot deny that some people—no doubt more inspired by a great light than I was besotted by in my spirit —did not care at all about Courage; instead of honoring her they held her in contempt and persecuted her. It is true, this sharpened my imagination and taught me to meditate, philosophize, and reflect on the why's and wherefore's of my life. But by this time I was already drowning in avarice and the vices attending it so that I remained completely unchanged, never trying to reach the firm ground of salvation; and so it still goes with me. I say all this, Simplicius, to put a crown on your reputation, because you boasted in the story of your life that you had enjoyed yourself in the spa with a lady whom in truth you did not know.

In the meantime, my store of money grew ever larger and became so great that I lived in almost constant fear for my possessions.

Listen to me, Simplicius, I must tell you once more that you would not have been caught in my net when we saw each other playing our games at the spa, if only you had been worth anything and had been under God's protection against me, the owner of the *spiritus familiaris*.

CHAPTER XIX

THERE is something else you ought to know, Simplicius! It was not only I who lived the way I have described but also my Skipinthefield— whom you have praised in the story of your life as your best comrade and a mighty good fellow; he had to follow my lead. And why not? It was not so miraculous, if you remember that loose women like myself induce (and note that I say "induce," not "force"), their dissolute husbands —if I may speak of "husbands"; I almost said "good husbands"—to engage in all kinds of chicanery, even though they have not made the sort of wedding agreement that Skipinthefield had. Listen to my story!

When we camped in front of famous Casale, I and Skipinthefield went to a nearby, neutral border town to buy victuals and take them back to camp. Since on such occasions I never went out merely to bargain like a descendant of the citizens of Jerusalem but also to seek gain in the manner of the virgins of Cyprus,* I had adorned myself like Jezebel† ready to seduce Ahab or Jehu or anyone else. I went to a church, since I had heard that in Italy most love affairs are instigated and begin at such consecrated places because amiable, beautiful women are not permitted to visit elsewhere. It so happened that I found myself next

* Virgins of Cyprus: Cyprus was the island of Aphrodite, where the virgins in order to earn their dowry sold themselves to visiting voyagers.

† Jezebel who tried to seduce Jehu was the wife of King Ahab (II Kings. 9:30).

to a young lady, whose beauty and jewelry aroused my jealousy, especially since a young man who gave her many a longing glance never so much as looked at me. I confess it vexed me deeply that the gallant preferred her to me and seemed to despise me because of her. This vexation and thoughts of revenge were my only devotions and prayers during the whole service.

Before it ended, Skipinthefield came to join me. What made him come, I do not know; I am not inclined to believe that he was driven by fear of God, for I had certainly not taught him that, nor was it a quality native to him; finally, neither the reading of the holy scriptures nor listening to sermons had implanted such fears in him. Nonetheless, he took his place next to me and I whispered an order in his ear that he should spy out where the lady lived so that I could get possession of the very beautiful emerald that she was wearing on her neck.

In accordance with the obedience he owed me, he behaved like a loyal servant and reported to me that she was the distinguished wife of a wealthy gentleman whose palace was situated near the market place. I explicitly told him that he would not enjoy my favor or touch my body again until he had handed the lady's emerald over to me; later I would give him further instructions about the most opportune occasion and the best ways and means toward this end. At first, it is true, he scratched his ear, and seemed taken aback by my demand, as though I were asking the impossible, but after a long palaver he declared himself ready to give up his life for me.

In such manner, Simplicius, I trained your Skipinthefield like a spaniel. He was the right man for it, perhaps more than yourself, but never would he have become such an arrant rascal by his own effort, without having been to my school.

At that time I was just about to have a new handle put on my hammer which I used both as a weapon and as a tool for opening the peasants' chests or boxes whenever I got a chance. I had this handle made hollow so that I could stack ducats or other coins of a certain size away in it. For, lacking permission to carry a sword and not being able to fulfill my desire to have a couple of pistols on me, I used to carry this hammer with me at all times and I intended to fill it with ducats against any sudden misfortune, of which there are many in war. When the contraption was ready, I tried out its bore with a few Swiss coins that I planned to exchange for other money. They fitted exactly into the hollow of the handle, although I had to force them a little, but not so much as is necessary to load a mortar. Since I did not always have enough coins to fill the whole handle, it sometimes happened—when the coins were lying against the hammer and I was holding the iron head in my hand, using the handle in lieu of a walking stick—that the coins slid up and down inside, producing a strangely muffled sound, a mysterious jingling, and no one could tell where this sound came from. Do I need to bore you with a prolix description? I gave the hammer to my Skipinthefield and taught him how to obtain with its help the lady's emerald.

Skipinthefield disguised himself, put on a wig, dressed himself in a borrowed black coat and spent two whole days standing in front of the lady's palace eyeing the building from its foundation to its roof, much as though he wanted to buy it. Further I hired a drummer by the day and let me tell you that this archrascal could have outdone all other rascals. His sole job was to stroll about on the square ready to come to Skipinthefield's assistance; for the latter knew no Italian, while the drummer spoke it as well as German. As for myself, I had prevailed upon an alchemist to let me have a liquid (no need to name it to you) capable of corroding, if not dissolving, any metal in a few hours; this I put on the crossbars in front of the cellar opening.

On the third day when Skipinthefield was still gaping at the house like a cat at a new barn door, the lady finally sent somebody to inquire about the cause of his continued loitering and spying in front of her house. Skipinthefield called the drummer over to serve as an interpreter and replied that somewhere in that house there was hidden a treasure big enough to make the whole town rich, once he, Skipinthefield, had unearthed it. Thereupon the lady asked both Skipinthefield and the drummer to come in. As she listened once more to Skipinthefield's lies about the hidden treasure, her desire to get at it grew stronger. She asked the drummer about Skipinthefield's profession; was he a soldier or what, etc.?

"No," this devil of a fellow replied, "he is said to be a bit of a necromancer, and stays with the army only for the purpose of finding hidden things. I have heard that in Germany he managed to locate and bring to light whole iron troughs and chests full of money." Otherwise, the drummer said, he was not acquainted with Skipinthefield.

In sum, after a long discussion, the business was settled; it was decided that Skipinthefield should search for the treasure. Thereupon, he asked for two consecrated wax candles and lit a third one, his own, which he could extinguish at any time by means of a brass wire inside it. With these three lights the lady, two of her servants, Skipinthefield, and the drummer searched the house while the

[181]

master was away. Skipinthefield had declared that his candle would go out when he reached the place where the treasure lay.

After they had explored many nooks and crannies walking about like a procession with Skipinthefield murmuring strange words whenever they reached a new spot with their lights, they came finally to the cellar where I had moistened the iron window grating with my *aqua regis*.§ There Skipinthefield stopped in front of a wall and while still in the midst of his usual ceremonies, snuffed out his candle. "There it is," he told the drummer to repeat in Italian, "here walled up lies the treasure." He murmured a few more strange words and hit the wall with his hammer a few times, whereupon the coins tumbled inside and made their usual sounds. "Listen," he exclaimed, "the treasure is once more about to bear fruit, and this happens only *once every seven years. It is ready and must be removed,* while the sun is still in the sign of Scorpion, otherwise all will be in vain until another seven years have passed."

Since the lady and her two servants would have sworn a thousand oaths that the jingling had come from inside the wall, they trusted my Skipinthefield fully. The lady asked him to remove the treasure and was prepared to come at once to an agreement with him about the reward. But he replied that on these occasions it was his habit not to make any demand and to accept whatever he was given as a token of good will. So the lady let it go at that, assuring him that he would be well satisfied.

After that he asked for seventeen corns of frankincense, four consecrated wax candles, eight ells of the best scarlet, a diamond, an emerald, a ruby, and a sapphire which had

§ *Aqua regis*: liquid capable of corroding metal. Grimmelshausen has only the abbreviation *A.R.*

been worn around the neck by a woman both as virgin and as wife; next, he was to be left alone in the locked cellar and the lady herself could keep the key with her so that she need not worry about her jewels and her scarlet and he must not be disturbed or talked to until he had brought the treasure to light. Thereupon he and the drummer were given refreshments and the latter a gratuity for interpreting. In the meantime, the various things that Skipinthefield required were all fetched and locked up with him in the cellar, from which it seemed impossible for anyone to escape; for the cellar window which looked out on the town square, was high and in addition secured with iron bars. The interpreter was dismissed and came at once to tell me about the whole course of events.

Neither I nor Skipinthefield slept through the appropriate moment for action (that is, when others were in their deepest sleep); it was then that I broke the bars off as easily as carrots, let a rope down the cellar to my Skipinthefield and pulled him up with all his trimmings, including the beautiful emerald I wanted so much to have.

My booty gave me far less pleasure than did the artifice itself which had turned out so well. The drummer had already left town the same evening, while my Skipinthefield in the company of others, astounded by the cunning of the thief, strolled about in the streets the day after he had removed the treasure, while efforts were being made to apprehend the thief at the city gates.

Such was Skipinthefield's dexterity, Simplicius, all of it my work and achievement! I tell you all this only as an example. For if I were to relate to you all the roguish tricks and pranks that he had to undertake at my pleasure, I wager that time would hang heavy on your hands, however jolly my tale. Yes, were I to describe everything as

[183]

you have described your own foolish adventures, a book could be written that would be bigger and jollier than that containing the story of your whole life. But I do want you to listen to another little piece.

CHAPTER XX

HOW SKIPINTHEFIELD AND COURAGE ROBBED TWO
ITALIANS.

WHEN we realized that we were going to remain at the gates of Casale for quite a while,
many of us put up huts in which we were
better off in the long run than in our tents. Among the
sutlers in our camp there were two Milanese who had built
for themselves a wooden hut for the safekeeping of their
wares, which consisted of shoes, boots, jerkins, shirts, and
other clothes for everybody, officers and men, troopers and
foot soldiers. It seemed to me that these two Italians did
me a great deal of disservice and damage, since they acquired by trade from the soldiers all kinds of booty, silver
trinkets, and jewels, all for half and sometimes a quarter
of their true value. But for them this gain would have been
mine and since I lacked the power to cut off their trade I
planned at least to repay them.

Their wares were stored on the ground floor of their hut,
which served them as a shop as well; about seven or eight
steps up, beneath the roof, they kept their bedsteads. In the
floor boards upstairs they had left a hole, not only to hear
better in case a prowler broke into the shop to steal something, but also to be able to welcome him with the pistols
they kept ready for such an occasion. When I observed
that the door of the hut could be opened almost noiselessly,
I thought the rest easy.

My Skipinthefield was told to collect a truss of thorns,
almost the height of a man—it took indeed a man to carry
it—and I filled a pint-size brass syringe with strong vinegar. So equipped, both of us went to the hut, when every-

one was asleep. There was nothing to opening the door quietly, since I had studied it carefully in advance; this done, Skipinthefield laid the truss of thorns in front of the stairway, which was not closed off by another door. The noise awakened the two Italians and they began to stir. We expected that first thing they would look down through the hole, which was exactly what happened, whereupon I squirted the vinegar right up into the eyes of one of the fellows, so that in an instant he lost all his curiosity. The other in shirt and night-pants ran downstairs where the thorns gave him such an unfriendly reception that, like his comrade, he thought in his great fright that these unforeseen happenings were sheer sorcery, an apparition of the Devil.

In the meantime, Skipinthefield had got hold of a dozen jerkins that were tied together and had taken off with them, while I, satisfied with a piece of linen, turned and slammed the door shut behind us, leaving the two foreigners in their state of vexation, one no doubt still rubbing his eyes, the other extricating himself from the thorns.

See, Simplicius, that's how good I was! And that's how I trained Skipinthefield. As you see, I stole not from necessity or want, but mostly in order to avenge myself on those I found hateful. In the process Skipinthefield learned all the tricks of the trade so that he would have dared to pilfer anything that was not chained to the vault of heaven. I let him enjoy the loot and wished him well: he had his own bag and, since we divided our winnings, he could dispose of half of the stolen goods in any way he wanted. But he was very prone to gamble so that he seldom amassed a great deal of money; when it seemed that he was well on the way to having a goodly sum, he could not hold on to it, because fickle fortune pinched off the foundation of his wealth by means of the faithless dice. Moreover he remained faithful to me and obedient so that I could not possibly have found in the whole world a better slave. Now you are going to hear what he earned from all this, how I paid him, and how I finally left him.

CHAPTER XXI

TALE OF AN ENCOUNTER WHICH HAPPENED IN SLEEP.

SHORTLY before we took Mantua, our regiment had to move away from Casale to participate in the siege. Since there were more soldiers there than in the old camp, more water flowed through my mill. I had so many customers and so much work to do for them that my moneybag quickly grew bigger, enabling me to send several drafts to Prague and to other Imperial cities. So, while many people suffered from hunger and want, I and my servants were fortunate to be prosperous and to make huge profits every day, and because of this my Skipinthe-field began to live like a lord. It seemed more and more to become his habit only to eat and drink, gamble, be lazy, and to neglect altogether the sutlery and all opportunities for making money in other ways. Moreover, he had fallen in with several spoiled and spendthrift comrades who tempted him and made him unfit for everything I had taken him on for and trained him to do.

"Ha!", they said, "you are a man and let your whore be mistress over you and your possessions? It would be miserable enough if you had to endure such treatment from a bad wife. If I were in your shoes, I would beat her up until she minded my orders or else I would chase her away to the Devil," and so on.

All this came to my notice in good time and it annoyed and vexed me. Without giving him or his followers the slightest sign of alarm, I began to think about a way in which I could get rid of Skipinthefield. My servants, including four strong fellows, were loyally on my side. All officers of the regiment were well disposed toward me, the colonel himself wished me well, his wife outdid him in this regard; and I spared no presents to obligate anyone who I thought might be of help to me in the domestic war which I expected Skipinthefield to declare at any moment.

I knew quite well that Skipinthefield, as my *pro-forma* husband, represented the head of the sutlery and that I did my business, as it were, in his shadow. Without him at the head of it I would soon have seen the last of the sutlery, so I moved with great caution. Every day I gave him money for his gambling and lavish meals, not in order to encourage him to continue his way of life but to bait him into daring and unruliness toward me so that through some foolish prank, some gross insolence, he would become evidently unworthy of me—in a word, would give me cause for divorce. For I had already earned, raked together, and sent away for safekeeping so much that I cared little either about him and the sutlery or about the whole war.

But either Skipinthefield lacked the heart to heed his comrades and publicly demand obedience from me or else he simply preferred his dissolute life to any change. In any event, he appeared to be friendly and humble, never giving me a sharp word or even a sour look. I knew very well what demands his comrades had stirred him up to make. But his behavior gave me no clue as to whether or not he had decided to dare me by carrying out any such plan. In the end, however, he happened to offend me in a strange way so that willy-nilly he had to part from me.

One night I was lying next to him sleeping peacefully since he had come home drunk, when suddenly his fist struck my face with such force that I was more than awake: blood was running from my nose and mouth, my head spun round and it still astonishes me that I did not lose all my teeth from this blow. You can imagine what sort of devout jeremiad I prayed for him: I cried "murderer" and called him by all other similar and honorable names that came to my mind.

In turn he said, "You mean cur, why don't you give me my money? Didn't I make it honestly?"

He was determined to beat me again so that I had a hard time protecting myself, especially since both of us were sitting up in bed engaged in a kind of wrestling match. He repeated again and again that he wanted money from me until I boxed his ear so that he resumed a prone position.

Then I escaped from the tent, raising such a hue and cry that everyone woke up and crept out of their huts and tents to see what was going on: not only my mother and the servants but also the neighbors, that is, all those persons of the staff, who are usually given their lodgings near the sutlers in the rear of the regiment: the chaplain, the regiment's mayor, the regiment's quartermaster, the commissariat officer, the provost, the hangman, the supervisor of the whores, and so on. I told all of them at length how my fine husband had treated me without cause or fault on my part, and this was apparent enough: my swelling milk-white bosom was covered with blood and of my face whose lovely features used to charm everyone, Skipinthefield's merciless fist had made such a terrible mess that Courage could be recognized only by her pitiful voice, although nobody had ever heard her wail on any other occasion.

They asked what had been the cause of our dissension and the ensuing battle. When I recounted the course of events, everyone present thought that Skipinthefield must have lost his mind, but I believed that he had played this game at the instigation of his comrades and drinking companions in order that I might lose to him first my pants, then my authority, and finally all my money.

While we squandered our time chattering and some women were busy stanching my blood, Skipinthefield came creeping out of our tent. He joined us at the watchfire which was burning near the colonel's bivouac and could not find words enough to ask my and everyone else's pardon for the fault he had committed. All that was wanting was for him to fall down on his knees before me to beg my forgiveness, mercy, and favor. But I was not willing to listen; I closed my ears to him.

Finally our lieutenant-colonel came from his rounds, and to him Skipinthefield offered to swear under oath that he had merely had a bad dream: he was sitting at a gambling place when someone tried to cheat him out of a considerable stake so that he had beaten him, thus hitting his dear innocent wife in her sleep, entirely against his will and intention. The lieutenant-colonel was a cavalier who hated me and all whores like the plague, but was not ill-intentioned toward my Skipinthefield. For this reason he told me that I should get back to my tent at once and keep my mouth shut, or else he would drag me to the provost for a flogging, which I had long since coming to me.

"The Deuce take it, that is a harsh sentence. I would not like to have many such judges," I thought, "but it doesn't matter, although you are a lieutenant-colonel and impervious to my beauty and favors. There are others—and more of their kind than of yours—who can be beguiled and will pass judgment in my favor."

I was as quiet as a mouse, and so was Skipinthefield, who was told that if it happened again, he would be punished once during the day in such a manner for what he had done to me twice at night that he would not come back a third time. The lieutenant-colonel ordered both of us to make peace before sunrise so that he would have no reason next morning to appoint an arbiter whose decision would make us lose sight and hearing.

So we went to bed again, both of us with our kicks and blows, since I had spared Skipinthefield as little as he had me. He protested once again, with a holy oath that he had been dreaming, but I warranted that all dreams were false, although his had nonetheless procured me no false slap in the face. He wanted to prove his love by his actions but the blows I had received—or rather the fact that I wished to be rid of him—made all my compliance vanish. Furthermore, next day I did not give him any money either for gambling or for drink, nor any kind words. I handed the cash that I kept at home for our business to my mother so that he could not get hold of it. Day and night she wore it sewed next to her skin.

CHAPTER XXII

THE REASONS WHY SKIPINTHEFIELD AND COURAGE GOT
DIVORCED AND WHAT SHE GAVE HIM AT THE END.

VERY soon after our nighttime battle, Mantua
fell to a strategem. Then, as if the war were to
be ended by this event, peace itself between the
Roman Emperor and the French, between the Dukes of
Savoy and Nevers, followed quickly.* Having left Savoy,
the French again stormed about in France and the Imperial troops in Germany to see what the Swede was doing; and I went along as if I were a soldier. Either in order
to give us a pause for recuperation or because plague and
dysentery were raging among us, our regiment had to
camp for several weeks out in the open near the Danube,
in country belonging to the Imperial crown. For me this
was less comfortable than had been our stay in noble Italy,
but I managed as best I could. With Skipinthefield who
was more humble than a dog toward me, I had made peace
again, but only *pro forma*, for every day I awaited with
impatience an opportunity to get rid of him.

I shall now relate how my ardent wish was fulfilled.
The incident shows that a cautious, reasonable, and even
innocent man, whom neither Woman and World nor the
Devil himself can get at when he is awake and sober, may
lose his welfare and happiness and be plunged into misfortune and disaster by his own purblind infirmity when
overcome by sleep and wine.

Just as my heart was vengeful and unrelenting whenever I felt that the least offense or wrong had been done to
me, so my body proved to be unhealing when it was in the

* Peace: 1631.

[193]

least hurt; I do not know whether it irritated my heart or whether my skin and body were so delicate that they could not take rough treatment the way a Salzburg lumberman can. While in our camp at the Danube I still had the black eye and the other marks which, with his fist, Skipinthefield had put on my delicate face in the camp near Mantua.

One night when I was again sound asleep Skipinthefield grabbed me around the middle, lifted me on his shoulder and ran with me clad only in my shirt toward the colonel's watch-fire into which to all appearances he wanted to throw me. When I woke up I did not know what was happening but I realized the danger I was in, since I was naked and observed that Skipinthefield was hastening toward the fire. I yelled as though I had fallen into the hands of murderers. Everyone in the camp woke up; the colonel himself, lance in hand, jumped out of his tent and so did several other officers. Everyone knew there was no danger of enemy action, so they all came to do something about the uproar, instead of which they found themselves facing a ludicrous sight and a most foolish spectacle. I imagine that it must have been extraordinary and amusing to watch. The guards received Skipinthefield with his angry and screaming burden before he could throw it into the fire; and when they saw it in its nakedness and recognized Courage, the corporal had enough sense of honor to throw a coat over my body. In the meantime a whole group of high- and low-ranking officers, who almost died laughing, had assembled, among them not only the colonel but also the lieutenant-colonel who on the earlier occasion had threateningly warned me and Skipinthefield to make peace.

When Skipinthefield ceased pretending to be mad or when he had collected his wits (I really don't know which was the case), the colonel asked him what on earth was on his mind with all this foolishness. Then he replied that he had dreamed that Courage had been covered with poisonous snakes, so that he had thought it best to save her by flinging her into water or fire. So he had been running here with her loaded upon his shoulder, and he now felt sorry for this from the bottom of his heart. But both the colonel and the lieutenant-colonel shook their heads and after everyone had laughed enough about the incident, they ordered him to be taken to the provost and me to go back to sleep again in my tent.

Next morning, our trial began and it was finished in short order, because during war trials usually do not take as long as they do in some places in peacetime. Everyone knew quite well that I was not Skipinthefield's wife but his mistress; for this reason it was unnecessary for us to go before a consistorium in order to get a divorce, but a divorce from him I wanted to get because my life was not safe in his bed.

All the assessors supported my case for this reason alone and thought there was sufficient cause to divorce any marriage. The lieutenant-colonel, who had been on Skipinthefield's side at the time we besieged Mantua, was now entirely against him, and everyone else from our regiment sided with me. I produced my contract according to which Skipinthefield and I had promised each other to live together until we entered marriage honestly, and I exploited and magnified the fear for my life in which my spouse would hold me in the future. So finally sentence was passed: if we wanted to avoid punishment we had to separate; we were to stay together only until we reached an agreement on how to divide between us what we had gained and won together.

I objected, however, claiming that the last stipulation violated the terms of our first accord and that ever since I had been with Skipinthefield—or to put it more bluntly, ever since I had taken him into my household and opened the sutlery—he had squandered more than he had earned, which everyone in the whole regiment knew and could verify. At last, it was pronounced that should we fail to reach a settlement that was equitable in the light of these circumstances, judgment would be passed by the regiment.

I was more than content with this sentence. As for Skipinthefield, he was satisfied with little, being unaware of the money that I had stacked away and having observed that I had lately no longer treated him and the servants as generously as I had done in Italy. Since more recently he had been paid out of our current profits, he thought that considerably less was left over than I in fact still had in my possession, that our funds were running out and that Hunger was stalking our house. It was only natural that he did not know the truth since he did not guess why I had so obstinately withheld money from him.

Just at that time, Simplicius, the regiment of dragoons in Soest, in which you learned your A B C's, was being reinforced by young men, boys who had grown up serving the officers of various foot regiments and who did not want to become musketeers. In these circumstances, Skipinthefield was inclined to accept the following accord with me: I gave him my best horse with saddle and harness, plus a hundred ducats in cash and the dozen jerkins which he had stolen at my instigation in Italy and which until then we had not dared to show openly. We also agreed that he was to buy my *spiritus familiaris* from me for a crown, which indeed he did. And so I got rid of Skipinthefield and so I endowed him.

Soon, Simplicius, you will also hear with what kind of present I contributed to your own bliss, rewarding you for your folly at the spa. Be patient a little while longer and hear first what happened to Skipinthefield's *spiritus familiaris* enclosed in the glass. No sooner did he have it than his head was full of foolish conceits. He needed only to look at a fellow to be tempted to strike him down without any provocation. In all his fights he came out the winner. He discovered hidden treasures and many other secrets that I shall not mention here. When he learned, however, what a dangerous guest he was harboring under his roof, he tried to get rid of it. Yet he could not sell it because the price had already reached its bottom limit.† Rather than lose his own skin, he wanted to pass it back to me. Indeed, at the time the whole army assembled before we took off for Regensburg, he flung the thing down at my feet. But I merely laughed at him, did not pick it up and it was all in vain; when Skipinthefield returned to his quarters, he found it again in his pocket. I learned that several times he threw the bauble into the Danube, but it was always back in his pocket, until finally he threw it into an oven, which rid him of it. But while he was having his trouble I felt more and more queer about the matter. I decided to sell everything I had; I dismissed my servants and retired with my Bohemian mother to Passau there to await the end of the war in full possession of my fortune, since I feared that were Skipinthefield to prefer charges because of the purchase and sale of the bauble, action might be brought against me as a sorceress.

† Each time the *spiritus familiaris* had to be sold at a crown below the last purchase price.

CHAPTER XXIII

HOW COURAGE LOST ANOTHER HUSBAND AND HOW SHE
BEHAVED THEREAFTER.

I LIKED Passau much less than I had expected. It
was too priest-ridden and devout for me: instead of the
nuns I would have preferred to see soldiers, and instead of the monks, some courtiers. I stayed there nevertheless, because at that time the war had swept not only
over Bohemia but over almost all provinces of Germany.
Since in Passau everyone seemed very much inclined to
fear the Lord, I accommodated myself, at least outwardly,
to the prevailing custom.

My Bohemian mother or nurse was fortunate enough to
go the way of all flesh in that splendor of godliness which
we had assumed in this devout place. I arranged an im-
posing burial for her, as if she had died at the gate of St.
James in Prague. But I considered her death an omen of
my future misfortune, since no one was left in this world
in whom I could confide and whom I dared to trust with
my possessions. For this reason I hated the pious place
where I had been deprived of my best friend, wet nurse
and governess. Yet I remained there patiently until news
reached me that Wallenstein had taken Prague, the capital
of my fatherland,* and returned it to the Roman Emper-
or's dominion. In the light of this intelligence, at a time
when everyone in Passau lived in fear of the Swede, who
was then the master of Munich† and of the whole of Bavaria, I left once more for Prague where I had deposited
most of my money.

* Wallenstein took Prague on May 4, 1632.
† Gustavus Adolphus, King of Sweden, entered Munich on May 17,
1632.

[198]

But scarcely had I made my home there to reap pleasure and enjoyment from the fortune that I had gathered together toiling and moiling—nay, I had not yet fully settled down in this large and presumably so very secure city—when Arnim defeated the Imperial forces at Liegnitz,§ and after the capture of no fewer than fifty-three standards marched on to threaten Prague. But the most illustrious Ferdinand III, while himself besieging Regensburg, sent Gallas to assist us, which succor compelled the enemy to withdraw not only from Prague but from all of Bohemia.

I realized then that large and mighty cities, for all their ramparts and turrets, walls and moats, could not protect me and my possessions against armies that camp in the open, in huts and tents, and rove from place to place. So I decided to join again just such an army.

At that time I was still quite smooth and attractive, though no longer nearly so beautiful as I had been a few years earlier. Yet by applying myself and making use of my experience, I succeeded once more in finding in Gallas's relief forces a captain who married me, just as though it were an obligation or ordinance of the city of Prague to provide me at all costs with husbands, and especially with captains. The wedding was held in lordly style, but no sooner was it over than we received orders to proceed toward Nördlingen, which was being besieged by the Imperial army that had just joined the forces of the Spanish Cardinal-Infant Ferdinand, and taken Donauwörth. The Prince of Weimar and Gustavus Horn made an effort to

§ The battle of Liegnitz, in which the Saxonian Field Marshal Arnim was victorious, took place on May 13, 1634; that is, two years later than the events referred to in the preceding paragraph—probably an error on Grimmelshausen's part.

relieve Nördlingen, and this led to a bloody battle, which because of its course and consequences will not be forgotten until the end of time.**

While our side was fortunate everywhere in this battle, personally I suffered harm and misfortune through it: during the first attack it deprived me of my husband, who had barely become warm at my side. Moreover, the good luck I had had in other battles deserted me this time. I did not gain any booty on my own, partly because others beat me to it. I took all this as an omen of my ultimate undoing and for the first time in my life I suffered an attack of real melancholy.

After the battle, the victorious army was divided into various contingents to regain the lost German provinces, but these were being destroyed rather than taken and held. With the regiment in which my husband had served, I followed the corps that took possession of Lake Constance and Württemberg. So I had an opportunity to visit the fatherland of my first captain (whom Prague had given to me and Hoya had taken away) and to look after his estate.

** The Imperial forces took Donauwörth on August 16, 1634, and began the siege of Nördlingen two days later. On September 3, 1634, they were joined by the Infant Ferdinand, commonly called "the Cardinal-Infant," who was the brother of Philip IV and both cousin and brother-in-law of Archduke Ferdinand, King of Hungary and Bohemia. Under the two Ferdinands, the Imperial forces defeated the outnumbered Protestant troops of Prince Bernhard of Saxe-Weimar and of the Swedish Field Marshal Horn in the Battle of Nördlingen on September 5-6, 1634. The Catholic League, which had suffered a shattering blow at the battle of Lützen, in November 1632, inflicted a momentous defeat on the Protestants. "It looked like the end for the Protestant cause and the German Liberties; it was the end for Sweden." (C. V. Wedgwood, *The Thirty Years War*, Yale University Press, New Haven, 1949, p. 377.) The Catholics claimed that 17,000 enemies had been killed and 4,000 taken prisoner. Oxenstierna, on the losing side, estimated the total loss, killed and prisoners, to be 12,000.

Both my inheritance and the neighborhood pleased me so much that I established my residence there in an Imperial town,‡ feeling certain that there I would be safe for the rest of my life from the enemies of the House of Austria; they had been driven across the Rhine and dispersed far and wide. I wanted to stay away from the war, since after the great battle at Nördlingen, the countryside had quickly become everywhere so impoverished that I did not think the Imperial forces could expect to acquire much booty.

And so I started a new life on a farm. I bought cattle and land, hired men-servants and maids and behaved altogether as though the war had been brought to an end by this battle and peace concluded. I withdrew all my money from Prague and the other large cities where it had been lying and spent most of it on my farm. So you see, Simplicius, according to my account as well as your own life story, both of us turned into fools at the same time, I with the Swabians and you at Hanau. I wasted my money and you your youth. You got into a miserable war while I had my delusions about a peace which still was far away.

Before I had struck any roots, troops came marching through and demanded winter quarters, but did not exempt us in any way from other burdensome contributions. Had I not possessed a goodly amount of money and been prudent enough carefully to conceal my wealth, I would have been ruined in short order. For no one in the city was fond of me, not even the friends of my late husband, because his estate which was mine to enjoy would have been theirs by inheritance, if—as they put it—a bad hailstorm had not blown me into town. Small wonder that the contributions imposed upon me were very heavy and

‡ Imperial town: Offenburg in Badensia.

that despite them my house was not spared being assigned as a billet. In short, I fared like the widows whom everyone abandons.

But I don't tell you all this to complain, nor do I want consolation, help, or pity from you; you should rather know that I did not mind any of it or worry very much but rather enjoyed myself whenever a regiment was billeted in town. Then I quickly became familiar with the officers, and day or night there was nothing but dining, wining, and whoring in my house. I did whatever they wanted, and once they had taken the bait, they had to do what *I* wanted so that they had little money left to carry out of their quarters when they departed for the field. Disregarding those who counseled restraint I took every possible advantage of them.

All this time I kept a few maids who were not a hair's breadth better than I was, but I proceeded with so much care, circumspection, and caution, that the magistrate, my beloved authority at that time, had more reason to look the other way than to mete out punishment to me, especially since the chances of their wives and daughters remaining respectable were all the brighter for my presence and for the snares that I was busy laying in town.

I led this kind of life for several years without suffering any harm. Every summer, when Mars took to the field again, I prepared my estimates and accounts of what the war had cost me during the preceding winter. Usually I found that my prosperity and income exceeded the expenses incurred through the war.

But now, Simplicius, I must finally tell you what a sound rating I gave you. For this reason I will no longer talk to you but to the reader. You may just as well listen, however, and if you think I am lying, don't hesitate to interrupt me.

CHAPTER XXIV

AT the Swabian border the French-Weimarian forces
and troops of the electorate of Bavaria were tan-
gling with each other and because of these fights
we had to resign ourselves to having a large garrison in
our town. Most of the officers were very much inclined
toward that which, for a fee, I was glad to provide, but
partly avarice and partly my insatiable desires made me
all too reckless. I was accessible to almost anyone so that
in the end I got something I had deserved the last twelve
or fifteen years, namely (asking your pardon), the French
disease. I broke out with rubies and was embellished by
them as the earth by its many beautiful flowers in the joyous and gay time of spring. Fortunately, I had means
enough to be made whole again, which happened in a
town on Lake Constance. But my doctor told me that my
blood was not completely purified and advised me to take
the waters at a spa in order to restore my health fully. So
I equipped myself well with a fine calash, two horses, a
manservant and a maid who was altogether of my kind
except that she had not yet been plagued by my gay illness.

I had been at the spa for less than a week when Herr
Simplicius paid me his respects, for "birds of a feather
flock together" said the Devil to the collier. I pretended
to be a noblewoman, and took Simplicius in all his pomp
and with his many servants for a respectable nobleman
himself. I tried to throw a rope round his horns and, following my practice, to make him my husband. Everything went according to my wishes: he came sailing full
blast into the perilous harbor of my insatiable desires and

[203]

I treated him the way Circe did the wayfaring Ulysses. Before long I was confident that I had him firmly under my thumb and yet the bird escaped me because he found a different wife, much to my shame and to his own detriment.

By means of a shot from an unloaded pistol and of a water syringe filled with blood he made me believe that he had shot me, in consequence of which not only the barber who wanted to dress my "wound," but everyone at the spa, young and old, looked me up and down. Later they all pointed their fingers at me, gossiped about the case and made such a laughing stock of me that, unable to endure their derision any longer, I quit the spa and its waters before I had finished my treatments.

In the story of his life, Book V, Chapter 6, Simplex, the fool, calls me wanton and says that I was more mobile than noble.* I admit both of these charges. But had he been noble himself, nay, had there been a single redeeming feature about him, he would not have attached himself to so wanton and shameless a wench as he believed me to be, and least of all would he have disclosed and proclaimed to the whole world his own dishonor and my shame.

Gracious reader, what honor and glory has come to him from gaining right off—to use his own words—free passage into my house, and all the pleasures he could possibly desire from a woman whose wantonness he now abhors, yes, from a woman who had barely finished with the charcoal treatment of her disease?† The poor devil gained tre-

---

* More mobile than noble: Grimmelshausen has *"mehr mobilis als nobilis,"* using the Latin words because the play on them cannot be made in German, as it can in English.

† Charcoal treatment: of syphilis by drinking a brew made from various kinds of wood.

mendous honor indeed from boasting about something which to his greater honor he should have passed over in silence. But this is the way such stallions behave. As the huntsman follows every head of game, so like unreasonable brutes these stallions pursue every animal-in-veils.§ He says I was smooth of skin. But he should know that at that time I did not have even one-seventeenth** of my former beauty. I had ample recourse to paints and powder, and he kissed plenty of it off my face! But enough of that. Fools must be deloused with clubs. I have hardly begun my story yet and now will tell the reader how in the end I repaid that man.

When I left the spa, I was vexed and greatly annoyed because Simplicius had treated me with so much contempt. This is the revenge I took: my maid had been as

§ Animal-in-veils: woman.

** One-seventeenth of my former beauty: Siegfried Streller who has examined the occurrence of number symbolism in Grimmelshausen's Simplician novels, is of the opinion that "17" has been suggested by the author himself "as the key to his work" (*Grimmelshausens Simplicianische Schriften*, Berlin, 1957, p. 90). Streller, who overlooked the use of "17" in *Courage, the Adventuress*, points out that this number occurs no less than five times in *The Enchanted Bird's-nest*. (It occurs more often. For a particularly interesting use, see Introduction, p. 74, and below, *The False Messiah*, p. 227.) In addition, the chronogram on the title page of Grimmelshausen's *Teutscher Michel* which, according to contemporary custom, contains the date of publication, is 1673, a number whose digits add up to 17. (Chapter 4 of *Teutscher Michel* contains a fairly detailed discussion of gematria and of the symbolic significance of certain numbers in the Holy Scriptures.) It also so happens that the number of letters in the name "von Grimmelshausen" is 17. Streller rightly rejects the Augustinian meaning of "17" as a symbol of blissfulness for Grimmelshausen's work (*op.cit.*, p. 90) but is unable to suggest another meaning. In 1940 M. Koschlig pointed to the use of 17 in *Bartkrieg* as one of the indications that this pamphlet was a work by Grimmelshausen ("Der Bart-Krieg—ein Werk Grimmelshausens," *Neophilologus*, Vol. xxiv, pp. 42 ff.).

active and sportive as I had been but (since the poor fool always got the short end of the stick) had for a pittance burdened herself with a little son, whom she had happily brought into this world on my farm outside the town. I ordered her to have him named Simplicius, too, although Simplicius had never touched her in his life. As soon as I learned that Simplicius had married a peasant's daughter, I told my maid to wean her child. I dressed him up in fine swaddling clothes, silken blankets and bands, so as to make this lovely deception I was planning look more convincing. Then, accompanied by a farm hand, my maid carried the child to Simplicius' house at night and deposited it in front of his door, leaving with it a written statement to the effect that this child was his and begotten with me.

You cannot imagine how much I enjoyed this fraud, especially when I learned that Simplicius was being called to account by the authorities and that every day his wife put sharp mustard and horseradish on his bread. I really made the good simpleton believe that I, the barren one, had given birth to a child, as though, even had that been possible, I would have waited for him instead of doing in my youth what he believed I had done while approaching old age. For at that time, I had already seen more than forty years, and was hardly the right match for a fellow like Simplicius, bad as he was.

CHAPTER XXV

COURAGE IS CAUGHT IN HER EVIL DOINGS AND BAN-
ISHED FROM THE CITY.

PERHAPS I should break off my story instead of
telling you more about my life, for by now it must
have become clear enough what sort of lady it was
whom Simplicius boasted he had deceived. But just as
there is no doubt that nothing but shame and disgrace
will come to him from everything I have so far said, so
the continuation of my story* will not redound to his glory.

In the rear of my townhouse there was a garden, full of
fruit trees, herbs, and flowers. It made quite a show and
there was nothing like it in town. My next-door neighbor
was a man, with a wife much older than himself, who was
adulterously fond of other women.† It did not take him
long to realize what kind of person I was, and indeed,
neither did I mind availing myself of his help in a pinch.
We met often in my garden, picking flowers like thieves
in very great haste so that his jealous wife would not notice anything. There was no safer place for us to meet than
this garden where the thick green foliage and covered
ways hid our shame and vice from public view, if not
from the eyes of God. (People with a conscience will think

* A story resembling the adventure related in this chapter can be
found also in Antoine de la Sale's *Cent Nouvelles Nouvelles*, No. 46.

† Adulterously fond of other women: Grimmelshausen has "ein alter
Mechaberis oder Susannenmann," which means literally: "an old Mechaberis or Susanna-man," *Mechaberis* being derived from the Latin text
of the sixth commandment, *non moechaberis* ("Thou shalt not commit
adultery"), and *Susannenmann* referring to the two elders who lay in
wait for Susanna, the wife of Joakim, while she was bathing in her
garden, according to "The History of Susanna" in the Apocrypha.

[207]

that the cup of our sins must have been overflowing or that God in His goodness would have called us to reform and repent.)

Once, at the beginning of September, we agreed to meet in the warm lovely evening under a pear tree in the garden. It so happened that two musketeers from our garrison had planned to steal their fill of my pears the same evening, and they had already climbed the tree, and had started their work before I and the old man entered the garden. It was quite dark. My lover came a short time ahead of me, but when I arrived it was not long before we turned to the same business we had transacted there before. Good Heavens, I don't know how it happened, but one of the soldiers must have moved in the tree in order to observe our jugglery better and carelessly dropped his pears. In any event, when they fell down on the ground, I and the old man thought that nothing less than an earthquake had been sent by God to keep us from our shameful sins. We said this much to each other and ran away in great fright. The two in the tree could not help laughing, but that only increased our fear; in particular the old man believed that a specter had come to plague us. So each of us ran into his own house.

Next day, when I went to the market, a musketeer cried loudly, "I know something." Another asked at the top of his voice, "What is it you know?" The first one replied, "There has been a pear-quake." And they shouted more and more loudly. It was easy for me to understand what I was in for. I blushed, although I was not prone to feelings of shame. From the beginning I expected that I would be up against a pack of hounds, but I did not anticipate that they were going to tear me to pieces. When the street urchins knew our story and talked openly about it, the magistrate could not but arrest me and the old man. Each of us was put in a separate prison. Like witches, we denied everything, although we were threatened at once with the hangman and with tortures.

They made an inventory of my possessions and sealed up everything. They examined my servants under oath, but that led only to contradictions, since not all of them knew about my loose conduct and my maids were faithful to me. In the end, I myself gave the truth away. The chief magistrate came often to visit me in prison, pretending to pity me greatly and addressing me as "Madam" and "Cousin." But in truth he was more a friend of justice than he was my cousin. When he had persuaded me in all his false familiarity that my old lover had confessed to adultery and to having repeated it many times, inadvertently the words slipped out of my mouth: "May the hailstones bash his teeth in; why couldn't the old fathead keep quiet!" And I begged my presumed friend to help me. But he delivered a stern sermon instead, and then opening the door pointed to a notary and some witnesses who had heard and taken down the whole conversation.

After that everything went topsy-turvy. Most of the town councillors were in favor of putting me to the rack so that I would confess to more such crimes and then, having been found a useless burden to people on this earth, be beheaded, all of which was expounded to me at great length. On my part I declared that they were not seeking to enforce law and order but rather to confiscate my wealth; indeed, were they to adopt such harsh proceedings, many people held to be honest burghers had better hold their own funerals or join me in mine. In this way I chattered away like a lawyer with words so cunning and protestations so sharp that I succeeded in shocking the more reasonable men.

The result was that I had to promise under oath to quit the town forthwith without redress, and to leave behind, as a more than well-deserved punishment, both my lands and all my movable possessions, which included well above a thousand Imperial taler in cash. They let me have only my clothes and whatever I carried on my body save for several jewels which were taken from me and found their way into various hands.

What could I do? Had they chosen to treat me more sternly, I would have fared worse. But, well, this was in the midst of the war and every man (I should say "every woman") thanked heaven that the town was getting rid of me, no matter how.

CHAPTER XXVI

COURAGE BECOMES THE WIFE OF A MUSKETEER AND
CARRIES ON A LOW TRADE IN TOBACCO AND BRANDY.
HER HUSBAND IS SENT AWAY, FINDS ON HIS WAY A
DEAD SOLDIER WHOM HE STRIPS BARE AND WHOSE LEGS
HE CUTS OFF SINCE HE CAN'T GET HIS TROUSERS OFF.
HAVING PACKED UP HIS LOOT, HE STAYS IN A PEASANT'S
HOUSE OVERNIGHT, LEAVES THE LEGS THERE AND RUNS
AWAY——ALL OF WHICH LEADS TO A HILARIOUS FARCE.

I WANTED to rejoin one of the Imperial armies, but none was stationed anywhere in the region at that time.* In view of this I decided to throw my lot in with the Weimarians or Hessians, then quartered in the Kinzig valley, and to see whether I could find another soldier to marry me. But alas, the first bloom of my great beauty was gone, faded like a spring flower. My recent mischance and the worry it caused me had disfigured me, and my wealth, which often helps old women to get husbands, had vanished too. Of my clothes and the jewels that the authorities had let me keep, I sold whatever I could and got about 200 guilders for them. These I took with me and set out on my way in the company of an army messenger to try my luck. But I met with nothing but misfortune. Before I reached Schiltach† we fell into the hands of a party of Weimarian musketeers, who beat up, plundered, and chased away the messenger and took me along to their quarters. I pretended to be the widow

* At that time: 1644. The only troops stationed near Offenburg, in the Kinzig valley, were remnants of the forces under the command of Bernhard von Weimar.

† Schiltach: a village on the Kinzig.

of an Imperial soldier whose husband had been killed near Freiburg in the Breisgau, and persuaded the men that I had left my husband's country and was on my way home to Alsatia. Although, as I have mentioned, I was no longer as beautiful as I once was, my appearance was still good enough to cause one of the musketeers to fall in love with me. He wanted to make me his wife. What was I to do? I preferred to grant willingly to this man what he desired out of love than to submit under force to the whole band. In short, I became the wife of a musketeer even before the chaplain had married us.

I would have liked to set up as a sutler again, as in Skip-inthefield's time, but my purse was too light for such an undertaking. Besides, I was lacking my Bohemian mother; in addition, my husband seemed to me much too slovenly and lazy for that business. So I began instead a low trade in tobacco and brandy, just as if I were trying to regain half-pennywise what I had recently lost by thousands. I slaved. It was very hard on me, what with marching on foot, carrying a heavy bag besides, and sometimes not having enough to eat and drink; I had never before experienced any of these disagreeable things, let alone been inured to them. Eventually I succeeded in getting a fine mule, which could not only carry heavy burdens but also run faster than many a good horse.

When I had collected two mules—husband and beast of burden—in this manner, I took pains to feed them well so that both of them would be the more serviceable to me. I and my baggage were now being carried, I was a little better off and managed to get by, until at the beginning of May, Mercy§ dealt us some pretty harsh blows at Herbst-

§ Mercy was a leader in the Bavarian army that defeated Turenne at the village of Herbsthausen near Mergentheim on May 5, 1645.

hausen. Before continuing the story of my life, however, I want first to tell the reader of an adventure** in which my newest husband got involved against his will, while we were still in the Kinzig valley.

Prompted by his officers and with my consent, my husband agreed to disguise himself as a poor banished carpenter, clothed in some old rags and with an axe over his shoulder, to carry some dispatches to a place where no soldier could be sent because the Imperial troops made it unsafe. The letters referred to troop movements and other secrets of war. Because of the severely cold weather we had at that time, everything was frozen stiff and solid, so that I almost pitied Stupid on his journey, but he had to go: there was a good deal of money to be earned, and he did indeed accomplish everything without mishap.

While he was on his way back, however, he found, on one of the side roads with which he was familiar in that region, the body of a dead man. There was no doubt that he had been an officer, since he wore a pair of scarlet trousers trimmed with silver stripes, the kind of garment then favored by many officers; jerkin, boots, and spurs as well pointed to an officer.

My husband looked at his find and could not figure out whether the fellow had frozen to death or had been killed by some people from the Black Forest, but it made no difference to him how the man had died. My husband liked the jerkin so well that he stripped it off. And having that, he longed also for the trousers, but to get them he first had to pull off the boots. He succeeded in that, but when he tried to strip off the trousers, they did not budge; the moisture of the already decaying body had collected about

** An adventure: The story that follows rests on an old farce also to be found in Heinrich Bebel's *Facetiae*, 1506.

and below the knees, where the trouser-bands were tied at that time, and had seeped into the lining and the cloth so that legs and trousers were frozen together like a rock. Now my husband did not want to leave the trousers behind, and since this dunce in his hurry could not think of any way of separating the trousers from the legs, he took his axe and chopped the legs off the body. Then he packed up the trousered legs and the jerkin. With this bundle on his back he was lucky enough to find a peasant who let him sleep for the night behind his warm stove.

Unfortunately, during the same night one of the peasant's cows calved, and because of the severe frost a servant girl carried the calf into the house, putting it for the time being on a small bundle of straw near the stove right next to my husband. Toward daybreak the captured trousers were already thawed free from the legs, whereupon he took off his rags, put on the jerkin and the trousers, the latter turned inside out, left his old rags and the legs next to the calf, climbed out through the window and returned happily to our quarters.

Still early in the morning the servant girl returned to look after the calf. Seeing two legs and my husband's old rags and a leathern apron lying right next to them, she began to scream as though she had fallen among murderers. She ran out of the house, slamming the door shut behind her, as though the Devil were chasing her and the clamor woke up the peasant and all the neighbors. Thinking that there were soldiers about on one of their expeditions, they either took to flight or grabbed their weapons.

In the meantime the peasant had found out from the girl, who was trembling with fright, why she had screamed, to wit that the poor carpenter they had put up for the night had been eaten by the calf—all except his legs—and that the calf had looked at her with a frightful face; had she not fled, she believed, it would have leaped on her too! The peasant was about to kill the calf with his short pike, but his wife did not want him to run such a risk, nor did she want him even to enter the room. Instead, she prevailed upon him to ask the village mayor for help. He in turn had the bells tolled for the whole community to assemble in order to take the house by storm and to exterminate this common enemy of mankind before it could grow up into a cow.

Now you had the extraordinary spectacle of the peasant's wife lifting her children and her household furniture, piece after piece, out through the bedroom window, while the peasants stared into the main room through the window and, seeing the dragon and the two legs lying next to it, believed themselves to have sufficient evidence of the immense horror of it all.

The mayor ordered the house to be stormed and the terrible, fabulous beast to be slain, but they all wanted to guard their skins. Everybody said, "What about my wife and children if I were to die?" So finally upon the advice of an old peasant they decided to burn down the whole house and with it the calf, whose mother had perhaps been covered by a snake or a dragon. The owner of the house was promised aid and indemnification from the common purse. Everyone went to work with gusto, the remaining qualms banished by the thought that it could have been thieving soldiers who burned the house down.

This story led me to believe that my husband had great talent for tricks of this kind. Why, I thought, if trained like Skipinthefield, what could he not accomplish! But the dunce was too much of an ass that was going to the dogs, as it were, to learn anything. Besides, soon thereafter in the engagement near Herbsthausen he was killed, for he was one of those who always get the short end of the stick.

[215]

CHAPTER XXVII

AFTER HER HUSBAND IS KILLED IN AN ENGAGEMENT, COURAGE ESCAPES ON HER MULE. SHE MEETS A BAND OF GYPSIES, WHOSE LIEUTENANT TAKES HER AS HIS WIFE. SHE TELLS THE FORTUNE OF A YOUNG LADY IN LOVE, PURLOINING FROM HER IN THE PROCESS ALL HER JEWELS WITHOUT BEING ABLE TO HOLD ON TO THEM FOR LONG; SHE GETS A GOOD BEATING AND IS FORCED TO RETURN THEM.

I ESCAPED from the engagement I have just mentioned on my good mule, abandoning my tent and the least valuable part of my baggage. I withdrew as far as Kassel along with the remainder of the army under Turenne. Since my husband was dead and there no longer was anyone whom I could have joined or who would have cared for me, I finally took refuge with the gypsies that had left the main Swedish army with the forces under the command of Königsmarck, the latter having joined our troops at Wartburg.

A lieutenant of the gypsies observing that I had some money, a real talent, and a clever hand for stealing, and other virtues useful among this kind of people, lost no time in making me his wife. For me, this had at least the advantage that I no longer needed either oil, creams, or tints and powder to make myself up to look white and beautiful, since my social rank as well as my husband required that I be of the very hue which is called the Devil's favorite color. From smearing goose-drippings and various salves for lice on my skin and from the use of other unguents to dye my hair, I soon looked as hellish as though I had been born in the heart of Egypt. Often I was so struck by the change I had undergone that I had to laugh at myself out loud. Life as a gypsy, however, suited my temperament very well: I would not have changed places with the wife of any colonel.

In a short time, I learned fortunetelling from an old Egyptian grandmother. In lying and stealing I had been an adept before, save for my ignorance of certain gypsy tricks, but let me say bluntly that in a short time I reached such perfection that I could have passed as the Madam General of the Gypsy Women.

Although I pocketed more for my husband to waste in carousing than ten other wives could have done, I was for all that not smart enough to escape every danger and to avoid being knocked about. Let me tell you about one of my misadventures. On our march we camped for a night and a day not far from a friendly town, which everyone was permitted to visit in order to make his purchases. I went, too, although not so much to spend money as to ac-quire it by theft in the first place. I did not intend to buy anything except what I could obtain by trading with five fingers or by some other trick.

I had not advanced far into town, when a young lady dispatched her maid to me to tell me that her mistress wanted me to come and tell her fortune. From the little messenger herself I learned without any difficulty that the lover of her mistress was derelict in his affections and had become attached to somebody else. Profiting from this in-telligence, I saw the young lady and told her fortune so well that it surpassed all astrological almanacs, nay in the opinion of the suffering young lady, all prophets and their prophecies. Finally, she complained to me of her misery and asked me whether I knew a remedy for it and whether

I could cast a spell over her lover to get him back on the right track.

"I do, my lady," I said; "he will return and obey you, even were he protected by an armor such as the great Goliath wore."

Nothing could have been more pleasant to the ears of this fool; nothing did she desire more than to see me put my art into practice at once. I told her that we would have to be alone, and that there must not be any talking about what we did. Thereupon she dismissed her maids, enjoining complete silence upon them. I then went with the young lady into her bed chamber and asked her to give me a black veil that she had worn while mourning for her father, two earrings, a precious necklace she was wearing, her belt, and her favorite ring. Muttering various meaningless words, I wrapped all these jewels into the veil, tied several knots in it, and put everything in the bed of the amorous lady. Then I told her, "Both of us must now go down to the cellar."

When we got there, I persuaded her to undress to her chemise and while she proceeded to do so, I drew various strange magical signs on the bottom of a big wine barrel. Finally I pulled out the bung and ordered the lady to keep her finger in the hole until I had properly finished the magical procedure with the bung upstairs. After I had tethered, as it were, the little simpleton in this way, I went to fetch the jewels from her bed and left town with them forthwith.

But either this credulous, infatuated young lady and her possessions enjoyed heavenly protection or her jewels were not destined to be mine for some other reason. In any event, before I could reach our camp, I was seized by a noble officer of the garrison who demanded that I turn over my booty. Although I denied everything, he persuaded me to the contrary: I cannot say that he thrashed me soundly with a club but I can swear that he beat me up with his sword. For when his servant dismounted to search me and it appeared that I was going to resist him with my fearsome gypsy knife, the officer drew his sword and beat me with it over my head, arms, shoulders, and ribs.

For about a month afterward I had to attend to my bruises with ointment and treat the black bumps on my body with compresses. I believe that that devil would still be beating me, had I not given up my booty and thrown it down before him. So, for once, I got my just reward for the perpetration of an ingenious fraud.

CHAPTER XXVIII

COURAGE AND HER COMPANY ARRIVE IN A VILLAGE
WHERE THE ANNUAL FESTIVAL OF THE DEDICATION OF
THE CHURCH IS BEING HELD. SHE INCITES A YOUNG
GYPSY TO SHOOT A CHICKEN; HER HUSBAND PRETENDS
HE IS GOING TO HANG HIM AND WHEN EVERYONE
LEAVES THE VILLAGE TO WATCH THE SPECTACLE, THE
GYPSY WOMEN STEAL ALL THE FOOD THEY CAN FIND,
AND WITH CUNNING AND DISPATCH THE WHOLE BAND
TAKES OFF.

SOON after this struggle our gypsy band left the forces of Königsmarck to rejoin in Bohemia the main Swedish army, then under the command of Torstenson. I and my mule stayed with these forces until peace was concluded, nor did I leave the gypsies even when peace came, for I was unable to give up stealing.

Now I see that I have one more sheet of white paper left, so I will, in conclusion or as a valedictory, put down for you another fine story of a trick that I planned and executed. From this account the reader will be able to imagine what else I was capable of and how well suited I was for keeping company with gypsies.

One day toward evening, we reached a large village in Lorraine, where we were refused permission to stay overnight because the village was celebrating the dedication of its church and we were too large a troop of men, women, children, and horses. But my husband, pretending to be a lieutenant-colonel, promised most solemnly that he would make reparation for any injury that might possibly be done by paying out of his own pocket for anything damaged or stolen; besides he promised to see to it

that the culprit would be put to death. So after much trav-
ail we were finally admitted to the village.

The whole place smelled deliciously of roasts and pas-
tries especially prepared for the festival. My mouth watered
for the food, and the idea that the peasants were going to
eat it all by themselves vexed me greatly and so I thought
of the following design for us to get possession of it.

I told one of our smart young fellows to shoot a chicken
right in front of the inn. It was not long before people
came running to my husband to complain about the culprit. My husband pretended to be terribly angry and ordered a man who served as our trumpeter to sound the
alarm for assembly. When both peasants and gypsies were
all together on the village square, I passed the word in
thieves' slang about my design and told the women to get
ready to grab whatever they could. My husband tried the
culprit quickly according to martial law and sentenced
him to be hanged, since he had disobeyed the orders of his
superior officer.

Soon the whole village was buzzing with talk about the
fact that the lieutenant-colonel was going to hang a gypsy
on account of a chicken, some considering such a procedure too rigorous, others praising us for keeping strict dis-
cipline. One of us acted the hangman and tied the offender's hands behind his back while a young gypsy girl, pass-
ing herself off as his wife, came running with three borrowed children to the square. She pleaded for her husband's life and begged for mercy in the name of her small
children, her wailing presenting a spectacle of utter despair. But my husband refused to listen to her and when
he saw that the entire village was assembled to watch the
poor sinner hang, he ordered the evil-doer to be led toward the woods so that the sentence might be executed.

[221]

Indeed, all the inhabitants—young and old, men and women, servants and maids, kith and kin—left the village with us. All the while, the young gypsy girl with her three borrowed children continued to wail, cry, and plead, and when the crowd reached the woods and the tree where the chicken-killer was apparently to be strung up, she looked so pitiful that first the peasant wives and then the peasants themselves all pleaded for the offender; nor did they stop until my husband finally relented and for their sake granted the poor sinner his life.

While we were playing this comedy outside the village, our women ransacked it to their heart's content. They pulled the roasts off the spits, emptied the meat pots, and loaded a great deal of other booty on our wagons. Then they left the village and came toward us under no less a pretense than that of trying to incite their men to rebellion against me and my husband, for wanting to hang the poor man and turn his wretched wife into an abandoned widow and his three innocent children into orphans, all for a mere chicken. At the same time they told us in our own language that they had taken a lot of loot, and that we had better get away before the peasants discovered their loss. Then I called out that a part of our band should pretend to disobey my husband and to run into the woods so as to get away from the village. My husband and those who had remained with him pursued the others with drawn swords. There was even an exchange of fire, but without the least intent to hit a single soul.

The peasants, expecting a bloodbath, were terrified and rushed home, while we continued the shooting on the run and maintained the pursuit deep into the forest where we knew every nook and cranny. We were on the move all night. In the morning we divided the booty and broke up into small groups, thus evading all danger and escaping from the peasants with our loot.

With these people I have since roamed all over Europe, planning and executing many roguish pranks and thefts. To describe them all would require a whole ream of paper, and probably more. All my life nothing has astonished me more than the fact that so many countries put up with us, although we are of no use to God or man and do not want to serve either of them, but to the detriment of both the country folk and the great, whom we relieve of many a head of game, live on nothing but lies, fraud, and theft. I'll pass all over this in silence in order not to bring us into more disrepute.

Besides, it seems to me that I have said enough to put Simplicissimus to eternal shame by showing the kind of person his bedmate at the spa—of whom he boasted so greatly in public—really was. I believe that on other occasions as well when he believed that he was amusing himself with a beautiful lady he was generally being deceived by a French whore, or even by a witch, and thus became the Devil's kin.

THE AUTHOR'S POSTSCRIPT*

NOW, then, you modest young men, you honest widowers, and you married men, too, who have been on guard against the Chimeras, have escaped the horrible Medusas, plugged your ears before the damned Sirens, and renounced or fled from the profound, bottomless Belides— let yourselves not be blinded in the future by these she-wolves! For it is only too certain that from the love of whores comes nothing but filth, shame, scorn, poverty, misery, and, above all, a poor conscience. Only too late one realizes what he has got, how filthy they are, how infamous, lousy, scurfy, impure, stinking of breath and of their whole body; how inwardly they are full of the French disease and outwardly covered with pock marks;

so that in the end one feels ashamed of himself
and complains when it is much too late.

* This postscript was taken by Grimmelshausen verbatim, and hence perhaps tongue in cheek, from Tomaso Garzoni's compilation of learning, *Piazza Universale*, which had appeared in German translation under the title *Allgemeiner Schauplatz* (1619); see also above, Introduction.

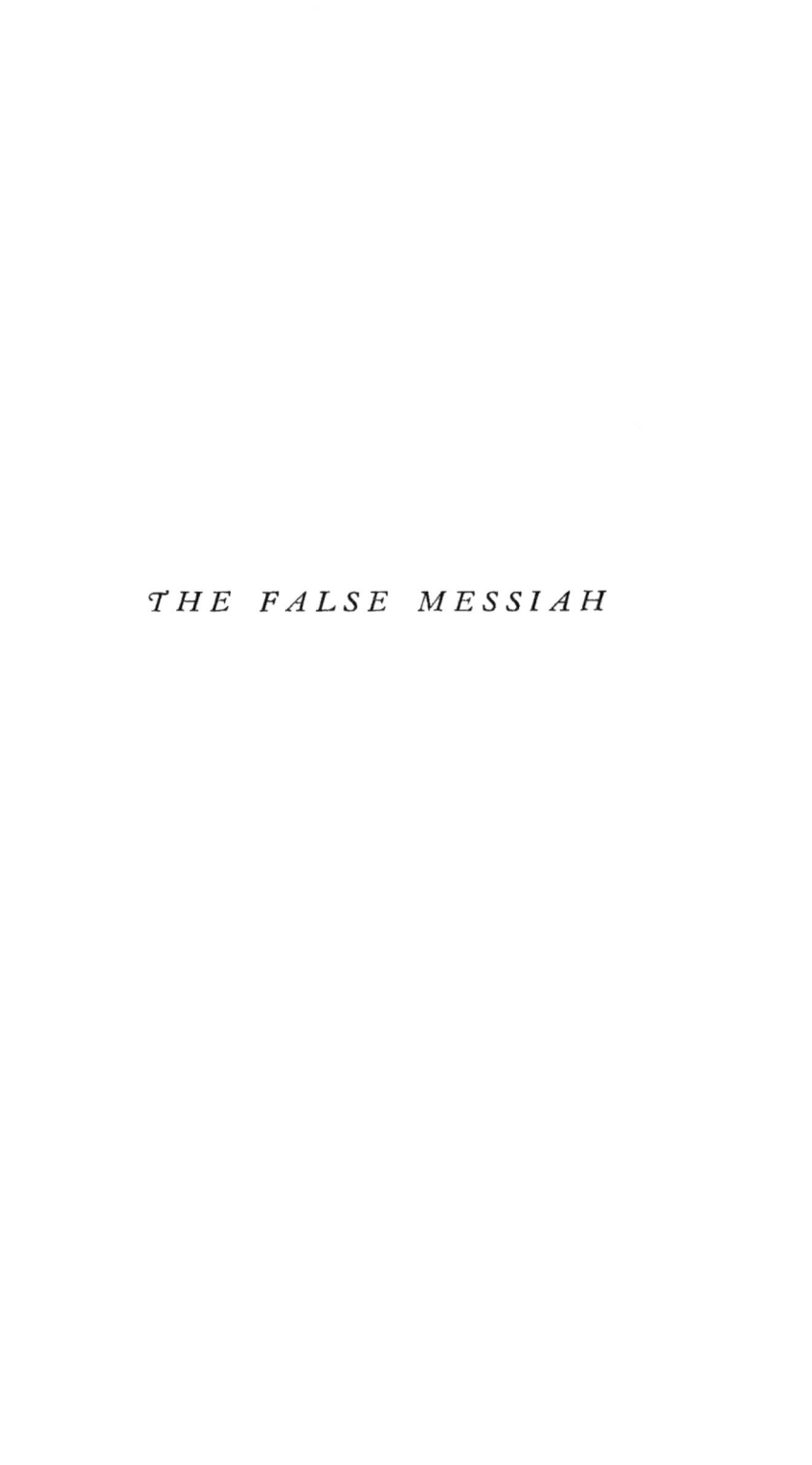

THE FALSE MESSIAH

PREFACE*

... Since man shrinks from committing acts of shameful vice in somebody else's presence (although the other is a sinner, too, and perhaps more godless than himself) how much more will he abstain from evil, nay from the smallest sin, if he heeds the teaching of *The Bird's-nest*, which is that he be aware of being watched everywhere by the All-Holy, who hates sin, the All-Just who fails neither to reward goodness nor to punish evil, the All-Mighty from whose hand and divine power no one can escape.

It is true the author has treated very serious matters in his usual jocular style and included many jests in this work, just as he did in the biography of *The Adventurous Simplicissimus*.† Perhaps only one in every seventeen readers will understand the author's meaning and intent, while the others will think that he produced his writings to while away their time. But this will not make him stray from his old chosen path. He trusts that the kernel of truth will be discovered by sensible people who can use it and benefit from it. It is well known that patients do not like to swallow bitter, if salutary, pills but easily take them sugar-coated. Thus, imitating a careful physician the author has coated and sweetened the galling bitterness of his censorious writings so that the unsophisticated reader may well fail to take them for helpful medicine and enjoy them instead like unhealthy dainties. . . .

* This "Preface" is taken from the Preface to Grimmelshausen's last novel, *Des wunderbarlichen Vogelnests zweiter Teil* (*The Enchanted Bird's-nest*, Part II), published in 1675. The meaning of the Preface is discussed in the Introduction, above, pp. 72ff.

† *The Adventurous Simplicissimus*: Grimmelshausen's most famous work, published in 1669. See Introduction, above, pp. 3ff.

CONTENTS

[229]

CHAPTER I

THE BEST WAY TO SURVIVE WAR IS SOUGHT AND FOUND
BUT THE WORST IS CHOSEN*

I HAD been thinking long and hard how to escape safely from the perilous war between France and Holland which most people felt was in the offing and might well spread until it engulfed all of Europe. I remembered, too, that an old astrologer had said that war would break out about this time in Germany and eventually come to an end in France, and that the Holy Roman Emperor would deal six hard blows to The Most Christian King.† I believed, therefore, that the whole Empire, my fatherland included, would be drawn into the fighting. This made me quite anxious and I pondered how I might amass for my viaticum a nice sum of money in gold that could be packed in small compass and be whisked away along with me and my belongings to a good safe place. I thought that I could surely attain this end with the help of my magic bird's-nest that made me invisible at will. Without delay I set my sights on a Portuguese Jew who was so rich that he was commonly held to be unable to tell the sum and total of his large fortune.

On my way to his house I heard someone sing the following opening of a song, which I took for an unfailing

* Chapter I of *The False Messiah* corresponds to chapter XII in *The Enchanted Bird's-nest*, Part II. In the first sentence of the translation five words of the original have been omitted, since they tie the opening of this chapter to the preceding chapter in the novel. In the original, the second paragraph opens with a sentence that begins "I made myself invisible. . . ." In the translation this sentence has been shifted to follow the comments on the song.

† The Most Christian King: the King of France, at that time, Louis XIV.

omen that we were indeed on the threshold of war; and this made me all the more eager to fill my purse quickly. The song began:

1

Simplex§ has no money left,
Skipinthefield** is all bereft,
Worries they have many,
Credit hardly any.

2

Brothers all! The sun will shine,
Circumstances, they'll be fine.
Smell it, you can't miss it.
War's acoming, bless it.

The other stanzas told of the godless lives of sundry persons of high station, and the final conclusion was that without war, pestilence, and hunger, the world could not be bettered. While the rhymes were artless and old-fashioned in the manner of Hans Sachs, the content was so sensible that I could not help taking them to heart as a sure prophecy, although I am usually not too superstitious.

I made myself invisible and entered the Jew's house to poke about for the places where his treasures were hidden; not being in my own home I was careful not to make any noise, lest despite my invisibility I be noticed and my project come to naught. Prowling about the house—I could just as well call it a palace—I found it larded with everything rich people usually have. I did not see any ready cash, however, simply because it was kept, along with many jewels, in a vault guarded by several strong locks.

§ Simplex: See p. 89, note †.
** Skipinthefield: See above, Introduction, pp. 6ff.

While I was searching the whole house for the keys, I discovered, in one of the rooms, a maiden who was embroidering a shoulder belt with gold, silver, and pearls, and I was stunned by her incomparable beauty. She was so extraordinarily and indescribably fair that I will never believe or be persuaded that a painter can be found anywhere in the whole world capable of painting so fine a picture. So radiant were her black-brown eyes that their lovely glances would have ignited the whole world into flames of love, if only she had been looking at the eyes of men and not at the fine pearly work of her alabaster hands. For she found joy and great pleasure in her unusual work, or rather work of art, and looked at it as if it were something she loved dearly. She was smiling, and if other eyes had caught her gentle glances they would have gone right through to the innermost heart binding it by chains of love, even had that heart been made of hard steel or of cold crystal and diamond.

While she was sitting there, motionless and absorbed in her work, I saw how artfully and fairly combined and distributed were the lovely, radiant white and rose colors of her finely formed face and how her lips shone as if painted with Spanish vermilion. I believed that the whole picture might be the work of some great master like those images—life-size, waxen, magnificently dressed—which used to be taken through German lands to be exhibited for money. But when she moved again and resumed her embroidery I was overcome by no less astonishment than Pygmalion must have felt when Venus poured a living soul into the beautiful virgin image that he had so ardently fashioned of ebony. There I stood enchanted, or to speak more truthfully, infatuated, unable either to drink in enough of her ravishing beauty or to recover from my astonishment. I did not notice anything Jewish in her features except for a suggestion of her well-formed nose, but to my eyes this was more a lovely embellishment than the key to a Jewish physiognomy. The jewels in her hair, around her neck, the pendants dangling from her ears, her ring and bracelets—all were of great value. Her slippers like her clothes and the shoulder belt she was embroidering were of a fabric such as no ordinary person wears every day. The sweet spheres of her bosom were tightly laced so that their rise and fall, as she breathed, gave me great joy. While I thus let my eager eyes have their fill, I failed to notice that I was drinking the sweet poison of love in very large draughts. I remained unaware of it until I wanted to leave and found that I could hardly tear myself away from this extraordinary picture.

I was already married and had served many a lass in my day—usual enough when love is stirring—and at the time when I was chasing the girls love and its passions had troubled me more than enough. But compared with what I was now enduring, everything in the past seemed a mere joke and child's play. Once I had looked at this Jewish maiden, I had no rest day or night. No sleep settled upon my eyes, all gay company repelled me, much as I sought it in order to forget my trouble. All I did was live on my pain, drag along the weight of my gloomy thoughts, exhaust myself with laments, futile efforts, vexations, deep musing, and a thousand kinds of fantastic follies and mad plots for possessing my love. To my regular business and all my affairs I bade goodbye. And just as my wits and reason became dull and useless, so my body and physical strength dwindled away, as though consumption had seized me by the throat. Thus only late in life did I learn the nature of really ardent love, although as a married man I should have reflected on Virgil's useful teaching, when he says:

> Vina sitim sedent, natis Venus alma creandis
> Serviat: hos fines transiluisse nocet.

That is:

> Wine for thirst and Venus for creation.
> He who balks them spurns elation.

My condition, worsening every day, would have worn me out by and by and eventually sent me to the grave, but it seemed that so merciful an end was not to be. Mine was a more cruel fate. The unsurmountable obstacles which kept me from stilling my desire were so immense that they threatened me with hopeless despair. I began to wish for my own death and might well have cried with that Italian:

> O notte, o cielo, o mare, o piagge e monti,
> Che si spesse m'udite chiamar morte!

That is:

> O night, o heaven, o sea, o mountain and vale,
> How often you hear my wish to suffer the
> torment of death!

Indeed, I went even further and seized upon the ultimate desire of bitter and despairing lovers, to wit, that heaven and earth collide, so that I might see the end of my misery. Alphenus Perusinus spoke of this desire in the Italian tongue as follows:

> Piouan dal ciel con tempestosa furia
> Folgori ardenti, che ciascun sommergano.

Cantalicius translated it thus into the Latin language:

> Totum terribili quatiatur turbine cœlum,

Cunctaque dispereant corpora fulminibus,

which might run as follows:

> Heaven races upon rushing earth to crash,
> No one can flee from that disastrous smash.

That my love was a Jewess caused me the least qualm
and trouble; for if one's conscience stoops to regain lost
money with the Devil's help, how much less will it care
whether one's animal lust is satisfied by baptized or un-
baptized flesh. Rather, I suffered my greatest anguish because I knew how strict and careful the Jews were in protecting their women, and especially their virgin maidens,
from downfall. Furthermore, it was not my least vexation
that gifts and gold which otherwise open all doors, level
mountain and valley, and score victories everywhere, were
of no avail in this instance, especially since it was commonly known that the girl's father, without depleting his
riches, could throw away as much as I could hope to amass
in all my lifetime. Thirdly, it was a sharp thorn in my side
that the Jews, both men and women, hate us Christians almost by nature. Compared with themselves—that is to say,
with those who believe that Abraham's seed was God's
people and chosen to dominate the entire world under the
future Messiah—compared with themselves they hold us
to be not better than dogs. Fourthly, my cheeks became
hollow and my hair began to turn grey because I had no
confidence that in this case I could make any progress even
with the help of panders or panderesses, against whose no-
torious cunning, malicious deception and daily renewed
plots, no virgin is sufficiently pure and chaste, no widow
too cautious, no woman too prudent, no resolution too stiff,

[236]

no intention too firm and no continence too enduring; nor is any rock hard and firm enough not to be moved by the steady heaving of these procurers; nor is there any hope whatever in employing force or fraud, wile or wisdom, speed, art, or skill against them. The more I thought about the cleverness of these panders, the more it pained me that I could not make use of them. Fifth, I found myself in a city where violence was of no use, because the Jews dwelt in it under the fullest protection; nor did I deem it possible to achieve anything by cunning, because, as I have told you, the Jews guard their women so closely. To introduce myself to her, however, and present myself as her servant, and then at some time to take her unawares with my skewer, this appeared to me flippant as well as perilous.

I believe that Satan tempts especially those people who habitually tumble from one sin to the other. He holds them in sway and assails them with more impudence than he shows toward those who are wary of vice. For indeed, it must have been by inspiration of the arch enemy that I asked myself, "How would you feel, if I let you be circumcised, which after all is nothing novel in Amsterdam?" No sooner did this notion strike me than I realized its horrible depravity. "No!" I cried, "such conceits and designs are of the Devil. You should rather die a thousand times than betray Christ, your Savior." If, at that time, I still had been sane and in possession of my wits, I would have easily reached the conclusion that my love of the Jewess, too, could have sprung only from the Devil's attempt to deprive me of my Christianity and thus of eternal bliss. Alas, I believed that I had done enough, and in fact had behaved like a Christian knight, by not denying Christ in public, even though I at no time suffered a single pang of conscience for ever adoring the image of

[237]

the Jewess in my heart and for offering up to her so many thousands signs of love.

The only refreshment in my miserable and gloomy life consisted in a walk that I took almost daily, going invisibly to see my love and to let my eyes rest on her wondrously beautiful face. But how can I call such folly refreshment, which was nothing but oil on my fire making the flames of love spurt higher all the while. Thus I loved without hope of pleasure, and tormented myself pondering on how it might yet be possible to allay my misery in some way or other. But there was no help except for hanging or drowning, neither of which I regarded as a pleasant way out.

In the meantime, I learned the names of the Jew and all the people who lived in his house; I became familiar with all the nooks and crannies of the house, as though I had been born and brought up in it. I discovered also the place where the Jew hid his ready money, his silver plates and gems, a veritable treasure so big that you would look in vain for anything like it in the homes of many a count in Germany and France. I left everything untouched, because the treasure I wanted now was not Eliezer's gold, silver, and precious stones, but Esther, his fair daughter.

One Friday evening,‡ I was again in Eliezer's house and after the prayers of thanks that they call Havdalah (meaning "separation," namely of the Sabbath from the other, profane, days) I watched Eliezer as master of the house, clad in his ermine-lined sleeping robe of damask, sprinkling wine from a large golden goblet throughout the house, saying all the while, "The prophet Elijah, the prophet Elijah, may the prophet Elijah come to us soon

‡ One Friday evening . . . : Grimmelshausen's mistake. Havdalah, "the end of the Sabbath" (as he says correctly, in chapter 11) is celebrated on Saturday evening.

with the Mashiah, the son of God and David; the prophet
Elijah," and so on. And these ceremonies gave me occasion
to think of that which later was to afford me pleasure in
my love.

CHAPTER II

WHAT THE JEWS THINK OF ELIJAH AND BELIEVE
ABOUT THE HOPED-FOR FUTURE MESSIAH

AT that time there lived in the city a fellow of Jewish
birth who, only a year before, had been baptized
and named Erasmus at that sacred ablution. He
was about twenty-four years of age, learned, of fine appearance and honest in his ways, rather poor and often so
much in need that he had to resort to sponging. In order
to make some sort of living he taught the children of various merchants to write and speak Hebrew. Some directors
of the East India Company had promised to employ his
services with the fleet at its next sailing so that he now had
some prospects of doing better than just making ends meet,
and even of becoming prosperous. Now, since this fellow
was well acquainted with both the Christian and Jewish
religions, hated the Jews and was mortally hated by them
in return, he disclosed their superstitious secrets to all his
friends who, for amusement, wanted to learn about them.
Once, I met him in the gay company of some young merchants whom he regaled with a lot of this silly Jewish
nonsense.

Since I did not dare to employ money, force, or anything
like that in my affair, I had decided to seek my salvation—
or rather damnation—by using cunning and fraud against
these superstitious, and hence so fatuous people; I thought
my invisibility would serve me well. I felt it necessary,
therefore, to cultivate this fellow Erasmus in order to learn
from him all about the Jewish faith, customs, and practices
so that I could set up and lay my fraudulent nets and snares
accordingly and cheat Eliezer of his daughter's purity. Pre-

tending that I was eager to learn to read and write Hebrew from him, I courteously invited Erasmus to my lodgings. Erasmus was a fellow as trusting as he was cheerfully willing to serve everybody as best he could.

Within two days, to my teacher's amazement, I knew the Hebrew alphabet perfectly and I continued to make rapid progress in my lessons. Whenever we ate together or went out for a walk, I made him talk about the faith of the Jews, their prayers, hopes, and customs. So much did I inquire about these matters that Erasmus asked me, jokingly, if I intended to become a Jew. I will not strain the patience of the most-gracious reader, however, and tell him only what I think will shed light on my story.

Most of the Jews, Erasmus told me, believe, though without foundation and only on the strength of tales inherited from their forefathers, that already in Abraham's lifetime Elijah had been his most faithful helper and the oldest servant in the house.* According to Genesis 24, he had fetched from Mesopotamia Bethuel's daughter, Rebecca, as a wife for Isaac. At the time when Sodom and Gomorrah were still standing, he had done much mischief and caused much harm to those cities to punish them for their ungodliness.

In addition to their other vices, the Sodomites were opposed to hospitality. They made it a law that the life of anyone be taken who invited a stranger to a banquet and treated him as a friend. Also, like Cacus,† the robber, they

* Elijah as Abraham's servant: According to Genesis 15:2, not Elijah but Eliezer of Damascus was Abraham's steward. Apparently, Grimmelshausen took the identification of Elijah with Abraham's servant from old Jewish legends in which it occurs.

† Cacus: the cattle thief slain by Heracles. Grimmelshausen confuses him here with Procrustes, the robber who was killed by Theseus.

had various bedsteads, some long, some short, on which strangers who came among them were forced to lie. Those who were shorter than the bed were stretched, and the heads or feet of those who exceeded its length were chopped off until each man fitted his bed properly. They had introduced these evil laws and manners in order to consume by themselves in lustful living the abundance of their country, the fattest part of the Holy Land, where milk and honey flowed. They wanted to share none of it with foreigners and neighbors. Besides, strangers might have made them feel a little ashamed; heated by wine, they could, after all, without them indulge in their filthy sodomies with less hindrance and greater abandon.

In order to play a trick on the Sodomites and to show them how much their laws lacked in wisdom, Elijah, Abraham's servant, joined one of their banquets. He ate and drank as though he were one of them. This angered the jealous and envious Sodomites so much that they resolved to put to death the man who had invited him or who at least was responsible for his admission and presence, and to mete out to Elijah, himself, according to custom, the punishment of the bedstead. When some of them asked him, however, who it was that had brought him to the banquet, he replied each time, that he, the inquirer, himself along with others had invited and introduced him, whereupon each one pulled back anxiously like a deaf mute. When night came, they wanted nevertheless to kill him, but he fitted all the beds, whether long or short, as if they had been made to measure for him. God, moreover, struck the Sodomites with blindness as He did again later in Lot's day, so that Elijah returned to Abraham's hut unharmed.

Many more such stories they tell of this Elijah. They

say that he had been ordered by God to be a faithful helper, prophet, and servant to Abraham and his kin, for which reason God had endowed him with a life that would last until Judgment Day. During the whole time that Israel was in Egypt, he had given them help and comfort, in visible as well as invisible ways and by assuming many different appearances. And although he had been transported to paradise in a fiery chariot at the time of Ahab, he was nonetheless still present every day at all Jewish circumcisions everywhere in the world, and each time there was kept ready for him a special, magnificent seat, which no Jew, no matter how pious, was permitted to occupy. In addition, he protected and shielded the Jewish people and diverted all misfortune from them. He favored especially those Jews who honored him with wine and certain ceremonies when they celebrated Havdalah, the end of the Sabbath; such piety pleased him so much that he would take the house under special protection and bestow his blessing on it. He was also supposed to bring the Mashiah, or future Messiah, and to assist him in his work.

In sum, the Jews esteem him more highly than the Catholics revere the Mother of God, and often in his honor invite the poor to their houses treating them to a full table and always leaving one seat empty for Elijah, because they believe that then he will sit down together with the poor guests to eat and drink his share invisibly.

Of the Mashiah and his office, Erasmus told me that the Jews believe that he will be a king of this world. With his great power and divine help he will miraculously bring them together again from all corners of the earth to which they were dispersed and will lead them back to the Promised Land. In this way, the Jews, hoping for a sort of temporal paradise on earth, confused the eternal life promised to the elect with the reign of the Mashiah or Messiah. They also firmly believe that God will awaken their dead; root out and destroy all enemies of the people of Israel; banish from among His people all trouble, hardship, and sickness; and rebuild with precious stones their holy temple in Jerusalem so that it will again look just as it did when the prophet Ezekiel had seen it. Thereafter the people of Israel will govern and rule over the entire world and possess all of its resources, treasures, and riches. God will rid them of inborn lust, of the desire and impulse to sin and do evil; indeed, he will dwell among them so that they will see Him face to face. God will lengthen their life span. They will reach Adam's or Methuselah's age, and he who went up to Heaven at the age of a hundred would be said to have died in early childhood. The Promised Land cleansed by fire of the uncleanliness with which heathens, Christians, and Mohammedans had defiled it, will become larger and a thousand times more splendid and fruitful than it now was; once again it would be as it was in the days when all twelve tribes with their twelve hundred thousand souls lived together there so well. Their Mashiah will govern forever, and at the beginning of his reign all Jews will be his guests in Jerusalem. At his table they will drink the most delicious wine, grown in paradise and carefully kept in Adam's cellar for just that purpose. The biggest beasts, birds, and fish that God had ever created, will be slaughtered, among them the ox Behemoth (Job 4), that crops a thousand mountains every day, and what he crops during the day grows again at night. His mate had been made frigid and barren by the Lord lest this breed of immensely big beasts multiply and ruin the whole world, but the ox himself had been castrated and fattened and preserved by Him for the pious Jews of the future. And so too, the great cruel bird Bar Juchne will be turned into roasts. So huge was she that a single egg which had once dropped from her nest felled three hundred cedar trees and, when it broke, flooded, drowned and carried away sixty villages. Of no less service would be the whale Leviathan (about which Job also speaks). In order to keep it from multiplying God had also castrated it; but the female He had done away with and salted for the table of those God-fearing Jews, who would return to the Holy Land with their Mashiah.

I was much astonished that the Jews, otherwise a learned, clever, subtle, and sly people, were silly enough to believe such nonsense and foolish dreams. But Erasmus told me that they doubted these tales about their future Messiah as little as a good Christian doubted that the true Messiah had already come. The Jews derive special, if unwarranted, consolation from the so-called Golden Ape,§ a verse from the end of the 26th chapter of Leviticus:

"And yet for all that, when they be in the land of their enemies, I will not cast them away, neither will I abhor them to destroy them utterly and to break my covenant with them: for I am the Lord, their God."

The promise of this verse had already been made and fulfilled by God at the time of the Babylonian captivity, but the poor, blind people do not realize that they live now under another prophecy, related in Deuteronomy, chapter 28, where no promise whatever is made of deliv-

§ The so-called Golden Ape (in German: *der güldene Aff*): Hans Heinrich Borcherdt (*Grimmelshausens Werke*, Vol. IV, p. 493) comments on this expression, "This is the name for the promise of Leviticus 26:44, because this verse begins in Hebrew with *Veaf*, i.e., 'And yet for all that,' and the Jews based all their hope on it 'as on a golden gem.'"

ery. They also take special consolation from Isaiah's message at the end of his 60th chapter by applying the prophet's words on the eternal life to the coming of their Messiah and his rule, to wit:

> Violence shall no more be heard in thy land, wasting nor destruction within thy borders; but thou shalt call thy walls Salvation, and thy gates Praise.

> The sun shall be no more thy light by day; neither for brightness shall the moon give light unto thee: but the LORD shall be unto thee an everlasting light, and thy God thy glory.

> Thy sun shall no more go down; neither shall thy moon withdraw itself; for the LORD shall be thine everlasting light, and the days of thy mourning shall be ended.

> Thy people also shall be all righteous: they shall inherit the land for ever, the branch of my planting, the work of my hands, that I may be glorified.

> A little one shall become a thousand, and a small one a strong nation: I the LORD will hasten it in his time.

They understand this to mean that at the time of the Messiah even the least of the Jews will become the head of a large family; nor do these blind people realize that this prophecy was fulfilled soon after it was made with great dispatch, as it were, through the disciples and apostles of Christ the Lord, since each of them, by virtue of his precepts and teaching, founded a large Christian community, an immeasurable multitude of many hundreds of thousands of believers in Christ. And all this happened indeed in very little time; for on a certain Pentecost the apostle Peter alone converted about 3,000 souls. But the aforementioned words (which read in Hebrew, *Ani Adonai B'itto Achyscheno*,** that is, "I, the Lord will hasten it in his time") are taken by them to mean that suddenly and in great haste God would send their Messiah, by post coach, as it were, and put them into the Promised Land as into an earthly paradise. They value these words far more highly than their Golden Ape because they believe this promise and prophecy—for them not yet fulfilled—must necessarily come to pass, that is to say, at the advent of their Mashiah.

All these legends and fables I kept in my head as if the salvation of my soul depended on them, and I believe that had I not yet learned the catechism, I could not have mastered it as quickly and as diligently as I did these tomfooleries. Erasmus told me a lot more than I have related here, but I shall not repeat all of it, since I do not want to burden the reader and because it is not needed for my story. The little I have told, however, the reader must, I believe, know, in order to understand my story clearly, how I used this or that part of what Erasmus told me for my purpose, and why I did one thing rather than another.

Let me end this chapter with what of all this foolishness seems to me the most foolish. The Jews believe that the archangel Michael will blow a big horn three times when their Messiah comes. At the first sound the Messiah, son of David, will appear with the prophet Elijah to reveal himself to the children of Israel. Everywhere in the world the Jews will hear the sound of the horn and know that God is visiting his people and the final salvation is near. The Christians and other nations, however, will know

** *Ani Adonai B'itto Achyscheno*: Grimmelshausen has *Oeni Adonai Bocitto Ochysche*.

only terror, lament, and misery, while the Jews girding their loins, will gaily get up and march in great joy with their Mashiah to Jerusalem.

Upon the second blowing, which will be a very long blast, all the graves in Jerusalem will open. God will revive all the dead; then, too, the Messiah, the son of David, and Elijah, the prophet, will awaken from his death the pious and poor Messiah Ben Joseph (who lived with the sick and the lepers of Rome and perished in an encounter of the Israelites). And the kings of all nations will lift the Jews who still dwell among them upon their own shoulders and upon their chariots to bring them to Jerusalem.

And when the archangel Michael sounds his horn for the third time, God will lead out the numberless Israelites who live beyond the rivers Gason, Lachlach, and Chobar and in the cities of Juda, and they will go to Paradise with the other children of Moses. During this exodus of the ten tribes of the Israelites God's glory and majesty will surround them like clouds, in columns, and yes, God Himself will walk ahead of them. In front, behind, and alongside will be nothing but fire and flame, and for the Christians and other nations on earth nothing will be left to sustain their lives.

I thought, "If so many thousand Jews believe these silly things about their future Messiah, and if because of him so many of them once wrapped their coats around their heads in Crete or Candia and threw themselves from the rock down into the sea,‡ then you should be able to persuade a single one of them that for the sake of their future Messiah he should let you sleep with his daughter."

‡ In the first half of the fifth century, Moses the Cretan, promised to lead the Jews back to the land of their forefathers. When he suddenly disappeared many of his disappointed followers committed suicide by throwing themselves into the sea.

CHAPTER III

ELIJAH ARRIVES AND DINES AS A GUEST, THE ANGEL
URIEL ANNOUNCES THE JEWISH MESSIAH, AND OTHER
GREAT PORTENTS

I PRACTICED copying in Hebrew those words
of Isaiah at the end of his sixtieth chapter, "*Ani
Adonai B'itto Achyscheno*," on which the Jews base
all their hope. My script was so fair and pretty that not
even the two scribes of Solomon, Shisha's sons Elihoreph
and Ahiah, could have improved upon it. Then I got a
few sheets of the most delicate vellum. I colored them
red, yellow, blue, and green and worked on them until
they became quite translucent, like glass, so that no one
could have recognized the material; it could have been
isinglass, parchment, or the kind of mica which the Muscovites use for their window panes. This heavenly paper
I cut into several hundred little pieces and wrote upon
them in golden Hebrew letters the words of Isaiah. In
addition, I had an alb cut out of snow-white Dutch linen
(this is a white garment used by Catholic priests at the
service) and out of a many-colored piece of material shot
with gold I had a surplice like a Levite's coat made for me.
Finally, I had two blow tubes fitted together. All these
things I needed to carry out the plan which I had conceived in the light of the useful information Erasmus had
given me.

With the tubes I blew all my little slips through a broken
window into the Jewish school on the very day when the
Jews with joyous voices were chanting the Golden Ape,
that is the twenty-sixth chapter of Leviticus. No one can
possibly describe the awe of the Jews, their reverence,

their amazement and deep delight, as they picked up the slips. You could sense their emotion when you saw how they trembled for joy as they read and recited the slips and even presented them to one another like gifts. It seemed as if each Jew had a lute in his heart which made him merry, for everyone now believed that beyond any doubt he had received a sure sign from heaven: the old misery and the dispersal of the Jews were going to end and the paradisaical life in the Promised Land was about to begin under the Mashiah who was already knocking at the door.

For several days after this I snooped around invisibly in various Jewish houses marveling at the great hopes and elation which my slips had kindled among these superstitious, silly, and blind people. They arranged banquets and holiday festivities and posted some of the slips to Poland, Italy, Germany, and even Asia, as joyous messages of certain redemption.

When pious Jews observe the custom of setting a table in their houses and inviting the poor to sit down at it, they leave the most honored place free and vacant for the prophet Elijah. They firmly believe that, though invisible, he is present at such banquets partaking of the food and drink. Now, ever since the day I had scattered my slips they took to this practice much more frequently, for they believed that Elijah would appear either before or together with the Messiah. My first step had been so well taken that when I went to Eliezer's house to feast my eyes on Esther's lovely face, and found that one of these banquets was being held, I dared it at last: I sat down at the table in Elijah's chair. Like the other guests I helped myself so amply that everybody, including Eliezer who personally attended to the serving, could see how the food wandered from the pots onto my plate and disappeared little by little, how my part of the bread dwindled and how my cups became empty. All this was observed with the greatest astonishment and received with still greater satisfaction and joy by Eliezer who poured for me not only the ordinary French and German wines, but also wines from Spain and the Canaries.

With this success, I became confident and bold enough to visit as well the houses of other rich Jews to attend in Elijah's stead not only the banquets given in his honor but also circumcisions. These great and hitherto unheard-of miracles soon became the talk of all the Jews in the city so that I decided that the time had come to venture further and proceed without delay to the execution of my real plot.

I asked a turner to make an instrument for me that looked like those humming-tops which young boys play with, except that the handle or foot of it was hollow like a pipe, and instead of the square openings on the sides which produce a humming sound it had a round one on top which could be opened or shut tight with a screw. This instrument I filled with cotton drenched in the most exquisite Indian balsam, liquid amber, musk, ambrosia, civet, and the most precious scents of flowers, herbs, roots, gums, and fruits. Now when I unscrewed the opening at the top and blew in at the bottom, I could in a moment fill any room with the loveliest odor anyone has ever smelled. The odorous object I took along with me when I went to Eliezer's house in the evening, invisibly but in full regalia: my alb and gilded cloth, a golden-blond, curly wig (easily worth a hundred taler) embellished on top by a green wreath of jewels, and my face made up with appropriate colors.

I hid in Eliezer's bedchamber. Perhaps because of the

prospective arrival of Elijah and the Messiah the room was adorned most remarkably; tapestries and precious draperies surrounded the bed and a wax candle large enough to burn through a whole night had been lit. I awaited with great impatience Eliezer's retirement and his first sleep.

When the proper time came, I stepped forward visibly, in my extraordinary make-up, in all my strange and bizarre appearance and borrowed beauty, and standing in front of the bed, I waked Eliezer gently from his sleep. "Let your heart not be frightened," I said, "and let your soul banish all needless fear! For lo, I am the angel Uriel, who stands before God's face. I have been sent by the King of Kings and His prophet Elijah whom you have served all your life in the fear of God, in order to bring you the glad tidings for which the house of Jacob has prayed for so long a time: The chosen people of Israel will be redeemed. For you are the branch, sprung from the root of Jesse and from Juda, of whose blood there shall be born the Mashiah, the holy savior and redeemer of his people, he who will lead them back from the diaspora to the Promised Land where milk and honey flow."

Here I paused a little, and when Eliezer had recovered his wits and wiped the sleep out of his eyes, he said: "True, everything is possible for the Lord, but how can this happen, when my Sarah is old and unable to bear children?"

I replied, "It is the will of the Lord and ordained by him that the Messiah be born not of you and your Sarah but of your daughter Esther and be conceived by her of the prophet Elijah. Lo, God has endowed her with virtue, piety, and rare beauty so that she be worthy to be the spouse of so great, holy, and wondrous a prophet and the mother of your long-expected Mashiah. Since the days of

David Elijah has preserved in paradise the seed of that king for the Mashiah in order to administer it to your daughter Esther on the third day of Elul (which in our calendar is September); on that day he will visit her bed-chamber—invisibly, as is his habit—and accomplish the work for which the house of Jacob has longed for so many hundreds of years. Thus it is that it is written: Elijah will appear before the coming of the Mashiah. For this reason, attend and see to it that your daughter be willing toward him. As for yourself, during the time he visits with her, you will not fail to treat him in the way such a holy prophet deserves, just as you have already done many times when you invited the poor to your table. For your reward and pleasure, after the birth of the Messiah, your little grandchild, you yourself will be reborn like Phoenix or the eagle, and you will live to your nine hundred and thir-tieth year in the Promised Land without want or sickness. The Mashiah will make you a great prince of the people, and you will have the joy of witnessing the decline and destruction of Israel's enemies and the elevation of your-self and your people."

Eliezer's curiosity was aroused, and being an inquisitive man, he wanted to know a few particulars about the entry into the Promised Land. In order not to lose credit with him I had to invent more lies in a hurry, that is to say, such things as he liked to hear and all Jews desire. So I told him that here, in the country where the Mashiah was to be born, war would break out and spread throughout the world. France would fight against Holland; the Holy Roman Emperor, Spain, and Holland against France; Sweden and Denmark against one another; the Poles against the Turks; the Turks against the Persians; the Muscovites against the Tartars; in sum, every nation

against another throughout the whole world. With the
ready help of sickness and famine, the successors to war,
each nation would so exhaust, shatter, and destroy the
other that the people of Israel would easily overcome and
enslave all of them. They would hardly need a single
stroke of the sword to attain that end, for, in the meantime, protected and blessed by God, they would have multi-
plied immensely. They would thus easily take away from
all the nations of the world their gold and silver, their
gems and jewels, their finest goods and chattels, household
furniture, merchandise and the like, carrying all of this
along with them to the Promised Land. Therewith I concluded my tall stories, telling Eliezer that it was not proper
for him to learn more at this time. He answered: "May
the Lord's will be done in exaltation of Israel and your
words be fulfilled on his people."

Thereupon I instantly made myself invisible again and
blew through my apple of scents in Eliezer's direction
such a powerful and delicious odor throughout the whole
room that the poor fool in his joy half imagined himself
already in paradise. With this seal I neatly certified my
lies as truth, for just as Eliezer must have heard or read
that evil spirits, after their appearance, leave a foul, hellish
stench behind, so he surely and firmly believed that after
the departure of good angels a paradisaical scent remained.
So I could not possibly be an evil angel or a false apparition; I had to be a good spirit, and this seemed all the
more certain since my prophecy agreed so well with the
tidings given by the slips in the synagogue. Eliezer's joy
and delight thereafter were indescribable, and no wonder: he saw himself in his imagination already as grandfather of the Messiah, and next to him as the greatest
prince in the world. He felt himself assured of a millennial

age, which he expected to spend with as little trouble as in Lubberland, and thereafter he would rise to paradise and that without the least trouble, and not like a cow trying to get into a mousehole.

Eliezer could not wait until daybreak to bring his daughter the good news. That very night she had to learn what the angel Uriel (I almost said her lover, Mr. Urian)* had spoken to him. She was, of course, delighted with the pleasant message, and I confirmed its truth for her by redoubling many times the lovely scent which she had found in her father's bedchamber.

At this point every good Christian should consider the danger into which my beastly desires had led my soul, or to put it better, consider the road to unfailing, eternal damnation, along which Satan himself had led me. No doubt, ever since I first availed myself of his help through the sorcerer,† he had increased his power over me. Through his familiarity with me and through his services he had established a claim, which at first he held in abeyance, but only in order to drive me later all the more forcefully into sin and the most heinous vices. It may seem merely a sport and a good joke that I cheated so cleverly the proud Jew— the arch enemy of Christ our Lord, of His church, and of all Christians—as well as his daughter out of her chastity. But no, my true, pious, Christian soul! I was much more irresponsible than appears at first glance. For first of all, I imitated the Devil, who in order to deceive man changes himself dissemblingly into an angel of light. In the guise of such an angel I committed lies not only upon the holy prophet Elijah, heretically imputing to him the

* Urian: a man who deserves little respect.

† An episode in the hero's life related in an earlier part of the novel; the sorcerer helped the merchant to acquire the bird's-nest that made him invisible.

[255]

most heinous vices, but also upon the just and true God Himself. With these terrible and blasphemous lies I did what I could to confound the wretched errors of the poor blind Jews making them still more obstinate and head-strong. God Himself beckons them to conversion, offers them mercy like a father, and after conversion more than willingly takes them into the womb of His church so that they may obtain salvation along with all those who are chosen. But I, by arousing false hopes with my lies, shielded and armed them so that a divine ray of mercy especially sent to enlighten them, might have altogether or very nearly failed to reach them. I made more wicked and evil those whose conversion should have been my concern. "Woe to him who causes offense," says the Savior. But everything I did was toward an evil end, for the sake of vile, short-lived lust, which severs the soul from God and condemns it to eternal death and damnation. The very worst, however, was this: I offended the supreme good, my true God, thereby declaring myself His enemy and forfeiting eternal life; I cruelly killed my poor soul anew, and moved much closer than I ever had been before to His left hand, the side of the Devil and his followers. O, how often do we wretched men err when we deceive our-selves and make light of our severe trespasses, regarding them as small infirmities, never as real sins. Unaware of our self-deception we sink quite imperceptibly into self-love and delusion and then through the vilest slime of the most horrible vices finally into the abyss of hell.

CHAPTER IV

A S I have already told you, I had got Eliezer and his daughter to expect Elijah to appear on the third day of Elul and I was joyfully anticipating the satisfaction of my desire and appetite. Still the suspicion had not entirely left me that perhaps, after all, the cunning Jews did not quite trust and believe me, but planned to undo me at the very moment I began my real work. For this reason, I stole about in Eliezer's house on the day before the third to see what they were up to. Were they preparing a bridal bed or a grave for Elijah? I found that these wretched people indeed wanted to be deceived and that the prophecy from the fount of all truth, which is recorded in the fifth chapter of John the Evangelist, was to be fulfilled: "I am come in my Father's name, and ye receive me not: If another shall come in his own name, him ye will receive." And woe to them who like the blind and stubborn Jews are deserted by God and without the illumination of a single glance from His merciful eyes remain impenitent and unconverted.

Who would ever have thought that the learned Rabbis of Amsterdam could be persuaded that the holy prophet Elijah would so displease God as to indulge in lewdness and beget in sin their promised savior, whom next to God they hold most holy? But these people, who think only of their well-being and the pleasures of the flesh, can imagine nothing but a fleshly saint. They have already

[257]

been seduced by nineteen false Messiahs; blinded and excluded from redemption they will surely continue to believe in more of the same kind, until they either all eventually disappear or little by little get converted; thus when the great day of the Lord comes few will be left of this large and once immeasurable multitude. Indeed, under the Emperor Aelius Hadrian, in the years 131 to 137 after Christ's birth, many hundred thousand Jews, men, women, and children, perished for the sake of their seducer Barchocheta* (which means "son of stars"). Rabba Bereshits Rabba,† folio 74, says that at that time eight hundred thousand died in the city of Bethera§ alone, which because of this they call "the bitter city." For this reason Rabba Juda Echa Rabthi** said on folio 71: "Henceforth, this man shall be called no longer Barkochba, a child of stars, but Barcostba, that is a child of lies." All this is related by Christian Gerson von Recklinghusen,‡ a born Jew and a baptized, reborn, Christian, in his refutation of the Jewish Talmud, book 2, chapter 9, where many other such false Jewish Messiahs are mentioned.

I shall leave it to others to say more about these matters and return instead to my story. Eliezer furnished his daughter Esther's bedchamber with bedclothes, chairs, pillows, and other decorations, as if a royal prince were to take his

* *Barchocheta*: later called *Bar Cochba*; he organized the rebellion during the reign of Emperor Hadrian (A.D. 76–138).

† *Rabba Bereshits Rabba; Bereshit Rabba* is the first book of the *Midrash Rabba,* a medieval Jewish commentary. *Bereshit* means "the beginning," the words which open *Genesis.*

§ Bethera: the town of Bethar, conquered by Julius Severus.

** *Rabba Juda Echa Rabthi*: commentary on lamentations of Jeremiah.

‡ Christian Gerson: a converted Jew who became a Lutheran minister, author of *Talmud Judaicum,* published in 1607.

lodgings there. He also provided his kitchen with the most delicious foods and an abundance of various sweetmeats so that Elijah would be well entertained and well fed and his business transacted in the greatest possible contentment.

I acquired a coarse, hirsute coat with a leather belt, so that my Esther would have no doubt when she touched me that I was Elijah in person. When I noticed how eager Eliezer as well as his wife and daughter had been to be obliging and how, ever since receiving the angel Uriel's message they had diligently adorned, painted, and bedecked their daughter, I donned Elijah's coat, took along my odorous top, made myself invisible, and entered Esther's room at the appointed time. Immediately I made my presence known by a gentle sound and by the scent which daughter, father, and mother had already experienced in Eliezer's bedroom. Thereupon the father and mother departed along with the maid servant, leaving Esther and me alone. She wore only a soft shirt and a sleeping gown made of damask and lined with ermine. Her arms and neck were adorned with large pearls and her hair was braided and beribboned, as is customary among Jewish brides. Various sweetmeats were on the table, and large, golden goblets, filled with wines from Spain and the Canaries, were not wanting. The bed was expensively furnished and embellished with silken draperies and a silk coverlet of the lightest feathers embroidered with gold and pearls; all the linen, pillows, and bedclothes were of the best Dutch materials. In short, everything was splendid and majestic enough to serve as a seat and wrestling-ground for the Turkish Emperor or the Persian Shah himself.

By now I was able to talk Jewish so well that anyone hearing me would have staked a fortune that I was a

Sephardic Jew born in Amsterdam. So I ventured to speak
to Esther although I kept my voice down lest I be heard
and understood on the other side of the door. I presented
her with a pack of fine lies (if lies can be called fine) that
made her heart leap for joy. First I brought to her from
paradise the greetings and congratulations of all the pa-
triarchs and prophets of the Old Testament, next a special
message from the King of the World (for this is the way
God is called by the most devout Jews, although we Christians following the example of our Savior use the title
"Prince of the World" for the evil spirit). The message
said that she would conceive by me, and give birth to the
Mashiah, and thus cause rejoicing among the whole heavenly host. Here again, every blessed soul can see the wanton, ungodly, and frivolous manner in which heaven itself
and its holy inhabitants became a matter for jest to those
who wade through the filthy swamp and mire of sin; nor
do these wretched people notice, mark, and reflect on, the
monstrous nature of the sins they commit, no doubt because they are struck with blindness by the Evil One. My
Esther took everything I said to be the literal truth, indeed
more readily than her forefathers accepted the truths an-
nounced to them by the prophets and by the gospel which
Christ Himself and His apostles had preached. She said,
"Fulfill on me what the Lord has commanded you to do,"
and already imagined herself seated beside her son in Jerusalem, a mighty Empress over the whole world.

There once was a Frenchman who, at the confessional,
admitted, among other things, to the following: "Had
some fun with the organ grinder's girl at the fair."—
"What more?" asked the father confessor.—"Slept with
her in the hay all night."—"What else?" the father confessor inquired further.—"Well," replied the Frenchman,

"I think the rest you can guess yourself." I will follow this example in my tale. Esther was willing, I was ardent in my desire, the bed was made, dusk had fallen, there was nothing to hinder us, so even a goose can fathom what we did to each other. Why should I spin a long yarn about it? Yes, I had a sweet, delightful night and did not have the least concern that these brief and base pleasures could drag me into eternal damnation. Had I dutifully thought of that, my pleasure would have been turned into bitterness or entirely destroyed.

I had worked hard enough during the night, so when daybreak came I told Esther that I had to attend various circumcisions that day, but I would return toward evening. I refreshed myself with some sweetmeats, drank some Spanish wine and at an opportune moment, after leaving behind me the usual agreeable aroma, departed in order to sleep my fill at home. I carried on in this way for several days and nights until I tired; I found that I had had enough and had grown weary of the game, while my good Esther, as usually happens in such matters, had become pregnant. On the last evening, when we parted we gave to each other a precious ring as a keepsake.

After all that had happened Esther did not exactly consider herself a nobody. Not only she, but also her parents, boasted of her good fortune. Although the rumor of the strange impregnation got about among the Jews they kept it a secret from the Christians for fear that something untoward would happen to the issue (which, they believed, would destroy Christianity) or indeed to all the Jews and perhaps an Herodian play be enacted. Among themselves, however, they freely exhibited their joy, gloried in their ancient faith, wished one another bon voyage to the Promised Land, extended invitations, exchanged gifts, and honored Esther as if she were a goddess. The baptized Erasmus, too, got wind of it all from his old confidants, and it almost made him waver in his newly adopted Christian faith; but about that I shall tell you in the next chapter.

Now as the time approached for Esther to give birth to their savior and thus bring their joy to a climax, the louder became the jubilation of the Jews. She had been cared for like a princess, and now preparations were made for a royal childbed. Not only the most experienced Jewish women who attend such occasions came to the delivery; the most distinguished and richest Jews of the city and the most learned Rabbis of the synagogue were also present so that they could, at his very first gasp for breath, kiss the newborn savior whom they had already adored in the womb, and present magnificent gifts to him.

I had persuaded Esther, poor fool, that she would have a painless childbirth; but in fact, when her time came, she began to moan like all other women; and when she was delivered of her burden, they found (and this, o Adonai, was the bitterest for the Jews) instead of the Messiah—a little girl! Now, jaws dropped to the ground and everybody left with a long face; and yet the most learned of the Jews were so foolish, so blind and so bent on the Messiah's advent that they would not believe their own eyes. So they asserted and eventually persuaded everybody else to believe that it was really nothing unusual for a lass at birth to turn into a lad at marriageable age. Accordingly, it was decided that this little creature should be reared in grand style, albeit less because of an awesome birth than because of a wondrous conception. Who knows, they said, God's intention in hiding the male member at birth? Perhaps, it would be circumcised only in its thirteenth year, or else—who knows?—perhaps the Goyim learning of this birth might try to kill the Messiah in his tender youth, before he could work his miracles and assemble the house of Israel for their march to the Promised Land. In the guise of a girl he would be sufficiently obscure, and safe from such designs. One should let God do as He pleases; perhaps He was leading them into temptation just in order to try their faith and constancy, as He had done with their father Abraham.

CHAPTER V

BY this time I believed that my friendly visits and daily talks had won me Erasmus' confidence. My unsparing generosity had so obliged him, I thought, that I could bet my last taler that he would confide all his preoccupations to me. In many respects he did. The good fellow had, however, heard from some of his old acquaintances in the synagogue that the chosen people of Israel had recently received very satisfying assurances of the Messiah's imminent arrival. When in addition he learned of the message that clearly came from heaven (by means of those slips which I had scattered and about whose true origin he knew, of course, nothing), he was assailed by the deepest melancholy: here he had gone and deserted the Jews just when their misery was about to end and their greatest bliss to begin. He did not tell me about these grievous doubts; indeed, he tried as best he could to conceal them. I could nonetheless see from the sudden change in him and from his constant groaning, so contrary to his usual jolly self, where the shoe pinched, but I still left him to stew in his worries. Then came further news that Elijah had performed all sorts of miracles and that Eliezer's daughter was already pregnant with the Messiah. This so disconcerted him that he began to waver in his Christianity. Now it seemed to me absolutely necessary to do something about the faith of this new Christian, which my roguery had undermined. He had failed to seize a long awaited opportunity to go to the East Indies on financially favorable terms, and I suspected that he was all ready to leap back into the old saddle again. He had become reluctant to tell me as much as he used to about the errors and shortcomings of the Jewish religion, and I took this for another indication of the change in him.

In order to alter his mood and to do this without arousing his suspicion I brought our talk around to the false Messiah Sabbatai Zevi,* and his prophet Nathan, who had made their appearances anno 1666. If I could be assured of his discretion, I finally said, I could tell him of a trick I had played upon the Jews only recently. When he swore that he would keep his mouth shut, I told him the whole story about the slips which I had copied and blown into the synagogue. He could hardly bring himself to believe me, so I showed him some pieces of parchment and a few poorly written slips which I had discarded, and the long blow-tube which I had used. He was really taken aback; it was, he replied, very odd indeed, and yet it was nothing compared with some very strange news that had been occupying his mind for quite a while. He would tell it to me, if I, too, would pledge silence. It was my turn to assure him of my complete discretion. Whereupon he told me what I already knew better than he did, that Esther, the daughter of the rich Jew Eliezer, was pregnant with the Messiah whom she had conceived upon the divine order of a heavenly spirit. Further, he told me a lot of wild stories about various great miracles that Elijah was supposed to have performed; many of them had not been my work but issued from the imagination of the Jews. Finally, he added, it was Esther's pregnancy that had led him a few days ago to give up his East Indian journey; he had wanted to see whether the birth of the Messiah would be as miraculous as his conception.

* Sabbatai Zevi: see Introduction, pp. 6off.

I could readily imagine the doubts that tormented Erasmus, but while I would have liked to rid him of his worries, I did not dare to disclose to him exactly how I had got myself on top of Esther. Nonetheless, as I listened to him, I could not help laughing derisively. I assured him once again that nothing but fraud and false hope would come from this Messiahdom, as had so often been the case before. He, a firm Christian and well-read intelligent man, ought to realize that himself. Indeed, now jokingly, now seriously, I hinted at just enough to make him ponder the matter further, clever and subtle as he was. In the end he declared that if it was at all possible to deceive the prudent Eliezer and his well-guarded daughter, whose purity was watched over by a lynx-eyed mother, then only he was capable of such deception who had started it all by playing on the Jews the trick with the scattered slips.

I thought, "Well, my good fellow, you've guessed it," but again I just laughed and laughed as I listened to him. Thus I increased his doubts, and I left him in this condition, until Esther gave birth not to the Messiah but only to the little slit-piece. This put an end to the religious doubts which had been tormenting Erasmus, but it also increased from day to day his suspicion that I was somehow involved in the whole affair. Just in what way this was so, however, he could not, for all his cleverness, figure out since he knew nothing of my gift of invisibility and did not even dream of such a possibility.

In the meantime, I had taken him into my service. I overwhelmed him with favors and presents and soon felt that he would be faithful to me in a project for which I needed his help. I trusted him fully from the moment he began to let me share the innermost secrets of his heart and the most delicate concerns of his conscience. Indeed, he confided in me more freely than many people do when talking to their father confessor. Among other things I learned that he had adopted the view which the Jews were taking of Esther's daughter. Perhaps, he said, the Jews were right. Perhaps, God was protecting the Messiah by concealing from the Christians that she was really of the male sex; perhaps God had given him the form of a little girl, until he reached the age at which he could do the work for which he was born. You can imagine how much it amused me to hear the otherwise clever Erasmus talk like a simpleton. But since he had kept everything secret that I had told him about the slips and had passed many other tests of trustworthiness in matters even more confidential, I now made up my mind to disclose the whole enterprise to him. Believe me, I told him, no one else but I am the father of the slit Messiah. I asked him, however, not to be too inquisitive about how I had done it and about the resources and cunning I had employed to dupe both Esther and her parents. I was still hesitant to tell him more and merely promised that in time he should learn all.

"Oh heaven," Erasmus cried, "I cannot believe that a Christian reborn in baptism for eternal life, a man whose heavenly bliss has been purchased by the blood of Christ— I cannot believe that a Christian would mix his blood with a Jewess. Christians commonly say that the Jews are not much better than dogs, and they call them that, unless they have been cleansed in holy baptism and have become Christians. I have been told that in some foreign places there are avaricious Jews who supply lecherous Christian whore hunters with Jewish wenches pretending they are Christian girls. I know it is shameful for me to speak of this since I am a newly baptized Christian, but is it my

fault if there is wantonness among our brothers? Then
these Jews gloat at having so cleverly cheated and duped
those Christian sinners with the very riffraff they dare to
call bitches. If the girls really were bitches, the Jews say,
and not human beings like the Christians, a Christian
sleeping with a Jewess ought to find out soon enough that
he had to do not with a human being but with a bitch."
Erasmus added that he could not really believe that I was
unscrupulous and wanton enough to commit so grave a
sin which among Christian brethren was considered
sodomy.

Erasmus touched me deeply and moved my conscience
so forcefully that I was shocked. I could have beaten my
breast, for having scandalized this new Christian and for
having failed to consider and weigh my sin before committing it. Instead I had waited to learn its enormity from
a former Jew. But I gave him as my excuse the unbearable
love that had blinded me and forced me to sin. Erasmus
replied that I had loved God less than a creature that in
her present state was capable of eternal happiness as little
as a dumb beast. I had preferred a brief moment of base
lust to eternal, heavenly joy and therefore deserved eternal
damnation; and failing just atonement, I would surely
suffer damnation. A true Christian ought to fight with all
his power against such vices in order not to provoke his
creator, who offers His help so that the struggling soul
may conquer and be victorious and be crowned all the
more splendidly by Him, the just Master of all struggle.

I have already mentioned that I took this brief, but
stern, sermon very much to heart; but just as one does not
become a knave all of a sudden, but gets to be one little
by little and by degrees, so a sinner seldom makes amends
with his whole heart, unless God sends a special ray of

grace to enlighten him. Moreover, I was a sinner really drowning in all my vices. Thus I remained the man I was and put all blame on love, like other mad adventurers who fail to make serious and earnest efforts to conquer their appetite, that is to say, to conquer themselves.

CHAPTER VI

ABOUT this time I began to wonder what to do about Esther and our little daughter. I decided to get them away from Eliezer's power and to provide for both of them. I intended to place the burden of caring for Esther on that good fellow Erasmus so that they would not marry outside their own people. I wondered how I might put my hands on a sizable sum for a dowry. This should lighten, I thought, what most people regard as an absurd and odious burden and make it readily acceptable to Erasmus. For, my dear reader, do you think there is today any weight in this world of ours that cannot be outweighed by a lovely pile of gold?

I realized, of course, that Esther was of such rare and uncomparable beauty that many fellows, richer than Erasmus and of better family, would have been overjoyed, nay, would have considered it the highest bliss, to get her as a wife. But when I thought of my young half-Jewish urchin of a Messiah, whom she would have on her hands, and that I was the one person—Erasmus aside—who knew what spirit or flesh he was made of; and when I considered, too, that shelter had to be found for the calf as well as the cow, I had no difficulty in imagining with what affection and fidelity that indivisible union for life would be blessed, were not provisions made and everything tied together securely with golden chains of money. Nor was I so frivolous or wicked as to make light of the little creature, my own flesh and blood, something I was more certain of than is many a good husband of his child. Since I did not want to leave her to the Jews, I said to myself, "Get going, look around for some money."

I wanted to avoid depleting the funds which I needed for my own affairs. In this regard I behaved like all insatiable misers who the more they have the more they want and never rest until the flames of hell, seventeen furlongs high, close over their heads. I was much too lazy and considered myself too important to make use of my invisibility and steal by the pound until I had a hundredweight and thus give the dowry of a million to my wild offshoot and its strange Jewish root. Instead, I thought up a new project, which I am now going to tell you about.

Little by little, I had become acquainted with a good many people in Amsterdam. I did not care whether I spent my time with the rich or the poor, with good and honest people or with the wicked and worthless. The well-to-do I treated respectfully. I always kept in mind their station in life and their habits in order to win their affection. The friendship of the needy I gained with little effort by my generosity. The former I imposed upon and separated them from as much of their wealth as possible; the latter I used for all kinds of needful services. There were also some fellows whose company I sought merely for fun. One of these trusted me more than any of the others and poured out to me the innermost secrets of his heart. Despite this I cannot regard him as a very good and faithful friend, because his friendship made me take a path that might have brought my life to a pitiable end and made me a horrible example of tragedy. The fact is, however, that I came off better than I ever deserved of God. Eventually, I learned to know myself, which is no small beginning to a good ending; but this I was to owe not to this man's friendship and the arts I learned from him, but only to God's goodness.

In the first lesson this fellow gave me he taught me how to make a special kind of gunpowder that did not emit a sharp report on shooting, but only a muted sound. To be sure, such powder befits furtive highwaymen and poachers more than honest people, who deserve to be punished more severely for using it if they get caught. The next lesson concerned another kind of gunpowder for shooting birds. They were not harmed by it but merely became weak so that one could pick them up as if dead and then have them come alive again. Thirdly, he taught me to mix something with the gunpowder that produced the same effect on human beings. If you aimed at someone's head a rifle or pistol loaded only with this powder and no bullet, he would lie as if dead for an hour or two and not be injured otherwise in the least. This last lesson, like the first two, was of no use to me, since I did not plan to amuse myself with birds and people or play the compassionate highwayman who wants his victims to be dead just long enough to rob them and get away with the loot. Still, I was eager to be able to do all these things; my curiosity spurred me on to master these first tricks, and in my folly I regarded them as not at all evil, since I thought the preparation of all three powders something perfectly natural, when it was in fact the ABC of the art that is called the black one. And that art is the road leading straight to the Devil.

When my instructor noticed my keen interest and saw how eager I was to learn more, he offered me still more lessons, proceeding from the natural to the unnatural arts. Once, he and one of his companions took me to a lonely place to try out a device that produced invulnerability.

This was a piece of fine parchment with some words of a strange, unintelligible language written on it in bat's blood; it had to be fastened underneath the left arm. We had carried a cat along to make a test. I intended to use my trusty musket, which was at the ready loaded with ball, but when I tried to shoot at the tethered cat, which had the parchment slip fastened underneath its left front paw, my musket failed me, although the powder burned away on the flashpan.

Ten times I tried it. Although I changed the flint several times, and primed each time, my good firearm did not give off as much as a single spark of fire. This made me so angry I wanted to break my musket against a tree. My teacher's comrade burst out laughing and made me try again, saying that for the fun of it he had blocked the barrel, bewitching my shot. Thereupon I shot at the cat so that her ribs resounded, but without hurting a hair of her fur, to say nothing of her hide.

No one was more eager than I to master these two arts as well. I promised my two companions everything I owned and more, but they replied that because of my generosity they would not accept anything, but would teach me these and still other excellent tricks gratis. Thereupon I took them to breakfast and afterward we went to their lodgings, where they showed me a book in which many natural and unnatural arts were described. Had anyone learned and practiced all of them he would soon have become famous and acquired the reputation of an arch-sorcerer. There were descriptions of how to make oneself invulnerable in various different ways and how to undo the invulnerability of others; how to cast a love spell on women; how to get game to stand at bay; how to extinguish great conflagrations; how to make oneself invisible;

[273]

how to put troopers in the field; and many hundreds of other things to boot. The two fellows gave me there and then some demonstrations of these tricks. They hung on the neck of a cock a mere blade of straw and a slip of fine parchment with a thread spun by a virgin on a Saturday night, and this made the cock look as if he were carrying a big beam. They also had a root, which would burst open any lock upon the merest touch. I was much taken by that; I thought it went so very well with my invisibility that I did not rest until they gave this mandrake root to me. Later, they showed me still more tricks, for instance, how to get three sure hits with a gun each day; how to cast bullets that would home on blood and undo all invulnerability; how to find and dig up hidden treasures; how to compel fortune in gambling. There were also the arts of catching fish and fowl by hand; of preparing coins which would always return to your purse after being spent; or the ducat that put underneath a hat over night would turn into ten; and this last one reminded me of the lucky purse of Fortunatus,* a wonderful trick if it could only have been done in good conscience. I heard about charms that would divert or call up heavy thunder and hailstorms, something I did not consider inferior to weather-making. In sum, I learned about diverse arts, some of which I liked while others made my hair stand on end, no doubt because I still was a novice unpracticed in such gruesome things.

* Fortunatus: see note*, above, p. 174.

CHAPTER VII

THE so-called mandrake root, which my two companions presented to me, seemed to be made of wood; for this reason and because I snatched about 10,000 ducats with it, I call it here my wooden fishing-rod. This is what happened.

I tried out the effect of my root on nearly all the doors and locks I come across, and whenever I touched them with the root, they all sprang open; unlike my musket, it never failed. Now this mandrake together with my gift of invisibility equipped me so well for thievery that I thought I ought to put them to use. I had in any case intended to find somehow enough money to take care of my Esther and her child. Now who was more obliged to provide a dowry for Esther than her own father? Had it not been for me, he would in any case have had to open his money bags in order to settle her after the Jewish custom in accordance with his wealth; he would undoubtedly have had to do so, had I not got the jump on whatever young Jewish fellow might have become her bridegroom and pulled the tasty morsel out from under his nose.

I took a bag along and proceeded invisibly in this just cause to Eliezer's house where I searched all corners for the hiding place of the Golden Fleece; I mean, of course, the core of his wealth, his ready money. To tell the truth, I was amazed at the extraordinary abundance of valuable household furniture, goods, and merchandise that Eliezer had in stock. I opened various vaults, some during the day, some at night, depending on opportunity and the need to proceed in secret, and I left no room unvisited. At last I came to the innermost cellar, where the jolly dogs I was after were sitting around. Not only was the collection of fine silver plate and big silver coins so extraordinary that it took my breath away, but there were also so many silver ingots stacked up like bricks that I really thought all the Portuguese Jews in the whole city had brought their wealth here for safekeeping. The iron chests, piled one on top of the other, were too heavy for me to lift. When I forced the top one open with my root, I found it heaped up with ducats like those baskets full to the brim that merchants empty into the buyer's sack. Because their lids were of such splendor I supposed that the lower chests contained precious stones, pearls, gems, and other valuables. It did not seem possible to get into them then. So I helped myself to what I saw in front of me, and filled my bag with as many ducats as it would hold and I could carry. I locked everything up very neatly, leaving it all as I had found it so that no one could have told without opening the ducat chest that anyone had been there.

Thereupon I returned with the loot to my room just as invisibly as I had left it the evening before, and I must frankly confess that never in my life have I carried such a heavy load. Eliezer would not have thanked me for my exertion, even had he known that I went to all this trouble solely to provide a settlement for his daughter.

After removing this large sum of ducats to a safe place—it was nearly a hundred-weight and a half of coins—I considered carefully how to get the two persons, for whose sake I had purloined all this money, out of Eliezer's clutches. I intended to do this with Esther's consent and to her contentment, and that required as much art and skill as trouble and exertion. As for Erasmus, for whom

I wanted to procure the Jewess, I did not think that once she agreed to become a Christian, much begging would be necessary. Either of the two baits, Esther's outstanding beauty or the remarkably handsome sum of money I had available should, I thought, be attractive enough to persuade Erasmus to close both eyes, let alone to wink at the deal. Now when you see what happened, you will realize that I was more correct in my calculations than even I had imagined.

Often when Erasmus thought that I had returned to my study I was not at home but instead was sitting invisibly in his own room, although he had just seen me leave it with his own eyes. For thus I could watch all his doings, observe what he was up to, and whether he was loyal or disloyal. Once, when he thought that I had gone out for a bite, an old hag—I mean to say, a Jewess—came to him, greeting him in a manner that was more Christian than Jewish. Since they seemed to be on very friendly and familiar terms, the thought struck me that she was a creature into whose hands Erasmus slipped the things he stole from me, although, to be sure, I had never noticed anything of that sort. As the saying goes, he who does not trust should not be trusted. I admit that this is true, and besides I had not the slightest reason to distrust Erasmus. It is also said, however, that blind trust rides away on your own horse. For this reason, I pricked up my ears, to hear more sharply what business these two had together.

"Where do you come from, my dear Josanna?" Erasmus said to her. "What brings you here? It seems like a century since I last saw you." "My friend," Josanna replied, "I used to come to you in the hope that our dear Esther, who was ready to abandon the Jewish religion, would go with me and you, as your wife, to the East Indies. Today, however, I have come to bring you quite different tidings about her. What a miracle has happened! Elijah made her pregnant with the Messiah, and she has already given birth to him, and what is more, in the form of a girl. For the Christians might learn about his coming and be fearful lest he destroy their empires and kingdoms. They might want to kill him in his tender and innocent youth, before he could do the miracles and other great works for which he has come into this world; and so he was born a girl child so that the Christians would be deluded into letting him live. As soon as Esther learned that the King of the World had chosen her to become the Messiah's mother and that Elijah had got her with child, she forbade me ever again to give her any messages from you, as I used to do. At first I could not understand why she behaved so proudly and suddenly despised you and the Christian religion. She used to honor and love you more than anybody else, and the Christian faith far more than the Jewish law. She was ready to leave her parents and their great wealth in order to go with you to strange countries abroad, to the very end of the world. Just before she became pregnant she assured me that she had decided to come to you with a lot of very valuable jewels which she had already packed. She was only waiting for a good opportunity to sail with you to distant countries so that she would be safe from her father's search. What will you do now, dear Erasmus? Your hope of getting Esther is now lost. The most learned Jews do not doubt that her offspring is the true Messiah; they and the most eminent Chachams* in Poland, Istanbul, and Jerusalem believe that it will change into a boy when it reaches thirteen and will then undertake the great work of redeeming Israel. Now if all this, my dearest

* Chacham: a sage.

Erasmus, is the truth, both Esther and I would be foolish to leave the chosen people of God and not share in their imminent salvation."

Erasmus replied: "I have never dreamed or believed that heaven, however kind it be, would vouchsafe to me the unearthly beauty of the gracious Esther, nor that fortune, however blind, would give so wealthy a daughter to me, a man of poor station and humble origin. All along I feared that some jarring turn of fate would sooner or later shatter my hopes even though they were nourished by Esther herself as well as by you. For this reason, I ought not to take what has happened too much to heart. It should be easy to bear the loss of that which has never been mine. If I hoped for more than was my due and more than heaven had ever resolved to give to me, I committed a folly. Instead of grieving for the loss of Esther, I ought to laugh at it all, although I confess that it is hard to see myself deprived of what perhaps after all I really believed I would possess. As for her offspring, which has shaken your intention to become a Christian, because you are being told it is the Mashiah, I must say that your blindness astonishes me greatly. If the Jewish people can imagine that a little girl in her cradle is the Messiah, it is no longer surprising that they let themselves be duped so many times in the past by swindlers who pretended to be the Mashiah. Don't you know yourself that even today women are not yet admitted to your sanctuary, your synagogue, as if their sex makes them unfit to worship? How then should a female child become the Messiah? But it is no wonder, it is only right, that such a people should take a woman for its savior, since in times past they honored the golden calf instead of God. Believe me, dear Josanna, I know the father of your Mashiah, who out of love for Esther pretended to be the prophet Elijah and presented her with a young daughter as a reward for her gullibility. Even if this child should happen to turn into a man when it grows up this would be nothing novel and hence no miracle, much less a reason for hoping that the Messiah has come. I advise you, therefore, dear Josanna, to carry out your old intention and, if Esther believes so firmly that her daughter is the Messiah, to wait no longer for her. She and her wealth on which you once relied will be of no help to you, but if through holy baptism you turn to Him, you will have God the Almighty as your refuge, and He will never desert you."

Josanna listened coldly to all this, in evident confusion and doubt. Nor would she believe that anyone but Elijah had got Esther with child, for Josanna knew how closely Esther was watched by her parents and guarded against consorting with men. Finally, she told Erasmus that she wanted to consider further what she ought to do. With a promise to Erasmus that she would talk to him soon again, she was on her way.

CHAPTER VIII

COW AND CALF ARE BROUGHT TO ANOTHER SHED

FR O M this conversation I understood clearly enough that Esther was in love with Erasmus and he in turn with her, and that had I not interfered with my skewer, they would have eloped and gotten married, not without having provided for themselves from Eliezer's chest. Realizing all this, I began to feel remorse for what I had done. I had injured Erasmus by skimming the milk for that good fellow. I had obstructed the conversion of both Esther and Josanna, and strengthened the silly hopes and expectations of the Jews. I decided, therefore, to reverse my course; although I could not restore Esther's virginity to the honest Erasmus, at least in compensation he would have my little daughter as his own.

When Josanna departed I left the room invisibly with her but at once returned visibly to Erasmus. I pretended that I had been on my way to him and had by chance met Josanna downstairs. I inquired about this woman who had visited him and about her business. Erasmus was such an honest and trusting soul that he told me their whole conversation and much more in addition.

For a long time, he said, Esther and he had been secretly in love, although they had never been able to meet, let alone touch each other. Instead, Josanna had served them as their Mercury. Ever since Esther had been a child, Josanna had been her governess teaching her not only all womanly skills, such as sewing, knitting, weaving, embroidering, and the like, but also to read and write German. Thus it was that they happened upon some Christian books, which gave them such a taste for the Christian re-

[281]

ligion that they resolved to embrace it and be baptized. There was no one, however, who could help them by either word or deed to set their good project afoot until Erasmus himself had turned from the Jews to the Christians. Then Esther found it in her heart to confide her intentions to him. Trusting him completely, because he had become a Christian, she sent Josanna to assure him that she would marry him if he could find a way for her to escape safely from her father; for she feared that he would use the power of his wealth to undo their project. They decided that all three of them would flee to the East Indies on the next boat bound for Batavia, and all this time Esther had been ready to sail and to take with her a handsome sum of money and many jewels. In the meantime, however, Elijah had snatched the bread, or rather the delicious morsel of meat, out of the very mouth of Erasmus and at the same time spoiled Esther's taste for the Christian religion, since she now thought of herself as the high and mighty mother of the Jewish Messiah. Some of Erasmus' old comrades had told him that Esther was honored like a goddess, and that her child was nursed and reared in nearly royal fashion. He had therefore lost all hope that he could now get her or that she would become a convert.

At this I asked him if he would still be willing to take her and the child if Esther became converted and a goodly sum of money were available for her dowry. He replied, "To begin with, I have never seen her, because she has always been protected from men like a valuable painting shielded from dust and smoke; how can I buy a pig in a poke? Secondly, if I had her, I would have to worry that the memory of Elijah would claim more room and love in her heart than myself. Thirdly, there might well be bad

blood in such a marriage, if one or both of us were to remember that someone else had picked the first and fresh-
est flowers. Fourthly, if would be hard to tend as one's
own someone else's plant. Fifthly, it is not likely that the
true mother of the Jewish Messiah will consent to become
a Christian. Finally, how could I escape from Eliezer's persecution with my bride and her child, on whom the whole
Jewish nation bases its hope of redemption? Eliezer's
powerful money reaches everywhere. It seems therefore
dangerous for me to try to take her now, unless someone
is smart enough to find a clever scheme that will remove
all the perilous obstacles which frighten me. Besides, I
really wonder who would want to give money to Esther,
an apostate Jewess, and, mind you, money enough for a
dowry."

"My dear Erasmus," I replied, "I will answer you on all
counts, whether you presented them to me in seriousness
or, as it seems to me rather, in jest. First, I can readily
believe that you have not seen her. For if you had seen her
or only once glanced at her beauty, you would know that
she is no pig in a poke; indeed, for her sake and in the
desire to get her you would regard all your 'perilous obstacles' as a mere sport and child's play. Believe me, dear
Erasmus, she is so formed that if it were my time to get
married she would never be yours. Secondly, as regards
your vying with Elijah, I know of an excellent medicine;
I will so arrange everything that Esther will never know
or believe anything but that you were the Elijah who sad-
dled her with a little daughter. And for my sake, it should
not be hard for you to love the child. As for the third
point, since Esther will regard you as the one who robbed
her of her virginity, it will be up to you to take your
worries on this score lightly or hard. Your fourth concern

[283]

is equally unnecessary, once she believes her child is yours, and if you love it for my sake. Fifthly, Esther's haughty conceit will vanish, if she comes to realize that instead of Elijah it was beyond any doubt Erasmus whom she held in her arms and that it was he who gave her a daughter instead of a male Messiah. This should make plain enough to her that she was deceived; and the very fact that such a deception occurred will tempt her anew to abandon Judaism and together with you to embrace the Christian faith. Sixthly, let me worry about handling Eliezer in such a manner that you and Esther as well as the child and Josanna will be safe.

"Now you asked also who would provide enough money for Esther's dowry. Let me tell you that I will be that person. It behooves you to care for her eternal happiness and to bring her to the Christian faith, because she relied upon you for this and to reach her aim confided in you alone. I, too, am obliged to do everything possible to provide for her and her little offspring, because I deceived her and got her with child. If you, my dear Erasmus, had done your duty, as your good luck invited you to do and your Christian religion obliged you to do, if you had hastened Esther's conversion, putting your trust in divine help and providence instead of worrying about your escape and other worldly concerns, then Esther would not have been deceived in her goodness, piety, and innocence, nor would I have become her deceiver and the false Elijah. But about what has passed one ought to say with the old proverb,

> Who's acquired wisdom? tell.
> He who makes things turn out well.

"Now, however, words alone will not do; so come with me and take a look at the money which I have gathered together as a dowry for the two of you and for my child's honest and proper upbringing."

Thereupon I took Erasmus along to my lodgings and showed him the 10,000 ducats I had pilfered from Eliezer's vault. I said to him: "Look, my friend, these I will give to Esther and her daughter as a dowry. If the dish, a treat in itself and spiced in addition so well with money, is not to your liking, I will find ten others who will lick their chops at it."

Erasmus was stunned either by my generosity or because he had never in his whole life seen so much ready money all in one heap. When he recovered, he swore that if I could only arrange it, he would marry Esther and would treat and bring up her child as his own flesh and blood.

Now that he had sworn his oath I told him what he would have to do. He was to ask Esther's old trusted maid-servant, Josanna, to come to his quarters next day. As for myself, that very evening, I let myself be locked in Esther's bedchamber, where she usually lay with her child, an old nurse, and the child's maid; I waited until they were all asleep. Then I took the little daughter away with me. She was wrapped like the child of a prince in sheets and swad-dling bands embroidered with gold, pearls, and precious stones. Eliezer's home was so well equipped with locks that no one else could have possibly gotten out, but I had no trouble because my mandrake root opened the way everywhere, and I was bold enough to take my time and quietly lock everything behind me as I went. When I entered my lodgings safely with my child, no one had heard or seen me.

In the meantime, Erasmus had procured a wet nurse to feed the child and was waiting impatiently for Josanna. Upon her arrival, he showed her my daughter in her princely swaddling clothes, and said, "Dear friend, here you see all in one your Messiah and my daughter at the mercy of both the Christians and her true father. She will not be killed as a Messiah but be baptized and brought up in the Christian faith, whether or not Esther decides to help her Elijah whose true name is Erasmus. Now what do you say, dear Josanna? Do you still hope that in time everything will happen as the Jews say and that the little girl will be changed into a boy? I wonder, too, what Esther will say when later she sees our child not as a Messiah sitting in the Jewish temple in Jerusalem but as a Christian praying in a Christian church to the true Messiah. Since you must realize that your Messiah has come to naught, I remind you of your earlier resolution and urge you to follow my example and embrace the Christian religion. As for my Esther who bore her child not of Elijah but of myself, if she will understand that her foolish conceit of being the mother of the Messiah is false; if she will agree to holy baptism, as I did, and will accept me instead of Elijah as her husband, then within twenty-four hours, she may come to me forever. I beg you to go to her and tell her all I have told you and ask her in my name to forgive me for having so cunningly deceived and betrayed her. Tell her that it was my love that made it impossible for me to wait for her to come to me from her father's house."

Finally, Erasmus gave Josanna the same ring which Esther had given to me as a keepsake on the last night I had slept with her, for I had given it to him to that end; he asked her to take it to Esther so that she would know him as her daughter's true father. And if he could speak with her face to face, he would offer her a still surer sign of his fatherhood by telling her what she and the presumed Elijah had talked about on the night the Messiah was made.

When Josanna saw the child and the ring and heard what Erasmus told her, she was utterly dumbfounded. She gladly agreed to deliver his message. She arrived in Eliezer's house where the Jews were consoling the good Esther about the loss of her child, telling her that no doubt Elijah had taken it to paradise. There it would be brought up among the angels and nourished with heavenly food until it came of age to accomplish the work of redeeming Israel and returning it to the Jewish land. Apparently Esther, as well as all the Jews who heard the news of the miraculous abduction, believed in it firmly, especially since they knew that all the doors, windows, shutters, and locks throughout the house had been locked. When Josanna brought Esther the ring, however, and told her what she had seen and heard, Esther abjured the Jewish faith. She felt ashamed that she had let herself be so tricked and deceived after all she had learned from her books about the verity of the Christian religion. So great was her impatience that she could hardly await the night to go to Erasmus; she packed her treasure of gold and gems as secretly as possible and stole off with it from her father's house.

After dusk she arrived with Josanna at my lodgings. Erasmus welcomed her and entertained her with the stories which I had instructed him to tell and which my plot demanded. She could not have dreamed for one moment that he was anyone but the pretended Elijah and her daughter's true father.

CHAPTER IX

I LET Erasmus behave toward the women he was to live with as a man who was his own master rather than my servant. In the strictest confidence, however, I urged him to rent for Esther and her child a special room, which had to do for Josanna as well, and to provide them with everything they needed. Furthermore, he was to look secretly for a trustworthy cleric who would fully instruct the two prospective Christian women in those matters wherein their knowledge of the Christian religion was still deficient; this cleric was subsequently to baptize them and the child in the presence of the proper number of witnesses, and finally to join Erasmus and Esther in wedlock. No sooner ordered than done. I was glad that in one stroke I had turned three Jewesses into Christians.

I was greatly upset, however, by the poor reward I received, for I could no longer enter where I longed to penetrate; Esther now seemed to me a hundred times more beautiful than before, and I was sorely tempted to be of service once more to that good fellow Erasmus. But I had to leave all that alone, if I did not want to be an arch-scoundrel, mortally offend the prospective Christians and spoil everything that I had arranged toward a good ending. I believe, moreover, that it was only through this mortifying abstinence that I made amends and became once more worthy of God's grace.

In the meantime, word had reached me that Eliezer had ordered a quiet search for his daughter and offered a sizable sum as a reward to anyone bringing him news of her.

Since money accomplishes everything one wants, it was both proper and necessary for me to protect those whom I had placed in danger. I pondered how I could secretly manage to give Eliezer a distaste for his search.

At that time a troupe of English comedians happened to be in town waiting for favorable winds to return home. I borrowed from them a terrifying devil's mask. It had a pair of ox horns, a pair of glossy, very fiery eyes, as big as chicken eggs; a pair of pricked-up ears like those of a horse; instead of the nose, an eagle's beak; a throat like that of Cerberus himself; a goat's beard; griffin's claws instead of hands; and, in place of toes, cloven cow's feet. It could spew terrible fire, if one wanted it to, and was all so horrible that looking at it made you feel faint or even ready to die. With this mask as a disguise I went invisibly to Eliezer's bedroom and waited for his retirement and the departure of the servant who helped him to undress. A wax candle burned in the room all night. When I thought that Eliezer had fallen asleep I made myself visible, stepped in front of the bed and said in a voice that struck terror: "Eliezer, if you do not stop looking for your daughter I will tear you apart. You old fool, why do you begrudge her the rest she has found? Lo, she is in Elijah's paradise to nurse the young Messiah. Beware, and don't dare to take his mother's breasts from him, or else I will be sent to you a second time and break your neck."

It was quite unnecessary for me to leave a stench behind when I departed, and yet I was the cause of one, for Eliezer, in dread and horror, shat in his bed so amply that the stench made me almost faint. Although I vanished before his eyes, I tramped about the house, in which I knew all nooks and crannies, now visible, now invisible, and made a terrible noise bursting open all doorlocks; but I shut them again, as I had done when fetching my daughter. After a while, I went out to the street and returned quietly to my lodgings.

In the meantime, Esther and Josanna diligently studied and accepted those Christian dogmas which they had not as yet learned; and the priest did not fail them in his industry and honest zeal. Soon he notified Erasmus and me that they were sufficiently instructed: the time was ripe for their baptism. We invited to the celebration a few of our best friends whom we needed as godparents and witnesses both at the holy baptism and at the wedding. Esther and Josanna kept their old names but henceforth were both to be called Mary in addition. The young daughter, however, was named Eugenia, although I can't imagine why Esther liked that name. The next day, the young couple were wedded by the priest's hand.

It pained me very much to observe Mary Esther's sweet friendliness toward Erasmus. I found it all the more trying and insufferable because I thought myself worthier than Erasmus of all those charming glances and amiable pleasantries. Had I not done much more to deserve them? No, you cannot imagine how bitter it was for me to watch this wedding which I had arranged myself with so much trouble and at such high risk. I believe, indeed, that had not everything already gone so far, I would never have let it come to fruition, for now my torment and the desire of my love for Esther were much more intense than they had been before I laid hands on her. And yet, I had to force myself to hide as best I could my unspeakable suffering, torment and anguish, all the while blaming myself for letting this beautiful bird fly into somebody else's cage.

The wedding was held secretly; few people in the house took notice of it, to say nothing of Eliezer and the Jews.

After the wedding, I gave the 10,000 ducats to Erasmus counting them out one by one in the presence of Mary Esther and Mary Josanna. I did not conceal from them that the ducats had been stolen for this purpose from Eliezer's treasure, because had he known of his daughter's conversion to Christianity he would have shirked his duty of giving her a dowry corresponding to his wealth. Since the bride, too, had taken along from her father's house a goodly number of gold coins, pearls, and jewels, the couple now had a considerable fortune. After turning over the 10,000 ducats I had a few hundred left which had also belonged to Eliezer; these I gave as a present to Mary Josanna. It seemed to me she had well deserved them through her faithfulness and also because she was the main cause of Mary Esther's conversion to the Christian religion. I stipulated, however, that she was not to leave the newly wed couple but should stay with them until they would otherwise provide for her.

At this time, the whole of Europe resounded with the news that the King of France was about to go to war against Holland. For this reason I quickly sent abroad the goods I still had in storage and settled all my affairs. Erasmus who was well-informed about my business helped me faithfully. Scarcely had we finished this work when I received a letter from home, my cousin, the apothecary, wrote that my wife had gone the way of all flesh. O heavens, has anyone ever suffered as much as I did? Not because my wife had died, but because the letter had been delayed on its way for three weeks. For had it arrived on time, Erasmus would never have gotten Mary Esther. But what could I do? It was too late; Erasmus was in luck and had won the bride.

I had been sufficiently upset and gloomy before because

of my rekindled and redoubled love for Mary Esther, but now I nearly turned mad. I had just provided Erasmus with the most beautiful woman in the world and made him a rich and happy man; now I wished him dead. I cursed both his luck and my misfortune and at last became so furious and insufferable that nobody wanted to be with me and nobody could get along with me. At last it occurred to me—whose inspiration it was I don't know, but surely not that of a good spirit—that I could sacrifice Erasmus and again take possession myself of Mary Esther. O horrible ungodliness! I believe that in the end I would indeed have done it, had God not watched over me and had not my fury and desire been curbed a little by some fleeting distaste for actually marrying a woman who by my own design had slept with somebody else. Meanwhile, the good Lord, who as I have said, watches his flock, opened Erasmus' eyes. He read my sullen face and guessed the cause of my raving madness and my intention as well, since he knew that my wife had died. He escaped at night with Mary Esther, her child, and Josanna, taking his whole fortune along. No doubt inspired by a good angel upon God's command, they sailed with some people who fled with their goods to Hamburg. From there he went to Danzig and thence to Lübeck, but about his further journey I have never been able to learn anything. Thus I was left behind on the threshold of utmost despair.

GPSR Authorized Representative: Easy Access System Europe - Mustamäe tee 50, 10621 Tallinn, Estonia, gpsr.requests@easproject.com